TELL ME
ANOTHER MORNING

TELL ME ANOTHER MORNING

AN AUTOBIOGRAPHICAL NOVEL BY Zdena Berger

with an afterword by the author

PARIS PRESS Ashfield, Massachusetts

First Paris Press edition, 2007.

Library of Congress Cataloguing-in-Publication Data
Berger, Zdena, 1925–
Tell me another morning : an autobiographical novel / by Zdena Berger.--1st Paris Press ed.
p. cm.
ISBN-13: 978-1-930464-10-0 (pbk. : alk. paper)
ISBN-10: 1-930464-10-X (pbk. : alk. paper)
1. Teenage girls--Fiction. 2. Jewish girls--Fiction. 3. Concentration camps--Fiction.
4. Concentration camp inmates--Fiction. 5. Holocaust, Jewish (1939–1945)--Fiction.
6. Theresienstadt (Concentration camp)--Fiction. 7. Auschwitz (Concentration camp)--Fiction.
8. Bergen-Belsen (Concentration camp)--Fiction. I. Title.
PS3552.E71915T46 2007
813'.3--dc22
2007000859

A C E G I J H F D B

Printed in the United States of America.

For those who did not see the other morning.

And for my husband, George Price,
who taught me how to laugh again.

Contents

TELL ME
ANOTHER MORNING

1

Cold held the city and the edges of the river were solid in the mornings along the banks. Under the bridges of fitted stones, where the sun reached in the afternoon, the loosened ice was like glass falling. Below the castle, water froze each night to level the hollow steps. Ice widened in the joints of the high trees on the hill and the limbs cracked before morning.

The borders had been lost. But the borders were far away and the ones living there were strangers. The people in the city ate their salted buns at breakfast. They poured milk in the coffee. They stood up in the trams with their papers folded. Sparta had won again at soccer and those who were for Sparta were happy. The shining girls walked at noon and in the park the gray nurses steered their prams in squadrons of four. Across spaces where the wash hung stiff in the lowered sun the women leaned and talked through their hands. Potatoes were smaller, fever had been checked in the suburbs, triplets had been born to a mother of fifteen.

With the lights going on the people bought chestnuts from the man with the fingerless mittens. The people warmed their hands with the chestnuts and ate them. The sky went out and the last rabbits were lifted from hooks in the market. In the bars the men turned the tall glasses in their hands and nodded to the voice in the radio. What happened on the radio always happened somewhere else. Then a waltz was played.

The last children were called from the courtyards. Neon rimmed Venceslav Square. The young walked up, smiling at the ones walking down. Beyond the statue of St. Venceslav they turned and walked down, smiling at the ones walking up. The restaurants were loud with voices and clicking glass. A space was empty on the menu: Goose liver had been removed. The tramway was crowded at theater-time. Laughter was louder from the orchestra seats. Small sausages were sold steaming at the corners. A word in white paint was splotched on the wall of the museum.

The children studied history, took their exams and were given a Spanish orange and chocolate raisins for good grades. Men in leather caps fished from the bridges. One of the signs in Venceslav Square did not light up one night. The shoes of the young shone bright in the square. The names of men were in the headlines. White flowers popped on the chestnut trees and the people talked of vacation. The trains did not go to the borders any more and the people, expecting a hot summer, bought more moth balls that year. The radio gave the news and many speeches and the people were singing: "We Are Afloat in a Boat on the Ocean of Love."

They had no ocean near but there were many rivers and lakes. In the summer the striped sails would again move like flags across the blown waters. The children were thinner, unbundled from their winter coats. The headlines grew taller and finally only the shorter names would fit and only the simpler words were used. Exports of shoelaces rose twenty per cent and an attaché had fallen from a window. A farmer had been imprisoned for feeding his cow mash from a brewery. Cobblestones were replaced by pavement on a street along the river. A hybrid rose was named for a queen and people were urged to unify and put away their differences. The people lined up for a movie in color: Holiday in Tuliptime.

One evening a neighboring dictator came to spend the night in the castle. The next day his armies moved on the city.

The family lived on the same street for fifteen years. The father went to his factory in the morning and returned at noon. As long as the family remembered, the father took a nap after his lunch. It was the tiptoeing time, until the door opened and he appeared, stretching his arms and shouting, "My tea! Where is my tea?" The mother brought him his tea and the children watched him sipping, one slice of lemon floating in the glass. The mother tied her blond hair in a bun on one side. Once a day, after lunch, with the father and children gone, she would call her friends on the new telephone, always wiping her hands dry before lifting the receiver. Then she would dust the piano, move the carpet sweeper across the front-room rug and prepare goulash or potato pancakes for dinner. In the evening the father brought home the newspaper, folded so that only the headline showed.

EARLIER DRAFT PLANNED FOR NEXT YEAR

The son was sixteen and would not come home for dinner sometimes. His sister was quiet, younger and thin. The mother and the father could not agree on which one she resembled. After dinner the family would sit in the front room and sometimes the mother would sing softly to herself at the piano, singing the old songs.

ALLIES STAND BEHIND GOVERNMENT

The girl and the boy would buy pots of flowers for Mother's Day and for her birthday flasks of eau de cologne that came from France. For the father they bought slippers, always brown felt with red tassels. When business was not good, they would move—the houses older and closer together—but they never left the street. Always there were the piano and the mauve curtains in the living room, always the smell of the mother's baking. They moved many times during those years, up and down the street, and only the view from the windows changed.

SMOKE SCREENS TO PROTECT CITIES

On their vacations they went to a village where the father was born. There was a river and they spent their time at the beach and the father would come on weekends from the city, bringing candy with him and they told him about each day, the colored ices they had eaten, the preserves the mother had cooked, and how far and how fast they swam in the river.

ARMS RACE CONTINUES

At the end of summer they moved back to the city. On Fridays the mother would heat the stove in the bathroom and one after another they would take their bath. On the door of the bathroom the father made pencil lines marking the growth of the boy and the girl.

PACT MADE. TALK STOPS.

There were two lines that showed the height of the mother and the father and these high lines above the children's heads marked the level of their future.

The Last Day

We are all quiet during dinner. Usually we talk a lot. My brother Karel is reading a book while he is eating. Father does not tell him to put it down. Grandma makes a noise in her stomach and leaves the table. Father does not take a second helping of the sugared noodles.

"Tania." Mother nods toward me. "Clean your plate."

Father folds back his newspaper, creases it and puts it behind him on the chair. Mother takes the dinner plates stacked to the kitchen, putting the forks and knives on the top plate. She brings the kettle and fills the pot; the tea ball rattles and steam puffs from the spout. She fills the cups. Into her cup she stirs one half spoon of sugar, ringing the cup with her spoon. Her head is bent and now her hand turns the small spoon—the spoon is up like a boat, down again with the dark hollow between the white tablecloth and the shine of silver. She holds up the spoon and the light bounces from the handle. She studies it as if to memorize what is cut into the silver—the letter A. A is for Andres.

"Tania, it's time for bed."

I say good night to them, standing at the door. They all lift their heads then. Father's face under the black hair, the nose long and slightly bent, his hand passes back and forth over his forehead. Mother smiles at me, gets up and comes over to kiss me on the cheek. Karel, sitting now under a lamp in the corner of the dining room, the white pages of the book in his lap, waves a hand that drops slowly to the book again.

I undress and lie in bed. Why did Father look so worried tonight? Because of the radio? The voices of the old newspaper sellers shouting their news in the street? Or is it because of the business? I do not understand why people would buy fewer shoes in spring than in the fall. There is always a little smell of leather around Father. Mother smells of yeast from making dumplings all the time. Maybe it is not the shoes. It is the other thing. And the gas masks on the shelf in the kitchen.

Grandma should get new teeth. Her mouth is all dark inside when she opens it. My friend Eva has the whitest teeth. She has breasts already. Did her mother hear us talking this afternoon? We didn't do the Latin. Only Eva knows about my poetry. One day, when I don't have to go to school any more, that is all I will be doing. I told that to Eva but she did not believe me. She is my best friend but we do not like the same things. If she had a pet it would be a crocodile. She doesn't like dogs, not even our Nora. They have weak characters she said and we had the argument about that again today. I brought my new jazz record with me this afternoon and she wanted to play Mozart for me. He makes me think of wigs and men in baggy pants. I turn in the bed but the dark does not turn. It is solid and takes the room away. What about now? We never talk about what is happening to the city now. I wonder why? I wonder why we do not talk about it. Eva always has many questions so that I feel stupid sometimes because I don't have the answers and they are not in the books I read. They are not in Caesar's *Commentaries.* "All Gaul is divided . . ." That was a long time ago. Karel would know the year. Karel knows everything. I wonder where he went today. I think he has a girl.

Mother's voice singing from the kitchen, ". . . Wait, you will regret, regret, regret . . ." Sometimes she sits at the piano and sings and the music sheets are very yellow. I hear Father closing the front door behind him. He is taking Nora for her evening walk. How big Nora is now. Maybe soon she will get mated and all the puppies will be here in their round fur. How many puppies does a dog have?

I wake up with Father's face close above me. The door to my room is open and the dim light from the hall seems far away. Father is dressed in his brown suit, his hand shaking my shoulder.

"Tania, dear. You have to get dressed. We will take a small trip."

I sit up in my bed. The feather bed clings to my body, my head already leaving the warmth. "Is it the . . . war?"

"No, not yet, but I don't like the late news. Now you better hurry!"

In the dark room I slip from my bed and look for the shoes. The woolen stockings I find over a chair. What shall I put on? The red sweater and the blue pleated skirt. I am cold now and I do not dare to make light in the room. What if they are going to bomb us? I take my coat from the closet and carry it over my arm into the hall. I am tiptoeing as if Father were taking his nap. Mother carries bundles in her arms and Karel is already downstairs. We descend the dark of the steps. I try to put my coat on but cannot find the right sleeve. Grandmother is already on the sidewalk sitting on two straw suitcases. Nora runs to the edge of the sidewalk, waving her tail back and forth with joy. I see Karel holding a book under his arm and a fishing rod in the other hand. There is only silence in the stone street.

A taxi pulls up and we cannot all fit in. Karel is in the front seat beside the driver and the rest of us and the dog in the back seat.

"I will find another car and join you in Kostelec," says Father.

So that is where we are going. The village where Father was born and where we spend our vacations. The seats of the car are red plush and there is a smell of dust. The driver has a black cap and he is old. We move away through the city that is dark and quiet. But I can feel the hidden lights behind the windows and people that do not sleep tonight. Crossing the bridge, I can see the Moldau moving with the low moon in it.

I am afraid. The sound of my teeth clicking together is loud in the dark car. Father said that if there is an air raid, we should all get out of the car, once we are out of the city, and lie down in a ditch. I am sure Nora will give us trouble. She will bark and they will throw bombs straight at us. She does not listen to anybody but Father. I wish he was here with us. The driver might kill us. He might think that we have money or jewels.

We pass other cars leaving the city. Their shapes moving with covered lights. And the engine sound rising and falling away as we pass them. I turn and see the city fading out. The road ahead is coming to me through the windshield. Karel is giving directions to the driver and he keeps asking us all the time how we are. Nora is fidgeting at my feet, growling in her dog's sleep. Grandma is falling asleep. She takes up so much space with her big skirts. She still wears at least three petticoats and I think that is unhealthy. She thinks it is still 1900.

There are trees now that move beside the car. We are in the country. The last time I was here we had a picnic. My cheeks burn and I don't feel good. I wish I could cry. It is too warm in the car and I have the heat in my skin. I would like to tell Mother. I look at her but she seems so distant. I was in my bed before. Now I am sitting here. Everything was nice before. Before the old newspaper sellers shouted in the streets. Everything will be different now. I feel I would like to stop it before it happens.

I am very sleepy now. The skin of my cheek against the cold window glass; I will sleep. Maybe I will wake up in my bed, and there will be no war. My head is heavy with the rocking of the car; I close my eyes. . . .

I am in a big pool. No, not a pool. A river. The river that flows through Kostelec. I am trying to swim across to the other shore. But the shore does not come closer. The water is so warm and it is getting thicker. I cannot part the water with my arms any more. I see Karel on the shore. I call to him. He stands there looking at me and I know that he cannot help me. . . .

I wake up with the jolt of the car crossing the bridge to Kostelec. I see the village as I have never seen it before, without lights at night. And entering the village, the feeling is there, the feeling of the dream, the warm river. It descends my legs. And then I know: It is only my first blood.

With the feeling that I am not the first one and that I am not alone, the thought: I cannot stop anything.

The Chain

We live in that small house at the end of the village. The windows have been shuttered since last summer and the air is old inside. It is almost like any other vacation, but it is spring instead of summer. Father works in the garden and talks in the evenings with the men of the village, sitting on their doorsteps. Mother makes fruit preserves and visits the pharmacist's wife, who is a cousin of hers. The tennis courts across from the house are empty, the red clay without prints. The movie house is opened only on weekends. The ice-cream parlor has been closed since winter and the owner plays cards in the village café.

Each day I go to the bathroom with the mirror. Holding it close to my face, I want to find the change in me. But I am the same, except for one new pimple on my chin. Sometimes Mother and I exchange the looks of two women who share their secrets and I feel very grown-up.

Sometimes I walk down to the river with Karel. The water is higher on the shore, the sand beach deserted. The wind sweeps dry leaves across the sand. The shades are flat color in the windows of the country club house, with a white square of paper nailed to the door: REOPENING JUNE 1.

"It's so different here now, Karel. Remember how it used to be in the summer?"

"It's better to be here than to go to school." Karel sifts the yellow sand through his fingers. "Maybe the war won't start right away."

"I hope not," I say.

"So do I. I want to be old enough to go."

"To go? Where?"

Karel wipes his hand on his trousers and lifts his head to me. "Where? To fight them, of course."

I cannot imagine Karel as a soldier. Maybe I do not try hard enough. He lies down on the sand, his head resting on his folded arm. I watch his face as if I had not seen it before. His skin looks smooth, no wrinkles showing; the nose is long and bent like Father's, the hair is falling on his forehead. The hand in the sand has long white fingers. He suddenly looks fragile to me, as if he needed to be protected. I want to tell him, but he turns on his side and watches something across on the other shore.

We are alone on the beach and, sitting here in this known place, I remember summer:

. . . The beach was loud with many voices and I walked away, turning to see the colored tents spreading wide their shadows. The sand burned under my feet but it was cooler there on the slope close to the water. I entered the river and swam away from the others. The beach more distant when I turned my head, I continued swimming for a long time, following the shore, with the trees hanging over and the water cooler in the shadows of the trees. . . .

I see clearly that day and I wonder why. Nothing happened, only that I went alone into the water. That was almost a year ago.

We stay one week in the small house and the radio tells us that there will be no bombing and no harm done. We return to the city and I find the houses taller, the streets more narrow. The apartment smells of moth balls.

One day, walking home from school—Venceslav Square dark with people and my steps faster—on the corner I stop. Standing on my toes, the schoolbooks falling from under my arm, I see the tanks and the green uniforms.

The sound of iron on the cobblestones and all the legs moving together. They march across the old square, under the stone man riding his stone horse, as if they had come home. The cannons are as long as the fallen trees I have seen in the country. The tanks move on an iron road that rolls around with no end to it. But the wheels that turn it are small as the wheels on a toy wagon.

People talk in whispers; some spit and shake their fists. One man, weeping, throws a flower. It falls under a tank. The crowd follows the sidewalk; the arms of the people tight to their sides, they whisper their curses. They are bad words, but I do not think they are bad now.

And I think, This is not possible. They cannot take us like that. It is too quiet. Nobody fights or screams or runs. I think of the French Revolution and guillotines. But this has nothing to do with that. Who was ever occupied?

A shopkeeper stands on the doorstep of his shop, his arms folded. A dog runs and stops at a lamppost. A newspaper seller sits beside his old news. In a restaurant, behind the glass wall, a fork still in front of his mouth, a man stops eating, his face white as the tablecloth.

I walk home, passing groups standing on the corners, the radio loud from open windows, the sound of dishes, the smell of a roast, and I walk faster and faster, past the travel agency with posters of lakes in the mountains. Past the Park of Roses, empty of birds, and green benches vacant behind the bushes. Past a blond woman, with her belly in front of her, and looking as if she had the world for dinner.

I hear the bells from the church and I feel them in my stomach. They keep getting louder now and I run and do not stop until my hands find the familiar knob on our door.

I shut the door behind me and my fingers close over the brass chain and I slowly let it drop in its slot.

The Star

It is a yellow star, rimmed with black.

At first, when Mother brought it home, I thought—I will never wear it. I prefer to die. I will just stay at home and not go out on the street. I don't like school any more. It is not really a school. We have our classes in a private apartment, each week somewhere different. It is as if we pretended and "played school."

I won't go to school. I will stay home. I can help Mother do something around the house. Grandma always says I don't do anything around the house. I can read. There are many books in Father's library that I still have not read.

I can play games with Karel. No, I won't play with him. I am sure Karel will go out and wear it. He will probably even be proud of it. Sometimes I really don't understand him.

Mother starts to sew it on my coat. It is a blue coat. Dark blue. I just watch. It really does not look so bad, the yellow against the blue. I still won't wear it.

At dinner Father talks about how there is nothing to be ashamed of. He talks about history and Karel joins him. I just don't feel like telling him right now that I won't wear it. Father always knows the answers to everything and he is always right and I love him. I think I will tell him in the morning.

In the morning I say, "I won't wear it!"

Grandma cries. She cries so easily. I suppose because she is so old. Father is in a hurry and is ready to leave. He bends down and kisses me on the forehead, longer than usual. And he squeezes my shoulder. Karel is leaving with him. I take another piece of bread and eat slowly.

All right, I will try it just once. See how it feels. I gather my books, kiss Mother. She smooths the star. There was a little wrinkle.

I put on the blue coat with the yellow star.

On the street I walk very quickly. As if the people won't notice so much if I walk quickly. I see another star approaching. It is a young boy who lives across the street. I like him but he never pays any attention to me. Today he gives me a big smile and a nod with his head.

I am slowing down. It is really silly to run like that. I have plenty of time. People don't look at me. In fact, they don't look at all.

I watch each face. Mostly they keep their heads down. Or look at something in back of me. I wonder what there is in back of me that they look at. Then I know that they are embarrassed. And I feel fine.

On the corner by the streetcar stop, another star. We look each other in the eyes. She is a young woman. There are other people waiting. I stand close to her. We both step into the last car. Because we are not allowed in the first and the second. Only the third.

The car is full of stars. It is a gathering of stars. They talk and laugh and read newspapers as on any other day. And I think, There has never been a day when so many stars could be seen. And at night nobody can see them—we are not allowed to be in the streets after dark.

I open my schoolbook. The Crusades. I can never remember the dates.

After a couple of weeks I don't even know I have it. But it is still there, sewn on my chest. Only it looks so shabby now. The black trimming is coming off in threads. Mother washes and irons the star and sews it back. We are issued two more stars. But they are not enough. Now, with summer coming, with each dress or blouse I have to change the star.

"Mother," I say, "why don't they give us more?"

"They will, dear," she says. "They will give us more."

The Saint in Stone

I change the stars. From blouse to sweater to coat. And again. Blouse, sweater, coat. More stars to wear and fewer wearing them. My coat is too short now. I wonder where the time has gone and all the people I have known. Now the waiting has ended and tomorrow I go where all the stars have gone.

Tomorrow we will leave. They sent us our green tickets. I don't remember if Karel's ticket was green. It has been six months since they sent him into the labor camp. His letters are short. He does not mention the packages we send.

Since noon I have been walking through the streets. The sidewalks made of snow, snow covering the stone cobbles as it covers the roofs of the houses and the saints on St. Charles bridge. The air is blue with cold. On the Moldau the ice is a white land between the two shores and the houses are darker with windows of frost.

Father went somewhere this morning to ask for a delay until Karel comes back. Mother does not have time to cry. She started a long time ago to put our things in order. Now she makes dry cakes that we can take with us. Bowls of margarine melted with flour and brown onions fill the kitchen table. "You just have to have that for a good soup," she says. Mother thinks she will be able to cook, wherever they send us. And that as long as she can cook we will all be alive. Grandma wants to come with us. We tell her that without the green ticket she cannot go and she cries.

The house smells of Christmas. But instead of glass balls and chocolate cookies wrapped in foil, the pink pigs with green clover stuck in their sugar mouths, there are green sleeping bags spread out in the dining room and heavy blankets. Instead of the smell of fir and berries, the open suitcases fill the room with the gray smell of cellar and mushrooms.

On the dark buffet, between the many Happy New Years and St. Nicholas, clipped together are the three green slips of paper. With the numbers in black: 682, 683, 684. I am No. 684. If Karel was here, I would be 685.

There are no gifts in the closet. I knew this but I looked anyway. And in the bathroom, there is no carp in the bathtub. I remember last year, the carp, as always, was bought a week ahead of Christmas and put in the tub. He was the nicest carp we ever had. We named him Joseph and he became very fat in a week and he would jump up for the bread crumbs we scattered on the green water. He did not like to be taken out and put in a bucket when we had our Friday bath. Just before Christmas Mother brought home another carp that was killed and eaten, because we just could not do it to Joseph. We had him for quite a while in our bathtub and I don't remember what happened to him. I think he died of indigestion.

The streets are darker now and Venceslav Square is wider without the high frame of neon lights. I climb the steps to the National Museum; the doors are closed. The snow is the only light between the dark stones of houses. I lean on a pillar and look down on the square. The tramway passes with rattling sounds and people walk down there, wool covering their ears and collars of fur, the white of their Christmas packages swinging on their arms. The cars move in one dark line, the snow pushed up round behind the wheels.

The knot on the tail of St. Venceslav's horse is a braided white ball suspended in air. He has been sitting there, St. Venceslav, the stone flag on a long spear, for hundreds and hundreds of years. Looking over his square.

I wish I were a saint. I would sit on a horse and watch over my city.

2

Once a week and sometimes more often, the streets of the city were filled with a procession. The morning light bent around the towers of beaten gold but the deep streets were dark. Feet slipped on the slick stones. Knuckles were blue at the end of sleeves. Steam puffed from the lips of the walkers.

They walked through the streets, carrying the numbered luggage of their final departure. A child held a stuffed toy, an old man shifted a bundle tied with a white string, a woman carried a suitcase with a tea kettle attached to the handle. They did not know where they were going nor when they would return. They did not understand why they had to leave a city in which there was enough room for them. They walked with a slow but steady pace. They did not have to stop for signals and slowly the street moved away behind them. The steel shutters were down on the shops and no waving hands lifted for the early travelers. A dog, a beggar. A prostitute buying a morning coffee—only these to keep them company.

They were many, the walkers; with a thousand eyes they saw the houses, the streets. They saw them as if for the first time. Down streets where flags had once blown like covers aired from windows, they passed under clocks where they had met before. Past cafés where they had spread their hands above the marble tables and sipped, through a sugar cube between their teeth, the black coffee. Past a park with the thick leaves white and the benches cushioned with snow. They saw the tower at the end of the bridge, the iron lamps with frost on the glass cage, the bronze man draped white, the iron spear leaning, the head held in one hand. The street bent over the bridge, snow in bundles on the parapets above the slow river. All in blue stone the city moved past their eyes. They walked under the pointed arch of the bridge tower and through the vaulting ribs, leaving behind the hollow sound of shoes. In the city no bells were swinging to mark the time. Only in single rooms did the private alarms cause a shaking under the warm quilts.

The people in the rooms were stretching their arms above their heads behind the drawn shades, their mouths open in a yawn, taking in their lungs the first conscious air. They rubbed their eyes and on the way to the bathroom and the shaving mug, the men lifted a corner of the shade and looked down on the street. Then they dropped the corner back in its place and walked away. The smell of coffee started filling the houses and the men sang in their bathrooms. There were the couples who entered the day by lovemaking and it was the woman, on the way to the bathroom, who lifted the curtain and pushed the hair back from her face.

The procession kept walking. Before entering the railroad station, the chosen ones turned their dark eyes once more upon the city. They captured in their wet eyes the last glittering towers.

They heard the first shutters being rolled back, the rattle of tramways. It was as if only now the city awakened. They turned finally to see the statue on the square. But the statue of the saint was hidden.

Those behind the windows pulled the shades up. Below they could see the unchanged streets. The city was clearer now in the bright morning light. It was a day like any other, now that the marchers were gone.

The Walled Town

The train stops and we step down. There is no railroad station and no man with a blue cap waving a red flag to the train. There are only fields under all this snow. Suitcases in hand, we wait to be put into a column. We stand then, quiet, and I turn and look back to see the long file of men, women and children. Father's eyes look as if he is angry; I watch them change color and become darker. The corners of Mother's mouth twitch. My feet are cold. I don't feel fear but impatience to see, to know already that place chosen for us.

The column starts to move. It is hard not to step on the heels that lift in front of me. Slow and long that walk, and with each step forward, the space between us and the train becomes wider. The train is already in a haze like forgotten things.

I see the town now that will be ours. The stone walls push up against the sky, steep above the deep ditch. Walls in a circle that close in that town. In the history class they taught us the name of the empress who built this place. I remember—the fortress that could not be taken.

But for us the iron gate opens. I see the big stone barracks built for the cavalry, the big square where they paraded on their horses. The cobblestones under my feet are pushed deep into the earth. There is an old church, doors nailed shut, and beyond the church I can see high walls the color of damp earth.

No people on the streets. We stop in the square. The men in green come and count us over. They are separating the men from us now. Father holds me tight in the circle of his arms; the smell of tobacco and damp fur around me and I want to stay like that, my face buried in his collar, so that I cannot see, but only feel the warmth and pretend I am somewhere else. He kisses Mother on the lips now and they look over each other's shoulders. Father's hand reaches to her forehead and slowly pushes one blond curl under the woolen scarf.

"Ella . . ."

"Yes."

"Take care of yourself. And of her."

". . . Keep your pullover on at night" are Mother's last words to him.

They lead the men away, the figures darker against the white of the snow, the suitcases hitting their legs at each step. The feet larger in the rubber overshoes. I still see Father, his shoulders straight, his head tilted to the right side, as when I would see him leave our house. A small man from the last row, his hands pulled longer by two bags, runs on short quick legs behind the rest of the column. A figure bends down to pick a dark object out of the snow and the rest of the men bump him from the rear.

But as I see the last of the men turning the corner of the square, I think, These men, they are my army; they are the conquerors of this town that could not be taken.

We are led to one of the stone barracks and separated into groups. We are fifty in a long room with two windows. My bunk is by the ceiling and Mother is below me. The room is filled with women of all ages and they seem to be in a hurry as they start to unpack their bags.

"I am very glad to meet you," I hear Mother say to an old lady. The introductions start and the women exchange polite smiles.

"Want some?"

"Yes."

A little boy across from me hands me a paper bag, one side of his face round with candy. My fingers find the sticky square and I push into my mouth a white peppermint.

"I like peppermint," I say, with my mouth full.

"Peppermint makes wind in your mouth."

"That's right. What's your name?"

"Peter. And I don't like to be called Pete."

"I am Tania."

He bends toward me as if he has a secret. "Do you think they have schools here?"

"I don't think so, Peter. Maybe all you have to do here is . . . play, or something like that."

"I don't like school anyway."

"You don't mind being here?"

"No, but I wish my friend was here with me. We could finish the plane we were building."

"I am sure, sooner or later, he will come here too."

"I hope so. We will build paper planes. Big ones."

"Do they fly? Your planes?"

"Sure. Higher than the walls even. You'll see."

"How do you make them fly?"

"With rubber bands. You hook rubber bands to the propeller and you wind them up real tight and you let the plane go and the propeller goes round real fast and the plane flies so high that nobody can even see it and nobody can knock it down. . . ."

"Did you bring rubber bands with you?"

"No . . . Don't they have any . . . ?" His lower lip bent and his eyes blinking, he looks as if he will cry.

I hand him back his candy. "Here . . . have some peppermint."

I turn to the window and look out beyond the street. The snow falls upon the empty street and the edge of the wall fits to the sky.

The Tree

From my upper bunk I watch the chestnut tree outside the window. I can almost touch the higher branches. It was covered with snow first, the trunk large with years, split on the surface into many dark lines and snow dented in the round notches. Now it has its first leaves, new in their pale greenness, the white knot of flowers tight in the center of the leaves. It is my tree and I watch the season change on its branches. I watch the slow growth of green. There are sparrows now: On short strokes they beat the air and the branches move under their steps. There are small ones, blind, in bunched twigs where the branch joins the trunk. Their beaks are open scissors that clip the dropped worms.

It is good to be suspended so high, with only the gray wall beside me. I have two walls and part of the ceiling. I would like to build a wall all around. Then I would not hear their voices high with anger or soft with complaint. Their coughs. And their loud dreams.

There are bugs here. They come marching in a long file every night. I wait for them and they come. I live in a fortress and these are a patrol of soldiers. They burn my body with a hundred bites. Each morning I follow other women with their covers to the gallery of open arches. There we try to shake them out. The bugs fall to the story below, upon the covers being aired there — and we get new bugs from the story above.

I am getting used to the life here. The day divided into a trip to the washroom and another into the kitchen. Cold water in streams over my naked body and warm water in gulps into my stomach. There are the free days when I work at night in the laundry house. From seven in the evening till seven in the morning. Another week

I work during the day. After a night's work I come back to a room that ripples with words, rings with dropped combs and mess kits, creaks with bunks, and I learn how to sleep in spite of it. There is no one I like to talk to but Ilse, a girl who works in the kitchen and gives a bigger helping to Mother and me.

Mother works in the hospital. Mother—always clean and somehow out of place; with a face smaller and whiter, as if she washed herself too much. She never sings to herself any more. In the evenings I sit sometimes on her bunk and listen to her quiet voice: "Remember when . . . ?" Only when she sees Father she becomes the one I knew so well.

One morning I look down from the gallery at the courtyard loud with counting and the march of women. The women stop and one face turns up and brings back a past for me: Eva. When she is led with the others to a room, I follow. She is taller than I remember. She used to bend like a question mark and walk so her small breasts did not show. Now she stands straight in the crowded room, turning as if to remember the walls. She sees me and we run to each other and embrace, repeating each other's names.

She opens a satchel and there are the schoolbooks. I find my own notes, question marks above a word in Latin that I do not need to know any more. We talk of the hours we spent in her bright blue room bent above these books, finding what we were looking for; and, when the search ended, we would talk of the world as if it were solid, touchable and we could close our hands around it, turn it and see all sides of it.

I show her our new home. I introduce her to Ilse. I tell Eva of the bigger helpings but Eva does not think it is right. She doesn't like my friend Ilse. They have nothing to say to each other. Eva thinks I only want to get more soup, that extra dip of the ladle at the serving window. That is not true. I do not know why I like Ilse. She is healthy and loud and laughs more than anybody else. Maybe I do count on a bigger helping.

One day I watch them walking together, carrying their blankets after shaking them in the gallery. Ilse takes up a lot of room when she moves. She is big and she doesn't move all at once. Part of her comes along afterward as an afterthought. Watching Eva, I think of a glass vase that might break if someone shouted too loud. When Ilse laughs her whole body laughs. But Eva does not laugh any more and when I am with her there is not much to laugh about. She makes me see what is happening and why, but sometimes I want to close my eyes.

Then Sophie arrives. She enters the room in a black dress with a lace collar, an easel in one hand, suitcase in the other. So small, standing in the door, saying: "Good afternoon. May I come in?"

The bunk below Mother's is empty and the little woman comes to it. I see the dark lines on her face, her hands long in their whiteness. "I am Sophie. Is this bunk taken? No? Good. Then I am home."

The days are full of color now as Sophie tells me stories about the times when she was known as a painter and she shows me the cutout pages of yellow newspaper, with her name in black letters and the names of art galleries. The circle of people meeting in rooms with high ceilings, under the lights of a crystal chandelier—the painters and musicians that were her friends. . . . There are days when Sophie just lies on her bunk, dressed in a gray dress with white ruffles around her collar. On these days she does not see us around her and she is not hungry. I wonder if she is ever hungry . . .

Once the green ones send a messenger. They want Sophie to come to the stables and paint a portrait of a horse. Somebody, in the house of the green ones, loves horses. The price will be paid in bread.

Sophie smiles and says: "I never paint horses. Never. I am very sorry."

Sometimes I go with her on the streets, holding the easel under my arm, and she beside me, so small, with the little steps, the gray hair bouncing on her forehead. She carries a small wooden bench that somebody made for her. She stops me with her hand, finds a flat space for the bench and settles down, spreading a clean gray cloth over her knees. I sit down by her and watch her sketch. She mostly draws the old ones. Sitting on a curb of a sidewalk, two, three figures in black, their white necks thin, with the narrow cords pushing out, their hands holding a piece of bread, the knots of gray hair moving as they nod and look into their hands. They come out in the charcoal, their eyes set deeper in the hollow center, their noses bent over the sucked-in mouths.

I hear soft steps below. I turn and look down into the smile of Sophie.

"Good," she says. "Is it a day off for you?"

"Yes."

Her eyes gentle, the small smile lifting the corners of her mouth. "I find hunger and misery every day. Today I want beauty."

"Will we go to the square?"

"We will go to the washroom and I will paint you."

"Naked?"

"Not naked, my child. Nude."

In the cold of the bathroom, I stand to be painted. I am very cold but I don't mind it. I am proud that Sophie chose me. I try to imagine all the aristocracy being painted by her and now it is me. The women come and go and watch me, but I don't look at them. My shoulders are stiff and I try to push my belly in but there is really nothing to be pushed in. My breasts are high, but in the old paintings they are always so full.

"We will continue tomorrow," says Sophie. "I am a little tired."

In the room Sophie lies down. Later I hear Mother saying, "It is a shame, Miss Sophie. You don't eat your dinner."

I am looking for a knife. "Sophie, may I borrow your knife? Somebody stole ours."

She hands me the knife and I climb with it to my bunk, where I settle down to divide bread for Mother and me, making a line in Mother's piece; beyond that line is tomorrow's breakfast and sometimes she forgets about it. Night is outside the window when I lie back to sleep and the tree is larger in the darkness.

It is still early when I wake up and all I hear is the breathing of fifty mouths. I bend down to see Mother. She lies on her back, her hand above her forehead, the blond hair spread on the bundle under her head. She is beautiful, my Mother, even here. I want to touch her and then suddenly I feel like crying. But I notice the foot of Sophie hanging out of her bunk; that reminds me of the knife. I should put it on the shelf above her head, so it will be there when she wakes up and wants to cut a piece of bread.

Halfway down the ladder, I bend over and give a light kiss to Mother's cheek. She is warm and smells of soap. Holding the knife in one hand, I step down to Sophie's bunk. And as I lean over her to put the knife above her head, I stop. . . . Why does her leg hang that way? I reach out my hand and even before the touch, I know . . . I know she is dead.

I climb slowly up again. I sit down on my bunk and see the knife still in my hand. I reach out toward the lock on the upper window and push it open. And my hand plants the knife in the bark of the tree.

The Rubber Bands

I wish his mother would come home and take care of him. But it will be two hours before the workers from the mica factory return. I touch Peter's forehead again. It is warmer than the bowl I hold in the other hand: the soup he could not drink. This morning the doctor said, "The hospital is full. There is no space."

The room is quiet; it is that part of the afternoon when everything seems to stop, that moment of waiting for the shadows to come out from the walls.

Peter looks at me. The words come slowly between the cracked lips. "Tania . . . when . . . do you think?"

"Soon, Peter. She will come soon."

"I would like a plum."

"It's not the time for plums now, but it won't be too long. Soon we can climb up the steps to the top of the town and look at the popcorn trees. Now, why don't you try to sleep?"

"I won't see anything then."

"You close your eyes and I will tell you things that you will see one morning when you wake up. All right?" He slowly nods his head. "One morning you will open your eyes and you will be in your room. What color was your room?"

"I don't remember."

"Close your eyes and I will make a room for you. Blue. The room will be light blue. And the first thing you will hear will be barking. You open your eyes in the morning and there on the rug is the puppy. His tongue is out and he wags his tail so hard, he shakes all over."

"Does he have a name?"

"He is brown and small, so you call him Peanut. You have a red ball under your pillow that you throw to him. He spins so fast he slides on the rug. You will run out of the house with him and roll down a hill that is all grass. He will chase the red ball." I look at Peter and say, "How do you like that morning?"

He smiles. "Tell me another."

"One morning you will wake up and there will be a bamboo fishing pole. You will go with the puppy down the hill to the river. And the fish will jump right up on the grass and they will be silver with dots of pink and blue tails."

"We will cook them on a fire. I will give the puppy half. Then what?"

"One morning there will be rain outside but you won't mind. There will be cups of hot chocolate and sugar cubes to give to the puppy. You will have a workbench by the window and blocks of white wood. There will be a new knife with a deer hoof for a handle. Sheets of tissue. Red like the ball and blue like the room."

"I know! I will build a plane. The biggest ever. Big enough for the puppy to sit in. I could do it tomorrow. When I feel better. There is some newspaper. I have wood from a box. And the knife. But . . . no rubber bands for the motor."

Suddenly I think of someone. Ilse.

"You wait, Peter. I'll be back."

I step down from his bunk. I look back as I walk away. Peter's eyes do not follow me. Once outside the room, I start to run. Along the corridor of arches, to the kitchen.

I push my head through the open window, into the steaming room. Ilse, her sleeves rolled high on the pink flesh, straightens with a pot, and leaning forward, sets it on the stove.

"Ilse!"

She pushes the wet hair from her eyes and turns to me, her face shining with heat.

"What's the matter, Baby?"

"I need rubber bands. You have to find me rubber bands."

"I'll be damned! Who eats rubber bands?"

She bites her lips, then walks to a man with a bare chest. She puts her arm around his shoulder and whispers something into his ear. He laughs. He scratches his head and calls to another man. They talk, heads together. Ilse comes back.

"It will take a while." She leans on her folded arms on the edge of the open window. "Cabbage and potatoes tonight," she says.

"That's what we had yesterday."

"Did you hear about the girl who jumped from the window?"

"No. Why?"

"Something between girls. I tell you, what a place!"

I nod my head. "You have a piece of bread?"

"Here." She pulls from her pocket a thin slice. I swallow one half and put the other half in my pocket for Mother.

"What's new otherwise?" I say.

"Nothing. Polio quarantine on the barracks next to us. I made myself a skirt from my plaid blanket. I look like an unmade bed in it. I have to go back now."

Ilse fades into the vapor of the kitchen. I lean against the wall and wait. He will be so happy. Why didn't I think of Ilse before? I look down at the yard below and through the open gate I see the dust turning in a gush of wind. I yawn. Soon my night shift again.

"Here you are, Baby."

Ilse's hands are filled with rubber bands. Red, green. I take them, and holding them bunched in one hand, I run back.

Peter's eyes are opened to the ceiling. Slowly he moves his head to me.

"Peter! Guess what I have for you?"

He looks at my hand, my fingers closed over the narrowed circles. "I don't know." His voice is tired.

"Look!" I open my hand. "These come especially for you from Istanbul. That's where they have carpets in the air."

His tongue crosses his lips. He does not say anything.

"Now we can build planes. Take them and put them under your head. And in the morning . . ."

With my hand out to him, I wait. He creases his forehead, the skin tightening on his face. His head rolls loose on the pillow.

"Peter!"

"I can't. . . ."

"You can. . . . They are yours."

"My hands . . . See? . . . I can't move them. . . ."

I see the thin arm lying stiff beside the pile of rubber bands that fall from my hand.

Peter looks up at me and whispers, "Again, please. Tell me another morning."

The White Night

In a column we pass through the gates of the town and the night is over the narrow road. We move toward that stone house with its tall chimney. The air is cold and the stars the only brightness.

The house will be warm, full of soap smell and vapor. If I could only sleep during the day, I would not mind the hours of the night. The twelfth hour of the night is as long as a day. We enter the lights and the warmth, the humming of the machines. Through white steam the other girls run to gather their things.

Eva and I separate from the group and walk to the other house, the quiet one, with hundreds of shelves, filled with clean cloth.

"I like the laundry, Eva. It's white and clean."

"One thing in this town, there is no shortage of dirt."

All night long we will carry the dried laundry in baskets and sort it by number, check it on the list and stack it on the shelves. All night the baskets will be filled and all night emptied, and each basket heavier than the one before. But it is warm in here.

"That flannel shirt is lost. No. 3485. I am sure of it." I talk with my head in the sweater, trying to pull it over my head.

"It might still come in," says Eva and rolls the woolen socks off her feet.

We are naked and put on only a thin work blouse. I sweat already. "You can tell when they are old."

"Flannel shirts?"

"No, the women. By their writing."

"If 3485 is old she won't need a flannel shirt. . . ."

I am proud of my row of shelves, the linen neatly stacked. The torn edges and the loose threads I turn to the back. I don't like to have pieces missing. I don't like it at all.

"Come on, let's go."

We run across the dark courtyard, the cold spreading high along our legs.

"A woman said she will give me her ration of bread," says Eva, "if I take her laundry with me."

"The guards check us sometimes. You know it."

"Still, a ration of bread . . ." she says.

We enter the main hall and find our baskets filled. In back of a machine I see the behind of Ilse round in the air, her head deep in a bucket of suds.

"You crazy? You should wait for the break!"

"I can't. I sleep during my break." And she pours clear water over her hair.

"What are you doing here anyway?"

Ilse is rubbing her head with a towel and shakes the wet hair away from her face. "I work here now. You see, the Bureau of Labor does not know about the kitchen. I am there quite illegally." She picks up the bucket and says, "Amazing, the suds I make, in such a small bucket."

"I think it's lack of imagination with Ilse," says Eva as we walk between the machines.

"What do you mean?"

"She just cannot realize where she is. And look at her! Big and healthy as a horse. I hate her."

"She is nice."

We start to fold the laundry on a large table.

"She is a whore."

I am folding a piece of a flannel cloth. My fingers press to the edge of the crease. Eva did not use to talk like this. I am glad Mother is not here to hear us talk. I pretend I am not shocked and look up to her.

"She is pretty and she likes men."

Eva strikes a towel flat across the table and her eyes when they are angry are green as old coins I used to save.

"Listen," she says. "We are not children any more. This is a big problem."

"What is a problem?"

"You know . . . that we didn't have . . . intercourse. And now there's Ivan. You will have to decide pretty soon. . . . Don't forget where we are. Things are different here. Don't forget that."

I don't want to talk about it. It is like something I want to keep separate. I think of Ivan. It was Ilse who introduced me to him. It already seems like a long time since we met and fell in love. It's been three weeks now. . . .

. . . We climbed the old steps to that high space of green, sometimes pretending the walls below were not there, saying, "Shall we take a walk in the fields?" Looking beyond the walls at the square fields. Bright colors swinging on the high stalks of barley. The land wide as two arms opened . . . To lie down beside him where he first kissed me and it was the first time I had been kissed. I did not tell him that. I did not know what I was supposed to do with his tongue. The searching in my mouth. My whole body strange to me, as if searched too by that tongue. And feeling warm from below my belly, I pushed him away, pushing away the hardness I never felt before, and afraid of his hands that shook and not knowing but being afraid of it. . . .

Eva is checking on her list the number of laundered pieces. She looks up at me, tapping her teeth with a pencil.

"I think I am going to do it. Sooner or later. There is nothing really wrong in it." She looks at me as if she asked consent.

If we had stayed in the city, how different she would be. Sometimes I walk through the town and feel the urgency of all the people, as if they have to hurry before time runs out, to live more by living faster. The coupled shadows in the evening, the exchange of bread for love, a new affair beginning on the leftovers of the old one. How strange that I already see it this way! Is that why Mother said the other day, "You are growing up"?

"You are free, Eva," I say.

"Free, ha!"

I lean over to her, with the table between us. "If I don't do what *they* are doing, then I am free. They pretend we are leading a normal life here. They even get married by the Council of the Elders. Children are born. I think you can even get a divorce. And every week a thousand are sent who knows where and another thousand come to fill the space. We do not have a normal life and I am not going to pretend we do. I am not going to do it with Ivan. Not here. I have nothing to hold on to any more. But I still have that."

"There is a song about that," laughs Eva.

"Maybe. I don't know the song."

We carry the next basket in silence. Eva is afraid she will lose her man. Maybe to Ilse. She lost the one before. The men here don't wait. They come and they take. There is plenty to take and there is not much time. Sometimes I think I hate men. But it is only because I fear them. I see them strong: working in the kitchen, working in the streets. Their bodies hard from work, as they bend above a shovel, the muscles tightening along their arms. Sometimes I want to touch them, to put my hand on the muscle, brown from sun.

During the break we lie down on one of the tables and Eva sleeps. She says something in her sleep that I do not understand. I do not understand her often when she is awake. Ilse says Eva thinks too much; when Eva thinks it is as if she were going to be sick, or had a splinter under her thumbnail. Eva lies straight on the table and that is the way she lives: straight. In all the crooked streets of this town, Eva lives on one straight chalked-out white line. She has drawn it herself and straight it runs and I cannot think of anything that could make her step to one side. Not even a piece of bread. Eva wakes, blinks at me, and says: "You know? I love him. We will get married after it's over. And maybe you are right. I should wait."

I jump down from the table and take Eva by the hand. "Let's take a bath."

We run across the courtyard, through the first light, laughing, passing a uniform and not slowing down. The light is green on the stones, a changed sky is over the town: down there, the town with its bunks, its fleas and its love.

We find a bucket and sit deep in warm water full of light suds. Back in that town, we will have a pot of black coffee and a few hours of sleep. And maybe Ivan will come.

The Window

When was it that we started to hear the hammering? Nobody said anything about it.

It is morning now. The room is the same. This long room, where each space is filled with a body. The old women with cups in their hands, the gray hair falling over the cup as the faces bend down to suck at that dark liquid. A little blond boy sits on the floor, a book of colored pictures spread over his open knees, and the saliva runs down his chin. The young women, their faces white, moving here and there like strange birds between the cages of bunks.

I walk to the window and look across the small square, toward the stone wall. It is in there.

"You know you are not supposed to be at the window today!"

"You will get us all into trouble," says another woman.

I press my head to the window pane. "We are already in trouble."

"Do you see anything?"

"They are coming," I say in a whisper.

"What?"

"They are coming. . . ."

The room is silent now behind my back. And they come, slowly. They are eight men. Most of them young.

"What are they doing?"

"They walk. What do you want them to do? With their heads down."

"Shh . . ." comes from across the room, as if to listen to their footsteps.

"How many guards?"

"More than ten."

And I try to imagine how it must feel to walk down there. In that deserted street. Walking toward that big wall.

"Where are they now?"

"They passed the big chestnut tree."

. . . Perhaps they are not afraid. . . . I am sure they are not afraid, but what does it matter? . . . What do they think, these men, walking with their heads down . . . as they are ordered to . . . ? Do they think of what they had, of what they will never have . . . ? And which is worse . . . ?

"Poor boys!" says a woman and blows her nose.

. . . It is this feeling of being alone. Already they do not belong anywhere but to this street. Nothing exists but the wall and the little door that will lead them behind the wall. The world is contained in this square. . . .

"Where are they now?"

"The door is open. They walk through the little door."

And sun, fast light in the black hair of the last man—the door closes.

"Are they in?"

"Yes . . . they are in."

Nothing moves in the street, but the leaves and the yellow light shifting from branch to branch.

The glass is cool on my forehead. I don't want to think about it. But the picture opens in my mind. The neck in the rope. The ground hinging away. The feet running in air. Then, while the legs swing slowly, the head hangs loose. And the bodies are longer.

"What time is it?" says a voice.

It seems that I have always been standing here. Waiting for something. I will leave the window now. Everything will be the same. We will wait for the soup and in the evening the couples will kiss under the arched windows. Nothing is changed. But for the eight men who do not need anything any more. The door opens now. The guards. They carry clothes.

"You see something?"

"It's nothing. Clothes. Empty clothes."

I turn my back to the window. I look at the small boy and his book. He turns the page to a white goose with a blue cap and a red, red muffler.

The Attic

It is evening in the attic room. The girls call it the mansard. I remember from the schoolbooks, Mr. Mansard, a Frenchman, who first built rooms under the roofs of Paris. I think of ivy-covered walls that overhang old houses, of squares of glass containing the last sun. Here, under the slanted ceiling, mattresses on the floor, no space between them. We moved up here weeks ago and left the rooms below to the older ones. It is hot by day under the metal roof and cold at night, but we are all young.

Ilse sits on her mattress, filing her nails. Where did she get the file? There are many things I wonder about Ilse. How can she keep looking so good? Maybe having lived in the country makes her stronger and healthier.

"I am going to stay in tonight," says Ilse and bites off a cuticle.

"What happened?"

She lies down, the blond hair spread out on the dirty laundry covering a suitcase.

"Oh, I have two dates and I can't decide which I should take."

"Can I borrow your comb, Ilse?"

She hands it to me, and lifting the corner of her mattress she pulls out a cube of sugar. I watch her. Sugar.

"Besides, the guy I like is waiting out there behind the nut house and that's too far." She sucks the sugar, pushing it out with her tongue and drawing it in again. "And how is my baby?" She leans over and pats my back. I hate to be called "Baby."

The voices of the other girls are loud and there is laughter from one corner. Someone is telling a dirty joke. What else is there to laugh about? But I know if I stood up now and went to the corner to listen, Ilse would pull me back. "That's not for you, Baby," she would say. "You stay clean . . . out of it."

"Why don't you be sick tomorrow, Baby? You work too hard," says Ilse.

"And let that horrible doctor check me all over with his filthy hands? That's what he did last time and all I had was a sore throat."

"Oh, he is a bastard all right."

There are many ways to pretend to be sick—rubbing the thermometer with the tongue or putting a finger in the throat, just before he comes, then vomiting on the floor. But it is too much trouble. Everything is too much trouble these days.

Ilse is singing now ". . . Paris is lovely by dawn; Paris is lovely by night; come to me my sweetheart; I will hold you tight. . . ." She lifts the corner of her mattress. "Here. Finish this sugar. The ants will get it anyway." She throws me the remaining cubes, gray with dirt, and I put them two at a time into my mouth.

"How is the kitchen?"

"Fine. The guys I work with are nice."

Everyone is happy to work in the kitchen because of the food.

"When I think I am wasting my best years here. Can you imagine? The best years . . ." She picks up the candle and the light brightens in her eyes as she lights a cigarette. Nobody has cigarettes here.

"You know, Baby . . . I think I was born at the wrong time. I always wanted to be a courtesan . . . say in France, 1890-something. Imagine, having all the men you want, and horses, and going to the opera, not that I care for operas, and all the men . . . Oh, my God, and they put you in one of those mansions and all you have to do is be pretty and make love to them. . . . It's funny, I can make love every day and I don't know, I just like it. . . . You don't understand

and I would not let a guy put a finger on you, but just think, where would we be without men and all you have to do is be just a little smarter than they are . . . and, oh, I don't know, life could be wonderful, just wonderful—except of course for the crap we are now in. . . ."

I look at her—this is the longest speech I ever heard her make. I turn to see if Eva is listening. But she is still writing that letter to her boyfriend in the next barracks.

With all the candles warming the room, I have the feeling of being at home. Home. What is home? I try to remember the color of our dining-room walls and I can't. But suddenly I can see the chandelier covered with green silk, fringes hanging loose and at each step the fringes moving and how Mother would hide the fudge there, right inside the chandelier, but we knew about it and just pretended we did not. . . .

". . . That's when I would have lived. Really lived." Ilse laughs. "Ostrich feathers all over. And you . . . go to sleep now."

I push my feet down under the cover, keeping my toes curled up, not to rip the thin blanket with my nails. Eva is still writing, Ilse is suddenly silent. I hear the other voices go out in the four directions of the room; the candles flatten.

"It stinks here and I am too warm." I hear Ilse's voice and another cover falls across my back. The new warmth spreads slowly over my body.

"Thanks."

"Shut up, Baby."

I hear the crackle of straw as she turns on the mattress. I fall asleep and dream of women in ostrich feathers, eating the dark brown fudge.

The Carnival

One day on the square they start to build a platform with three steps to it. And a large roof above. In one corner of the square they erect poles to hold swings and dump a pile of fresh sand, yellow and clean. There is a slide too. I try to imagine the children playing there.

In the evening we read the notices posted on each corner of the streets. A speech is given by the Elder of each barracks. We are going to have visitors. Everything will be spotless, in order. If questions are asked by them—about food, quarters—they count upon our co-operation. A list of punishments is read to us, starting with no portions of bread and ending with imprisonment.

Next day in the town there are the paper flowers stuck on the window sills. Passing shops, I see that the blankets no longer cover the windows. The people and their mattresses are gone. The windows are bright now with cardboard salamis, jars of mustard, shiny black coats and clean, thick blankets. Money is distributed to us—play money; it is very small, the paper thin. We can go and buy now whatever we want. Except for the mustard and the old clothes, there is nothing to buy. But we do look more prosperous.

On the square, some of the children are high on the swings, their thin legs kicking the air. Sitting in the sand, the other children hold red buckets tight between their knees. The sand sifts from their fingers and into the buckets, and once in a while they look up at those flying on the swings. On the platform, an orchestra practicing a march. After the march comes a round waltz.

The visitors arrive. Led by the green uniforms, they are shown the town. On a corner of a street Eva and I stand, watching them.

"Where do you think they are from?"

"Switzerland, I'm sure." Eva's voice is low; she hisses the *S*. "Look at the hats. And flowers yet. The bitches."

Yes, there are women too, in light summer suits, each with a flower pinned to her shoulder. They walk through the streets with long strides, their feet large in flat shoes.

"They should have a flag in their hands," I say.

The men bulge in their gray suits and walk in step. I imagine them sitting on a weekend, by a lake or on top of a mountain, saying: "My dear, let me tell you, it was spotless, absolutely spotless. The children . . . well, a little bit thin, but you know how children are, they grow so fast. . . . Yes, another schnapps please. . . . Anyhow, as I was saying, no luxuries, but good simple food . . . Yes, we did look into that other matter, but who are we to judge . . . ?"

So they pat the heads of the children, saying, "Isn't he cute?"; they look into our barracks and find them clean; into the prison and find the prisoners polite and well. They visit the various working places—and when they come in, there is a distribution of bread. God bless them, I say. And then they sit for a while in the late-afternoon sun and listen to the waltzes played by the band.

They go to the commandant's house for dinner. Later, we see them come out. They stand on the steps. Hands are shaken, there are some low bows, heels are clicked, friendly words are exchanged. It seems to take a long time. They leave.

As we walk through the darkened square, Eva points her finger. "Look . . ."

There, men are already at work, tearing down the swings and loading the sand on a truck.

And I wonder . . . how did they ever get the red buckets out of the children's hands?

The Scar

Karel arrives late in the summer. It is a long time since I have seen my brother. The day of his arrival Mother makes a small celebration on the bench in front of her bunk. She pulls from her suitcase an old matchbox and from it she takes out a rolled piece of tissue paper. We watch the unrolling in silence. Father leans forward; Karel sits with hands in his pockets, the long legs stretched under a bunk. With a proud smile Mother holds out her hand: on the creased paper the black heap of crumbled dry leaves and stems; a half handful of tea. The last.

"I was saving it all this time. I knew Karel would come one day." She bends above Karel, looking down at him.

Karel leans to her and kisses her. "You did not change, Mother. I must still be your favorite son."

"Maybe I did not change. But you . . . you have grown so much, you have grown . . . oh, my God . . ."

"Sure he has grown, Mama, that's good," Father says. "At his age, you know, they . . . never keep any fat on them."

"I will get the hot water," I say and walk out with a pot in my hand.

Outside the room I stop and lean, with the pot pressing into my chest, against a wall. That is my brother, that tall, thin man in the room; the face gaunt under the brown skin. He has the tan of a man of leisure with the hands of an old laborer. Even his voice has changed; it is deeper and he talks very low, almost in a whisper. I kick at the wall and then walk toward the kitchen.

The tea made, we raise our tin cups with the steaming liquid and make a toast: To Karel and us! May we all stay together from now on! Karel looks at all of us, as if to remember our faces. We ask him several times to tell us about the time he was away, but he says, "There is not much to say. It was just a camp. Like any other."

Father leads Karel into his barracks; there is an empty bunk in his room where Karel can live from now on.

Next day I walk into Father's room and find Karel washing himself in a bucket of water. He does not see me. I see the scar on the right side of that lean back, the deep line, hollow, purple, the edges of the skin red in uneven knots. A second scar, smaller, running down from the back of his neck. I back out of the room and run into Father.

"Came to visit?" Father puts his hand on my shoulder.

"Yes. It's my day off."

"We have to wait till Karel finishes with his toilet. My own son! Won't go with me in the washroom and I have to leave the room when he washes himself."

"He was always shy," I say.

Later I walk with Karel in the streets, showing him the town.

"You see, at first there were people living here. They had houses and shops and worked on the land. Then they had to evacuate the town for us. Sometimes I think of how they must hate us."

"They can always come back after the war," says Karel. "Houses and fields, they don't change."

"All the barracks have names of big towns. The black one there, that's where the Council of Elders is. They do everything there. They are the bridge between us and the green ones. They marry you and take you off the files when you die. They also send the notices . . . to the ones that are going to be sent away."

"How often do the transports leave?"

"It changes. Right now, very often. Two, three times a month. You will see how the town changes when it is known that they are preparing a transport. Everybody waits. And you are sorry for the ones that are selected and glad it was not you, this time again."

"Where are they sent?"

"Nobody knows."

We sit down on a pile of freshly cut wood planks, behind the barracks with iron bars over the windows.

"Prison?"

"No. Asylum. I did not know there were so many insane people. They come here from all over the country."

"And some went insane here?"

"Well . . . yes."

"Listen, do you remember what I once told you?"

"About what?" I turn to him.

"About God. I cannot believe in God. If there is a God, it is the chemical in your cells. The stuff that holds life together. And sometimes, like when you are hungry or something hurts you very much—imagine I take a knife and—well, there is nothing left inside you. God leaks out. The cells break. Just pain or hunger is left and no space for God."

"Do you remember, Karel, that summer in the scout camp?"

"Yes. That was a long time ago."

"You were so sick there, you had fever, and I was so scared because we were so far from home and I really prayed. It's silly. I thought you would die."

"What does it prove?"

"Well, you did not die. That's all."

A sound above us now. We look up. A face behind the iron bars, white in the dark of a room. I cannot tell if it is a man or a woman. They have their heads shaven in there. The face with the tongue stuck out at us, the fingers moving like butterflies, the thumb attached to the nose. We look away.

"How was it with Grandma?"

"Fast."

"That's good." He nods his head.

"When she came, she was so happy to be with us again. But they did not let her live in our barracks and they put her into a special one for old people. She was very angry about it. But you know how she used to be, always doing something and never sitting still. She brought with her a lot of provisions and a small alcohol stove that was not bigger than a matchbox. She would prepare a soup out of dry vegetables and we would go there in the evenings and she served us what she had cooked. She never said much about what she did after we left. Only that she spent a lot of time in the Park of Roses with Nora and she would tell us about the old people she met there. And how she had to give Nora away before she left. I don't think she was unhappy. But then she seemed to be getting confused about what was happening. And she ran out of her supplies."

"Poor Grandma."

"That was about two months after she came here. We were there in the afternoon, sitting by the window and talking. We ate the last soup. And during the night she died."

"Remember how we used to steal her chocolates?" says Karel.

"Yes, I remember. She would lock the drawer, the middle one in the brown chest of drawers . . ."

"And we would pull out the drawer above and reach in . . ."

"... And the chocolate would slowly melt into a sweet liquid, thick on our tongues."

Karel's body bends low; he coughs, his face redder. He spits under his foot.

"Let's go home," I say. "It's getting cold."

"Yes, let's go. Home!" And he spits again, in a large half circle.

Karel has to leave again. He is selected with two thousand others. This time the ones that have to go are all young. Ivan must go too. And Ilse.

Ilse sits on the floor, packing her suitcase. "Well, Baby, don't cry. That's life. You get settled in one place, you get warm, and then all of a sudden ... off you go."

"Maybe ... it will be better ... where you go," I say between sobs.

"Sure. Hey, your brother is going too, isn't he?"

At the sound of the word "brother" I burst out crying. "I want to go too, Ilse, I want to go."

"Don't be silly, Baby. You just stay right where you are. I am going to take care of Karel anyway, so you have nothing to worry about."

The thought comforts me. I know she will always have food. "You promise?"

"What?"

"To take care of him. He is so thin."

"Yes. I promise. Remember, where there are men, there is hope. That's my motto."

I think of Ivan. How he kissed me for the last time and said that he wants to marry me after it's all over and not to worry, everything will be fine and we will find each other again.

We spend the last evening with Karel. Father saying, "You write to us." Mother wrapping a ration of bread in a piece of white cloth. . . . She holds it on her knees and keeps smoothing the wrinkles. And I, just looking at him, seeing him changed again, the absent one, the one I will try to remember again. . . . How did he look when he was sitting here?

The stone yard between the barracks holds them in the early morning. I see Karel in the second row, the collar of his coat pulled up high on his neck. On their heads the first sun shines like water. The overcoats are gray and the feet shift in the dust, like the feet of impatient children in a schoolyard.

The soldiers count them. They speak in numbers. The loud voices reach the open arch where I stand. The men turn their faces. The overcoats move, the split hems flap. I see the dark hand of Karel move twice in the air and the hand drops.

Winter comes again with the streets of the town soft with snow. Sinking powder, hard crust, slush. The deep tracks fill, melt, go gray into stone. The last ice breaks under our shoes, opens and floats with the dust settling and the town regains its color of darkness.

The evenings long in the close-breathing room and the nights filled with coughs and the steady but distant murmur of the ones with fever. Ilse's place vacant. The barracks colder and the soup thinner. The voices louder. And spring comes. With the spring there is mud where snow was, typhus and polio instead of pneumonia.

It is in the early days of spring that the first mail arrives. The barracks loud with Did you get one? . . . Where is it from? . . .

What is the date? . . . All the postcards are the same; no stamps on them and all dated the same day.

A postcard from Karel, saying, “Keep your head up. Am thinking of you. Karel.” And the date, in very small writing, as if his hand shook. “March the 15th.”

That night I pray. Whispering to myself the old prayer, in Hebrew first, and, after I finish, continuing the translation as I learned it from the black book: *Shma yisroel adonoy elohenu adonoy echod . . . Boruch shem kvod malchuso l'olom voed:* Hear, O Israel, the Lord our God, the Lord is One. Praised be His name whose glorious kingdom is for ever and ever.

And I add: Thank you, my God. For letting him live and write to us. On that March 15.

The Long Train

And then there is the morning—always the early morning—the third day and the flashlight on my face. On the morning of the third day after the numbers are posted, I light the candle, fold my blanket and pick up my valise by the rope handle. In the attic the others snore loudly, pretending sleep. There are two of us from the attic: Eva and me. At the door each of us waits for the other to open and go first. I cannot understand the feeling, the need to stay. This is not my home; what more is there to fear in another room?

I look back in the room to the single light. A stub of candle stuck in the round pool of solid wax; the candle leans but its flame is straight. Nothing left under the mattress, no blankets hanging from the galleries, no wind moving the first leaves, no heat left in the stones of the street tilting down empty blocks to the gate of the town.

Before the gate we stand in deep rows. Father is on one side of me, Mother on the other, Eva is in another row. The guards count us; we are checked off on a list. Hinges bend in and the gate of our town opens. Outside we are on a road with the town going down below the hill. The trees move back beside the road. The trees have been cut at the top so they bush out in new green.

Below the hill the cattle cars are linked together. The cars have small windows, high and barred. A hand under each elbow boosts us up into our car, our bundles and bags are thrown in after us. I see Eva being pushed into another car. The doors roll together and a piece of wood is nailed over the window.

Soon the car jolts, the wheels grind, the couplings squeal and strain, and the long train pulls taut and carries us away. I sit very close to Father, who has one arm around me, the other around

Mother. With the slow movement of the train we lean together, our shoulders touching. Some light comes in through the cracks in the wood, and the edges of wind.

Now there is only now. There is the train, there is the motion, there is the dry tongue swelling in my mouth. I am not thirsty but my mouth is dry. I would like to say something, but there is nothing to say. There is only the feeling: Something is wrong, a mistake has been made.

The steady sound of iron wheels; hours pass. Sometimes the door is opened and we are given water or a piece of bread, and sometimes it is daylight outside and sometimes night. . . . My head spinning with the wheels: the sleep, the waking and from somewhere the soft murmur of a prayer or the crying of what could be a child but is a man.

The figures on the floor, sitting close as in a gathering, without room to stretch their legs. The women and their trips to the bucket in the corner. The men trying to find words to displace their fear. One old man starts to sing a song about a plum orchard and we all sing with him. As we finish, a woman starts to cry. And their words come, always the same: . . . If we just knew . . . what is going to happen . . . nothing . . . another camp . . . the war will be over . . . a year . . . never . . . no . . . yes . . . Mama, piece of bread . . . no bread . . . my belly . . . God eternal are You. . . . The bucket is full. . . .

The stories turn in my mind: trains that stop in the middle of nothing and there are woods and they lead you there and shoot you and then they walk back to the empty cars. . . . Perhaps if I pretend to be dead they will forget me there, lying under a tree. . . . I must tell this to Father; the first shot and we should all fall down. . . . I cannot keep my eyes shut without fluttering my eyelids; oh, my God, I don't want to, you cannot do that, you cannot, you cannot. . . .

Mother's lips when I kiss her feel very dry. It makes me cry. She rocks me in her arms and says, "Shh, shh . . . You know, Karel will be waiting for us." And Father says, "Yes, Karel."

Suddenly I find myself thinking about the outside. There is a whole world outside somewhere. The round globe turns under the white finger of my history teacher; mostly blue, so much water in the world, but there are lands too. And people. They don't know about this. About me sitting here. And where *do* we go? All those countries she used to talk about. To think that all those people . . . they just don't know. . . . Why doesn't somebody tell them? But then, how could they believe it?

The train stops. I hear the shouting of many voices and the doors open to strange men. They jump into our car and their heads are shaven and their bodies covered with a gray cloth striped blue. They take all the luggage away from us. We step out of the cars.

The sun is gone. I did not know it was night outside. I cannot see anything, but in the distance there is a great square of high lights, like many towers, wide as the night. There is a pattern to the lights and to the darker shadows below them. We walk toward the lights. The dark we carried inside the cars is spread over the land. The ground turns and I space my steps wide against that motion—but it is not the ground—the shaking of boxcars and turning of wheels is in my body now.

It is only now that I see the wire. Through a gate we walk into a square of wire, four towers and lights that move, slanting off the roofs of wooden barracks. We enter the first square, follow a road. Wire along the road. We come out to enter another square. And so we move through the night, crossing from one camp to another.

And I tell myself, Maybe they will put us on another train; we are only going to walk through here. I don't know why, but as long as we don't stop we will be all right. I want to walk, walk out of here, I don't want to stay. Oh, please, just keep walking, whoever you are that is leading us, keep going, go. . . .

The column stops. We are in the middle of a camp. We are counted again. Men separated. I am so tired. Mother's hand shakes in mine. In the barracks, bunks without mattresses. I lie down beside Mother.

"Mama, where are we?"

"I heard. This is ____."

"Is it . . . bad?"

"I don't know. But it is big, so big. . . ."

"We will find Karel tomorrow, Mama."

I see Mother smile; she looks almost happy. "Yes, tomorrow we are going to find Karel. I know he is here. I feel it. My son."

Mother falls asleep before I do and I listen to her regular breathing.

My last thought is . . . I forgot to ask her if she saw that big chimney. The flames at the top, in the familiar darkness.

3

The garden was set outside the wire, behind the Administration Building, between a road and a railway track. The road ran straight to a guarded gate; the rails curved in, split from a switch in the distance, to enter the camp. The spur line ended inside the wire, behind two squat stone houses. Beyond the two houses rose the chimney. Its shadow at sunset touched barracks a mile away.

In the garden the begonias were turning yellow. The pink had disappeared altogether, but the blooms were consistent. The peppermoths rose above the bushes. The black mutant was increasing now that the few birds, still circling in the sky, could not spot them on the sooty leaves.

The garden path ended at a high mesh fence. Beyond the garden, inside the walls of electric wires, as far as eyes could see, the landscape of a thousand roofs. Each block had its shared boundary of wire, watchtowers set at the corners of blocks. Every square neighbored with an identical square, except for those along the perimeter, protected from the outside by a doubled fence. Each measured view of the sky was the same; flat beneath the lowered sky, the many barracks were without conflicting color and no roof rose higher than another.

Beginning of another day: Fingers whisking his dove-gray breeches, the commandant strode between rows of begonias. The compact blooms stood high as his buckle, dull color of brass. An orderly walked with a broom two paces back of the commandant. The commandant half-faced, brought his heels together; his eyes fixed a pale-yellow bloom dangling from a stem longer than the rest. He drew from the belt of his tunic the chrome-bright shears. The left hand, taut in the black glove, flicked the opened blades. The flower fell to the gravel. The orderly swept the cut stalk into a dustbin.

The commandant glanced over the level line of roofs to the lifted shaft of bricks. The smoke twisted away from its top, and from time to time an orange flame pushed through the smoke. The chimney seemed to sway above the straight and quiet city.

Seven-twenty . . . *Turned about and walked back, toward the single, two-story building. The gravel spurted from under his fitted boots. A peppermoth, breaking from a bush, tossed above the shaking leaves. He stopped, tipped forward, slapping the air behind the black wings of the moth. In a sky drifting with soot he saw the moth grow small in the covering color of smoke.*

Seven-twenty-five . . . *Closed the door of the building behind him. Inside his office he went to a desk, removed his cap and pulled the gloves from his fingers. The shears he placed beside a pile of stacked files. He looked once at the clock set in the belly of a bronze Venus. His eyes rested on a frame with a picture in it. The photo was inscribed: "To Our Beloved Father, From His Family.* STRENGTH IN YOUR TASK."

Seven-thirty-five . . . *Began marking the files with a purple stamp:* CANCELLED. *Another stamp lay at a corner of his desk. When pressed upon a file, it read:* TRANSFERRED. *He did not use it very often. It was the job of the doctor-major to select the ones for a transfer. Recently the doctor had complained that it was getting harder to find, among the inmates, people able to perform good work; he had tried to convince the commandant that the transferred inmates, sent to a labor camp, must represent this camp as delegates.*

Seven-forty-five . . . *Looked again at the clock and compared it with his watch. There was a busy day ahead, one hundred barracks to clear. He calculated on his adding machine. Seventeen hours of steady work for the first stage. But he was right on schedule.*

The commandant leaned back in his chair and lit a cigarette. It was simpler when the train went directly in front of the chimney. There was not the bother with temporary housing. But he had to wait for orders. The idea of inaugurating a six-month plan in some of the blocks was a waste of time and provisions. When the last six-month plan ran out, he disposed of the two thousand the same night of the sixth anniversary. In the morning he received a telegram to select the able ones and send them into one of the major cities for work. It was too late and he had to write a long explanatory letter, suggesting a selection among the latest hundred thousand. But they understood and did not hold it against him. He was more careful after that. Waited one more day.

The phone rang. The doctor. Yes, he knew that the doctor was unhappy. That he did not have much time now for his experiments. No, he had no idea when the next train with some gypsies would arrive. Or twins. The commandant understood, but lately there were too many major assignments.

A knock on the door. The sergeant major. Eight o'clock on the dot. The commandant handed him the barracks list. He reminded him that today, before igniting the burners, he had better clean the gas jets. The doctor had complained and the commandant had posted a sign there: FOR SANITATION PREVENT ACCUMULATION. *He repeated his new slogan for the sergeant. The sergeant saluted and went out.*

The commandant lit another cigarette and continued stamping the files. It was an easy job at the beginning. Keep the population within housing capacity. Now, three years later, the trains kept coming every day and almost every night. An annex holding an additional hundred thousand was built to the main camp. The commandant reached to the radio and flipped a switch.

Trucks, a red cross on their sides, came down the road. The rattling of the sulfuric drums ceased as the trucks stopped at the gate.

From the commandant's office the notes of slow music came to the guards stiff inside the sentry boxes. The air was darker now and a thin sifting of soot settled on the straight, dry road.

The Rule

"Let's just ask somebody."

"Yes, Mother."

There is mud on the road that divides the long rows of barracks. The air cools and the gray fog shifts over the road. Above the roofs and the fog, the watchtower—the searchlight turned off.

We are seen by those we cannot see. All I can see is this road and the barracks and the wire. The men and the women, one like the other in the gray drift. The stripes they wear, fog color and blue, make them part of the weather. But I don't want to look at them. They do not look like us. What is it? And there are so many walking, each across the other's tracks. The air is quiet around the groups that stand.

A man stands alone by the side of a barracks, the striped clothes loose around his body, his arms folded under the jacket.

"Could you please tell us something?"

He looks at us with eyes blue, moving under water.

"You from last night?"

"Yes. You see we would like to know . . . that is if you by any chance happen to know . . . my brother . . . Karel . . . if he is here."

His back slides down the rough wood. He sits, legs stretched wide open. The skin of his head dark with roots of hair, the skin of his face pulled to cover the bones that seem to be growing in that head. He draws a fist out from under the jacket and wipes his eyes.

"That depends."

"What do you mean?"

"Well, you see, it depends: *When* did he come here? Time. It's all a matter of time."

Mother takes a sharp breath as always when she is excited and her head bends down to him. The words are pushed out, falling over one another. "September. He left us in September. And he is here somewhere. Could you help us?"

He rubs his eyes again, and looking at me with a smile, he says, "September, eh?"

"We told you already. Yes, September."

"I will tell you where he is all right. And all the rest of them." He stands up and leads us to the corner of the barracks.

"You see back there . . . far over there . . . that big chimney?"

"Does he work there? Is it a factory?" Mother waves the fog away with her hand.

"No. But that's where he went all right. Yes, sir, right in there. That is, if he came in September, as you say. You see, we have a nice little place here, ladies, very, very nice."

He chuckles and walks back to where he sat before. I take Mother's hand in mine. All I want to do now is go away from this man. He is insane. But Mother shakes my hand loose and it is the shoulder of the man she holds now.

"Could you explain . . . ?"

He wraps his arm in the jacket again and for a while does not answer.

"You make me laugh, you new ones. Always the same."

There is a wet stain on the jacket, where he wipes the water from his face. "Explain . . . always explain. And it is so simple. Look here. We have that big chimney. I showed it to you. All right?"

We both nod our heads.

"Now, you come here, you stay six months, and don't ask me why six months, I don't know. It's a rule. And after the sixth month is over, they take you out of here. I have three more months to go. You still have full time. You just started. Now is that clear?"

"No, it isn't clear!" I am shouting at him now and all the time I feel like when I was a child and was so afraid at night of the black in the room and if I just kept my eyes closed it would not be so bad, but I *had* to open them, to *see* the dark, to *know,* and all the time the fear, and all the time the need for it.

"Ha, ha. Always the same, you new ones. Just don't want to understand. Just don't want to, that's all."

Mother tries a different tone now on him. "Now, you said something about the chimney and then the six months. That they take you out of here. Could you please tell us: to go *where?*"

"Well, in the chimney, of course. They kill you there. Not in the chimney. No. In the little house with gas. It's very modern here. In the chimney they burn you."

I don't know when Mother sat down; she is sitting now by my feet, her back is warming my legs and it is very agreeable. I have cold feet. I am cold. She has both hands over her knees, rocking herself gently. How young she looks. . . . How old is she? . . . There is no sound from her, just the rocking.

"Well, I better go now. Anyway, you're lucky to be here. Six months. The other camps here don't have it. Hey, you don't happen to have a piece of bread for me? For the service?"

He is standing up and Mother also, and she tries to say something. "When . . . ?"

"When? The seventh of March. Remember it like today. I always remember the dates. I used to write it down before. I don't have a pencil any more but I remember. Just tell me when they came and I'll tell you when they went."

He slowly walks away, the elbow lifted to his eyes. He then bends down to do something to his shoe. Mother is hanging on my arm, pulling me. There are rounds of perspiration between the lines of her forehead.

"It is not true, Tania! It is not true! The postcard! See?" She laughs. "Tell him. That he wrote it on the fifteenth . . . So he couldn't . . ."

We run after the man. He turns to our footsteps.

"It couldn't be! We got a postcard from him. *After* that!"

"What, the date? Lady, they *always* make you postdate. That's a rule."

He continues walking; then the blue, watery eyes turn to us once more, in the middle of the muddy road, and he says, "You get used to it. You will see."

The Small Room

I sit on my bunk. I don't think about anything. Mother is somewhere outside. Eva's bunk is vacant. The others sit, or their narrow shapes lie under the thin covers. I would like to work. Or do something. Anything. I cannot just sit here and wait for six months. I don't know any more if I want the time to go fast or slow. I don't want anything very badly any more. Except food. I would like to eat. I wonder if they give you more food the last day.

I see Eva running through the open door; her face is red.

"Tania, Tania . . ."

"What?" I let my head roll over the edge of the bunk and look down at her.

"Come down! I have something to tell you. Unbelievable."

I step down the ladder and pick up my shoes. I sit down on the lower bunk and slowly slide one foot into a shoe, then the other.

"So, what's the news?"

"Come outside. I can't here. Hurry up!"

She takes me by the hand and we walk outside and turn the corner of the barracks. Her eyes wide, she brings her face close to mine.

"I saw Ilse!"

"Ilse! She is dead, Ilse!"

"I saw her. I am telling you. . . ."

I take her by the shoulders and shake her hard, her chin striking her chest. "She is dead! How could you!"

She moves out from my hands. "Sit down."

We both sit down and lean on the barracks. I don't feel very good.

"Listen. I saw her. Walking in the middle of the road. There was a man with her, a prisoner, but his clothes were clean. I noticed that. He must be somebody, an Elder maybe. And I heard her laugh. It's Ilse. Nobody laughs like her, you know that."

"But if she is here . . . maybe some of the others . . ."

"I couldn't make myself go to her. I was afraid. You understand?"

"Yes. We have to find her. . . . We have to talk to her. Right now. Let's go."

How easy it is to find her. The first person we meet, we ask her name. Yes, the last barracks. There is a girl leaning outside, her eyes following us.

"What do you want?"

"We want to talk to Ilse."

"What's your name?"

"Just tell her Tania and Eva."

"I'll see if she is not busy."

When she leaves, Eva starts to laugh. "I'll see if she is not busy. Did you hear that? Who does she think she is, a secretary?"

A door slams somewhere and Ilse stands in front of us. We don't say anything, just look at her. She is quiet too. Then she turns to the girl and says, "Get out!" The girl goes.

"Come in."

She opens a little door inside the barracks and we enter a small room with one large bunk. There is a small alcohol burner under the window. Ilse sits down on the bunk and spreads her hands on both sides of her.

"All right. Here I am! I know I am not supposed to be here, but I am. Touch me! I am here!" I never heard her shouting before.

"Why do you stand there, both of you? Oh, my God!" Suddenly she bends over and, hands over her face, she cries.

In two steps I am by her and, sliding down to the floor, I hold her knees. "Don't, Ilse! Stop it!"

"Do you mind?" Eva is holding a pack of cigarettes.

Ilse straightens, jumps to her feet. "No, go ahead." She looks as if nothing has happened. "Where is my head? You are hungry. Where the hell did he put that bread? Here it is." She holds a loaf of bread in her hands.

"Don't bother with the knife," says Eva. "Just break it in half."

"Shut up!" says Ilse. With a knife, she cuts the bread in two pieces, giving one half to each of us. My teeth sink deep in the bread and for a while there is only the sound of biting and swallowing. I put a chunk in my pocket for Mother.

"How did you do it?" Eva sits down on the floor, letting the smoke roll out of her mouth. There are some crumbs on her chin.

"Listen. There is just one thing I want you to know. He is not a green one. He is just like us. He is a prisoner himself, only he has some sort of a position because he has been here for a long time already. He managed to do it for me. That's all."

"Ilse . . . you couldn't . . . I mean you couldn't do anything for . . . one of them? Karel?"

"No. It was not possible. You have to believe me, Tania."

"Yes. I know."

"He would come here every evening. I gave him each night a ration of bread. I told you I would take care of him, didn't I?"

"How was it for them? Did he know?"

"Listen, Baby. It's all over now."

"Yes, that's true."

"Anyway, next time I go too. He said they won't do the favor twice. So. I will go there with you."

"Great!" says Eva.

"You know, it's funny when you think that I begged to get six more months out of it. For what? Of course, he thinks anything might happen until then. . . ." She sits down.

"How do they . . . how do they do it?" I say.

"It happened during one night. The trucks came and stopped in front of each barracks and the soldiers ran inside the barracks to get the people out. They have these dogs to help them, trained shepherds. I am sorry, but you might as well know." There is a hardness in her voice now.

Eva lights another cigarette and I take it from her fingers. The smoke is warm and bitter in my throat.

"He was not in the room the whole night and I did not know anything. I went with the rest of them. Up on the truck. Then I saw him running and shouting, with a paper in his hand. Then I was lifted down from the truck."

Her eyes are fixed to that small burner under the window. Her hands are folded in her lap, as if she is waiting. I think she forgets we are in the small room too.

We walk back through the darkened camp and Eva is quiet for a while and then she says, "You know? I like her better now . . . since she went through hell."

The Safety Pin

In the first weeks I did not notice how slow the soup line was. Now the line is long, long as the inside of the barracks. I hear Eva yawn behind me. Through her half-open mouth she says, "What is it today?"

"Cabbage, I think."

It does not really matter. The taste is always the same, the color sometimes different. With one slice of bread, or two slices of bread. One cabbage leaf, two cabbage leaves, floating between the metal walls of a mess kit, in a liquid sometimes brown, sometimes gray. Between mess kits the space is twenty-four hours long.

The line shuffles forward between the racks for sleeping. Bringing closer the smell of the barrel at the door. I put one foot in front of the other as the tall girl in front of me does. I feel full of hollowness. The round light space in the middle of my body. It hurts a little. If I could just not talk about it. Eva is always hungry very quietly.

"You know, we had beautiful trees in our street, Eva."

"That's good. Trees are very important. And streets too."

"Shut up!" says the tall girl in front of me.

Eva pats my shoulder twice. "They are all so stupid. Don't pay any attention."

"You know, it *was* a beautiful street. Not too long, just right. In summer, the trees had green light around them. And at the corner there was a candy store and on the other corner was an old woman with a pushcart selling pickles."

Eva does not listen any more. But I see the pickles. They lie green in the shade of the barrel, glistening, deep lines on their skins, and the round whites of onion spread in circles around them. . . .

"Maybe we will get the thick from the bottom today," I say.

But Eva knows better. "Everybody wants the thick and you know there is less thick soup than there is us. So!"

"If they don't change the barrel now, we are bound to get it, Eva. We are bound to."

"Sure."

I look down at my feet so that I cannot see the barrel. I wear big wooden clogs now. They took the leather shoes away. My feet feel small inside. I bend down and tie the rope more tightly, shoving my feet forward at the same time. When I stand up, I am in front of the barrel. I hand the girl my mess kit and try to smile at her. But she does not even lift her eyes.

I watch the ladle come down and part the gray liquid, then disappear. The soup moves in circles, then parts again, and the hand with the ladle is above my mess kit. And thick, thick is the soup. The potatoes come down with a round sound, one leaf of cabbage hangs over the side.

I turn to Eva and say, "I got it! I knew one day I would get it. *Straight from the bottom!*"

"I have the bottom too." And for the first time she smiles.

I push through the standing bodies, not seeing anyone. At the open door I stop and stand still. Here, as each evening, the group of men. Waiting . . .

I see my father. The skin of his face clamped tight from behind, giving him the false youth of the very wealthy or the very hungry. The color is gone from his hair. His eyes are empty. There was always pride in his body. Now there is an old man standing here. Shoulders jutting forward. Hands holding a tin can. Waiting.

I walk slowly through the men, toward the face, and I feel hate. That he has become like the rest of the men. Now he is everybody.

I stop in front of him, the steam of the soup spreads over my face, and through the haze I see the safety pin. The lapels of his jacket pinched together with that pin. That lock, for which any hand is a key, holding together the helpless—babies and the buttonless.

I hand him my mess kit and keep staring at the pin. He gulps down the soup and tries to work his mouth into a smile. My hand pulls at the lapel and I say, "Why do you have that pin?" And the jacket opens under my fingers. There is nothing. No shirt, no sweater. Only his skin.

I stamp my feet and shout, "Your pullover . . . the blue one . . . What did you do with it?"

He does not answer; instead his hand reaches in the pocket of his jacket. "I . . . I have something here . . . for you. . . ."

He looks as if he is counting to himself while he tries to find the thing somewhere in his pockets. Then relief on his face as the hand comes out.

There on his open palm—ten white cubes. Some specks of dirt cling to them. But otherwise they are solid, square-sided and bright—these ten cubes of sugar.

Father finds his smile. The smile is as I remember it. New as it always was, on his old face. "I made a good trade."

And the tears that come I swallow with the sweetness of the first cube.

The Road

There are no birds in the sky. Ever. And I think, Is it because of the air? . . . They smell it, the birds. The wise birds. Above the road then, only the birdless sky. Along the road I walk, as every day. There is nowhere else to go. Just this one road that ends at a gate. I turn there and walk back. At the other end are the lines of wires, crossing each other. The electric wires are wherever I turn.

On the road, the men are working. They make ditches. They carry stones. Always the men carry stones. For many days I watch and they carry stones from one end of the road to the other.

There is a man who nods to me. Sometimes he stops and smiles at me, holding a stone against his belly. I see him now on the other side of the road and I cross over to him. It is their lunchtime. But no lunch. Beyond the hunger in his eyes, there is something else. I notice a nerve that twitches the left eyelid. He speaks to me.

"You know, I keep waiting for you now."

"You do? Why?"

"You are the permanence for me. Since I am here, I have come to understand. The soup at a certain time, you walking by, even these stones. It is here, it exists. And that is the true permanence."

"What you are doing here, it makes no sense. You just carry them back and forth. The road always looks the same."

"But it is not. There was snow before. You haven't seen it. Now there is mud. And we are still here."

Yes, they are still here. I never ask him how long he has. I look at them, all these men, dragging their feet, sitting down on the piles of stones. They don't look at each other.

"You don't speak much to each other, do you?"

"No. But we all know the same things. That we carry stones. That we will get up in the morning. That we will be hungry. That we will get hot coffee all at the same time. That we will carry stones."

He sits down at the side of the road and I sit beside him.

"You know, I learned many things before," he says. "At the Charles University. About psychology and the hidden fears and all the theories of human behavior. I thought I was ready to teach. . . ."

I listen to his even voice. And I think, Nobody is intelligent any more. He still has words that are good to listen to. Because they are from outside of this place.

". . . I learned the secret. Look at them. How indifferent they seem. But there *is* hope in them, under the falling faces, under the dirt, under the stones. Yes, hope."

"We all have our time. I mean . . . to serve. Afterward . . ." I move my hand toward the high, dark pillar of brick.

"Yes, there's that. But there's more." He leans to me and in a low voice continues, "You see, the green ones think we will carry stones forever. No, not the same men, of course, but others. . . ." His eyes move to that far field. "Different ones. For them we are always the same. But we know better. We know that one day there will not be others to replace us. End. There will be the end of this. The end of this road. One day."

He stands up and says, "The only thing to believe is that you are in the last group that carries stones and makes this road—that finally will lead out."

One day as I walk along the road, I stop suddenly. The faces bent above the heaped stones—are new faces. I think of the sound of trucks in the night and the barking of many dogs.

He will not be there. Only the road.

The Blue Pen

The days follow each other, always the same. The feeling of loss, always there, and it is only that, the feeling of loss, over and over again. Wanting to stop time and start it all over. Wanting to be myself in somebody else in some other place. All the things I did not do . . . too late for any of them now. So many questions inside my head, but nobody to answer them. Never to know. And Ivan? Why didn't I? It is not a loss I feel. It is that I did not give when I could give. When I think about him, I see him somewhere on a mountain. They took him away, where I cannot get to him. I don't think of him as being dead. I *know* he is, but I never think about it. With Karel it is different. I would like to know. How did he feel? I picture him getting up and getting dressed. Why do you have to get dressed? What did he think about? I remember the men, a long, long time ago, walking to that small door, to be hanged. To think I will finally know how they felt. I don't want to know. Suddenly the French verbs come to me: *Je suis, tu es, il est.* I did learn many things. I am, you are, he is. I know it even in Latin. I know the start of Caesar's speech on the tomb of somebody. Maybe one day, when everything is over, they will make poetry about us. How we died here. Yes, I think they will make poetry. That's nice. What year is this? I can't remember the year of my death. I must ask somebody. October, it will be. We wrote many compositions about October. I think it was because of the leaves that fall, and their color on the sidewalks, orange and yellow. . . . We would go into the park and pick up the big chestnut leaves and make a bouquet out of them. On the way home we would throw them away and maybe next day we would go again. It was important to have dry chestnut leaves then. But I never liked October. A neutral month that does not belong anywhere . . . So this year will have only ten months for me. . . . Who started to divide the year in twelve? I think the Romans. They started everything.

Ilse comes running through the barracks. She rarely comes here. She climbs the ladder to me and says, "Listen. They prepare something."

"What . . . They can't. . . . It's too soon."

"I know. But I didn't see him the whole day and that means they are preparing something. I saw a green one walking with long sheets of paper."

My mouth is dry. "Maybe they are just counting us. Or something like that."

"Maybe. Anyway, don't say anything to anybody."

"I won't."

"If I find out more, I will come and tell you."

"Yes. All right."

After she leaves I feel very much alone. The place is changed. The corners of the room are closer. The edges sharper. I reach in the wall, into that crack of wood, where I keep a piece of soap. It is green and rough to touch. I pick up the piece of cloth that is my towel and climb down. I should wash my hair. . . .

I walk along the road. The men are working there as always. The camp is as always. I feel light-headed and I wonder why it is important that I should wash my hair. The washroom is empty. I bend my head down under the faucet and let the cold water run on my head. The soap does not make suds. This is a poor soap. I rinse my hair and feel the burning of my scalp. I undress completely then and wash my whole body. I look down at myself. The skin is smooth over my bones and white. I feel very clean and cold now.

Walking back, I hear a whistle. The shapes along the road start to run, disappearing in barracks. I run too, the wet cloth swinging on my arm. The soap slides out of my palm and I stop to pick it up. The air is cool on my head. I enter the barracks and find the women in a large group in front of the Elder. I press my nails into the gritty soap.

"Walk out by twos, toward the last barracks. And no talking on the way." The Elder goes away.

Mother's face is bleached. She looks at me as if I had the answer. "It's nothing, Mama. They are going to distribute something. I saw Ilse."

"Yes. That's what I thought."

We walk out and I see the green ones at the last barracks. We are put in a line and I cannot see what they are doing there, but the line shortens. I can see some girls now, with pens in their hands, the green ones telling them something. Ilse is among them. She too has a pen. It has a blue handle.

It is in front of Ilse that I finally stand. She smiles at me and whispers, under her falling hair, "It won't hurt, Baby."

She takes my arm and slowly the blue pen's point sinks into my skin. It burns a little. I watch. A number starts to show from under my skin. It was not there before. I have a number in my skin now. I walk away holding my arm with the other hand, and read again: B-4828. I am glad Ilse has such a nice handwriting. It is very small and neat. Between the B and the number there is a little dash, very straight.

Mother is walking beside me now. "Show me yours, Mama." It is not Ilse's handwriting and the number is big.

"I think this is very good, Tania."

"What? That they gave us numbers?"

"Yes. Maybe they want to . . . keep us. Why would they otherwise?"

"Maybe, Mama."

Mother stops in front of Father's barracks, to wait for him. I continue walking alone. And entering the smell of the barracks, I whisper to myself:

"*Je ne suis pas, tu n'es pas, il n'est pas. . . .*"

"I am not, you are not, he is not. . . ."

The Last Wall

Aram looks very much like Ivan, his brother. But older and bitter. Maybe because he has been here three months already. He is impatient with me sometimes, but still he comes to see me.

We sit behind the last barracks. The sun is in the sky and I lift my face to it.

"Still like a sun tan?" He is holding my hand, bending my fingers. It is agreeable and it hurts a little.

"You close your eyes and the sun makes red squares under your eyelids." I feel warm. I like the sun. It is so high and yet feels so close. It is like a thing from the past that still exists.

"Tania, I want to talk to you."

"Yes. You know, sun and maybe music. And books, of course. Yes. These three things are very hard to lose. Back home, when we couldn't go anywhere—no school, theater, movies—we could still read, we could still listen to music. And we had the sun. Now there is only the sun."

"Tania. Will you listen now? It's important."

"Go ahead. Although it cannot be important. Nothing is."

"I want you."

"I know."

"I don't know when it started. I just want you. I am not saying that I love you. We don't have time for that. I need you. That's all."

. . . I am in somebody's attic, listening to records. . . . Sitting on the floor . . . the smoke . . . the trumpet blowing. I get up; I stand at the window and look down. . . . I can see bridges and roofs and the cathedral with its golden towers. The city below me and the music behind me. I feel sad for some reason, for a reason not there . . . yet.

"... You can cheat them! You can take something away from them!"

Suddenly his mouth comes down to mine and his kiss is long and hard. He lets me go. We both hear at the same time the sound of a wagon that dumps something on the other side of the wire. The wagon drives away and the pile of dead is high under the sun. I shift a little to get more light on my face. I close my eyes and Aram continues: "I will go in three months. You a little later. Four months. That's all you have. So little time ... like scissors, cutting you off."

"When you think ... four months. Almost half of a school year. How long it seemed then."

"Here we are. You know it's all over. Making love is part of a life. You should live it. You should have all that's due to you! Remember the time."

"I remember the time...."

"It will be good. You will know what it is to have a man...." He holds my shoulders.

I look back at him and say: "This time is mine. As it is, whatever it is—that's all. It's important because there *is* so little. I can't change that. But I can keep myself inside of me. You say, 'Cheat them'—I say I can't cheat myself. What I have is all I have."

"I can't talk with you! You're insane! You make me so ... I could hit you."

"They hit me too. But they didn't change me." At once I am sorry. I start to say something but he holds up his hand to show me he understands.

He stands up. "Think about it. I will be behind your barracks tonight." He kisses me lightly on the forehead, as Ivan would sometimes do.

I continue sitting there. I am tired now. The sun is slowly going down behind the chimney. Why not? What does it matter? I couldn't even become pregnant. I am not a woman any more. Outside, yes. Inside, I have stopped being.

I follow the path behind the barracks. The sun is almost down. I turn and stand still, looking over the camp. Strange land with people in it, strangers to themselves and to others. All laws have fallen here and nothing has replaced them. We are all drifting, without the belief in anything. There is nothing to follow any more. We all look the same and we all act the same. The change is slow but, when it starts, nothing can stop it.

I know now that I will not join him behind the barracks. Who am I? What do I know about myself? The only thing that remains is the *I* in me. I find suddenly some strange pleasure in knowing that when I die I will die the *same,* unchanged, as when I was me. It matters very much. Yes, as I was.

Keep that last thing. Hang on to it as to the last wall.

The Riding Crop

I should never have believed them. It is mostly that feeling—of being cheated.

We stand in line in front of the last barracks. They told us to come out and we came. I see the men on the other side of the road, standing quiet. They are not working on the road today. And the word is said many times—I feel it hanging in the air round as a balloon—one word only and it takes up so much space:

Selection . . . Selection . . .

Mother stands next to me. She does not ask anything. It is strange how quiet we all are. We used to talk during the dinner at home, with Karel, and Father would say, "Be quiet."

The first ones enter the door now. Sound of wooden shoes against the planks of wood. It is a large hall. Nothing to fill it but us. We furnish all the corners and all the walls. I see Ilse pushing between the standing women. Her palm on Mother's shoulder, she brings me closer with her other hand. The hand feels warm, and the words, "It's for work. He said it's for work." Her eyes move over the room.

"You are a nice girl, Ilse," says Mother.

Then the voice of a green one, asking for silence. And in the silent room his voice carries two words to us: "Undress! Completely!"

The room stretches up, hands above heads, gray clothes offered to ceiling, hanging in that instant before the fall, then the room bends down, knees pull up, clothes now gray bundles lying bunched at the ankles.

When I start to undress, Mother is already naked, both arms folded over her breasts, and she seems too white and too naked. I pull my pants down slowly and I think how often I have imagined the first undressing before the first man. The silk falling away slowly, while the pulse goes faster; the curtains moving their edges into the dark room and it would be a summer night behind the open window and a soft wind. . . .

When I straighten up, it is as if I am not naked. There are many green ones, right across from me. As if I had something around me, not much, a net, something. They think they see me. But they don't really. I smile at Mother. But there is still that one thing: the hate that they have cheated. It was supposed to be six months. And it is not. That is all. That time that was due to us. That is all that matters.

The door opens. The sound of boot to boot—and the green ones raise their hands to their pink foreheads. In front of them stands a tall man, his head shaven to a blond skull. His uniform seems greener and his boots darker. In his hand, a riding crop. Beneath the stars and leaves, the sign of a stick with two snakes twisted around. The sign of a doctor. We are not sick. I am not sick. Doctors heal. . . .

. . . The white beard of Dr. Svoboda when he would come to listen to my chest. He always had candy in his pocket and the syrup was red and smelled of strawberries. His name meant Freedom and one day at noon he came and helped my mother in the big brown bed. There was no time to go to the hospital and she heard the bells of noon through her cry and I came, so fast, in a hurry to be born, to live. He was there, always, above me when I was sick, his head always whiter. I would hear his voice from the dining room, where he would drink a glass of tea with Mother, after closing the door of my room, and the last thing I would see would be the black-leather bag in the half-closed door. . . .

The women in single file, all the blank bodies moving slowly toward this man. He says nothing. But the black riding crop moves and moves again. Left, right. I see already two groups. Left, right. Right. Right. Left. Sometimes the hand stops, the crop lifted in a moment of quiet air. Then the crop moves quickly: Left, right. I can almost hear it moving.

We are very close. Ilse whispers to me, "Baby, want me to go first?"

"No. I . . . I'll go first, then Mother . . . and then you. She will be between us. What do you think?"

Ilse is frowning. "Wait, Tania!" My name sounds foreign. I am not Baby now.

I see Mother being pulled back by Ilse's hand. I turn, slowly back from the file. The women around me have their eyes straight ahead, as if drawn toward the man. Ilse is by the wall, searching through her clothes, her hand still holding Mother's. Mother stands there with so much patience in her face—she looks so calm, as when she would try to explain something to us and knew that we would not listen or would not understand. She stands, waiting, and I know she does not know what Ilse is searching for and it does not matter. Ilse opens her hand and in it lies an old lipstick, the yellow metal peeled off in many places, the shine gone, but the color there, under the cap. Slowly she spreads some of the red on her finger and she takes Mother's face in her hand. The chin of my mother rests in the hand of Ilse, as if she was waiting to be kissed. The red spreads on Mother's cheeks and Ilse smooths the last touches. Mother looks younger now and rosy.

Ilse laughs and whispers, "What do you say to that?" She turns Mother toward me.

Mother touches her face; she looks to the wall as if it were a mirror, and says in a small voice, "Do you think it is too much? . . . They will notice. Do I look nice?"

"Yes, Mama. You look nice. And they won't notice. You just look younger. It will be all right, you'll see."

She turns to Ilse and says, "You know, Ilse, I think this is the first time I have had rouge on my cheeks."

We are back in the file and there are only three women now in front of me. Two left, one to the right. I pull my belly in . . . so that I look young. . . . I *am* young. . . . I have no belly. . . .

I take a deep breath and start to walk. There is nothing in my head. Nothing. No wish or memory. My legs move under me. I know that, because first I see the left side of the man's forehead and then the eyes stare straight across from me. I look behind him, through the small window. Above the wire, a piece of sky. It is blue today. Noon. And I see only the black point of the crop, pointing to the right. I know where the right side is. The hand I write with. The clock. A hand from a green sleeve closes on my wrist, a white sheet of paper, a push, other women. How much time did it take and where am I?

I turn, the heart beating in my throat. Mother stands still, in front of the man. She is looking above the man's head, her face with a shine from the red. God, please, please, I will do anything. . . . The black leather of the riding crop is straight, his chin leaning on its point. The leather shines. I know the smell. Father's shoe factory. Mother looks at the window. The man looks at my mother. I close my eyes. God! The black points now toward the white flesh that is my mother, then is lifted. . . . Which way will it drop . . . and it swings. Right.

We are holding each other's hands, Mother's palm warm with sweat. We watch Ilse. The big body moving, the hips round. She stands then, her chin forward, looking into the face of the man. The black leather moves to the right, very fast. We are back together again and we look at the women in our group. They are young. There are young ones in the other group too. But not so many.

We are told to return to our barracks. We dress fast and run out of the door. There is another group waiting and I see Eva, standing to one side of the others. I walk to her with Ilse and Eva asks, "What's going on in there?" She seems as calm as always.

"It's nothing," says Ilse. "It's right or left."

"What are you?"

"Right."

"I will see you later."

I touch Eva's shoulder. "Good luck, Eva."

"Sure. Thanks. But you would have to know. Which way is luck?" She looks toward the entrance of the barracks. "I heard there will be potato soup tonight."

In the blue air I walk along the road. The sun has rolled from the top of the sky. Soon it will be time to eat. I see the camp as I have always seen it. It is there and there is nowhere else. I know every barracks and each watchtower.

It all seems so familiar. As if I had been born here.

The Circle

In the evening we wait for Father. To return from the selection. Leaning on the side of a barracks, we wait. It is the time of evening when the color of the sky is gone and the lights above the wire not yet turned on. The round white eye in the watchtower does not yet sweep its line of light, doubling, folding across the roofs.

Since the first day, the evenings have been waiting, waiting for soup and waiting for night. When I sleep I do not have the given dream any more. When did I lose it? I should know. I never know the exact moment of a loss. My sleep is heavy and if it had a color it would be purple. As a child my days had color. Sunday was red and Wednesday blue; yellow was the color of Saturday. Now I have a color for sleep. I get up in the morning as if the days were a continuation of the nights. I enter the first minutes as I would an empty room.

It is that time now when the hollow round in the center of my body becomes a growing circle of nothing, so heavy my body is filled with it. The time before the soup.

"What do you think will happen to Father?" Mother asks that again. I don't want her to say that. Nothing will happen. We will all go and work somewhere.

"I was just twenty when I married your father. In that little street off the square, that's where we first lived. I did show you that street, didn't I?" She is frowning, as if she worried about forgetting to show me that street. But I remember the street. She pointed it out many times. The gray house, the stones large and the windows high, in that narrow street . . .

Smoke blackening the sky. I watch it spreading over the broad space of air, rolling out over the fading clouds. They never stop, in the chimney. They work all the time, in the chimney, all the time.

I feel the strangeness of this day, this day that is so slow to end; a day like no other day. Mother has wiped the color from her cheeks and she is again pale. I could divide the day by Mother's cheeks. When they were red. When they were pale.

Earlier in the afternoon we saw Eva coming back from the selection and she waved her hand to us from far and I knew she went right. She stopped, her hand flattening her ruffled hair, and said: "It's all over. They decided for us. But we still don't know. . . . This is the first time that somebody knows something about me that I don't know. In this case, if we are going to . . ." She made a large circle with her arm, pointing to the sky, to the indefinite smoke.

"Why, Eva, you should not talk like that," said Mother. "You are always joking, aren't you?"

"Yes. I was joking," and she walked away, the thin body straight, and I thought, How much weight has she lost? . . .

. . . Now we wait for Father. Mother is still standing. I sat down long ago. After Eva left. I feel very tired—since Eva left.

"Won't you sit down, Mama?"

"No. Thank you. I will see him sooner if I am standing." After a while she says, "I met him . . . Did I ever tell you?"

She did, but I say, "No, Mama. Tell me."

"Right after he came back from the war. We ate at the same guest house. I was going to the business school and the city seemed very closed-in after the country I was used to. I remember that. How closed-in it seemed. I forgot about it after I started to go out with your father. . . . Did you know that he had a fight one day with a young man who wrote me a poem? It was a beautiful poem.

Your father never knew how to write a poem and that made him angry, I think. Besides, he loved to fight. . . ."

I see the jolt in her body now. I stand up. I see him walking toward us. His feet not slow or fast, as with a man in no hurry and with nowhere to go. His head tilts to one side; I see the two deep lines in his forehead. He stops in front of us and smiles.

"Where did you go?" Mother's voice even but the eyes move fast over the old face. These words, said many times, from above the pots, where she would lean to stir the evening meal—where did you go today?—the table white under the yellow light and the four plates, waiting, the napkins rolled in the colored rings—where did you go?

Father lifts one foot above his ankle, his head down; then the heel moves in the loose earth. He smooths the earth back in its place, watching the ground. He lifts his head, his mouth tightens.

"Oh . . ." as if he had forgotten. "Oh . . . left. I went left."

The watchtower light sways from right to left. The wire tightens and becomes a circle. In this instant the lights go on.

"He sent me left," says Father.

"Left," says Mother.

The world said left, the wire, the watchtower—written under the roofs. Left.

We stand there, looking at each other. We form a small circle with nothing in the middle. No center. There is something to be said, words, that could change this. Stop. Start again. I will go and talk to them. Tell them. He is strong and . . . *Ilse.* I see Ilse coming.

She stops and says, "It's for tomorrow morning. The right ones. And he said it's for work. We are going to be sent out to work, that's all he said." Her eyes lift up to Father; she reaches out one hand and the long fingers move over his shoulder. "And you . . . yes, I heard. . . . You are going to take it easy and wait here in the camp. That's all. The ones that went left are going to stay here. The six-month plan is off."

Mother does not say anything. We watch Ilse. And she has to explain more. "They just can't take everybody. . . . There is not enough work for everybody."

She takes a step away from him, and without looking at anybody, she says, "And you never know what they are going to do till the last minute. With us or with you."

Mother walks to Ilse. Their heads bend together. I hear words: ". . . arrange . . . volunteer . . . certain . . . of course."

Then Mother says, turning to us, "Ilse is a nice girl. She will try to do it for me." Ilse turns her head away, and without looking at me, she leaves.

And I ask, even though I know already, as if I had always known, and I know that Father knows, and this is the way it will be. Through their lives they left the decisions to God and the authorities. At this last and already familiar moment, I hear Mother make her final and first decision. "I am going to stay with Father. Here. We are both going to stay here. And wait . . . for you."

Already they are on the other side away from me. They are facing me, their shoulders joined, and I see their two hands, holding each other, Mother's fingers closed over the knuckles of my Father's hand.

"You are a big girl now," Father says. "If Mother wants to stay . . ."

I know that nothing can make Mother leave him behind. She will find a way to stay. There is more peace now on her face than

I have ever seen before. They both smile at me, still holding each other. I feel cheated. They made their decision. I wish there was a decision for me to make.

"Just remember one thing," says Father. "After it's all over, go to your Aunt Magda. She's the only one they didn't take. We will come there too."

"You remember the street?" says Mother.

"I remember."

"Fourth floor," says Mother.

"Number 19," says Father.

I try to see my aunt's house, but I cannot.

"I will say good-bye to you in the morning," says Father.

I leave them standing there and I don't know where to go. I turn and see them sitting now, leaning against the barracks, their hands still joined. I should have stayed with them. But I have to go. And there is nowhere to go. . . .

. . . I stand somewhere and watch the kettles of steaming soup carried into the barracks. People hurrying to their mess kits and to that liquid that will almost fill their stomachs for one night more. The right and the left ones. Eating. Some standing outside, their heads tilted forward, above the filled metal. Steam hiding their faces. I feel myself moving. . . .

I turn a corner and sit down, facing the wire. The dark lines of the wire cut into many squares the flames of the chimney. The wind is warm on my face and I close my eyes upon memory. . . . Father, in summer, with his newspaper, sitting on the small balcony, on a Sunday morning . . . the shadows of the railing crossing the printed lines . . . a brown housecoat, with twisted strings, the news blown by the slow wind and his hand striking that paper . . .

some words of Mother's song from the kitchen. Mother comes in and pours coffee into the white cup set at the base of the railing. I see the soft, round white in the opening of her dress as she bends down in front of him. They look at each other. . . .

. . . Their not speaking then was different from the times when they did not speak and did not see each other. The silence then made the rooms larger. Mother walking from room to room, picking up a book or knitting, to put it down in the kitchen. Father leaving after dinner and the sound of the door, a blow of air and the snap of the lock. The small brass chain moving slowly in the empty hall. Then there was the time when a new factory opened, the name flat as the shoes they produced. The stores had large square fronts and the prices ended in .95. Father's words were all of leather and the evenings were more silent. Mother's cooking was less good. There was the day when he closed his store. Before dinner he looked at the floor and saw my shoes. He told me to hold up one foot. The price tag was still on the bottom. It ended in .95. Father did not wait for dinner. . . .

. . . I should know more of the lives we had. I cannot remember more. Perhaps there was no more. I am losing my past now. Their past. What was it in their past that now they go together that way with their hands joined?

The fire does not reach into the sky; the smoke has colored the night. The colors of my days—Sunday fades to Saturday, changes to Wednesday, drops to the color of sleep. The colors are gone.

At the thought of my living now beyond them, I straighten my back against the barracks. All that there is of life, I have to go on living—alone. That is what they want me to do.

I stand up and start to walk. Before each barracks, the lights hang round. I walk through the white circles and under each bulb my shadow is short. But between them, the shadow grows. I hurry now to reach the next circle where, in the center of light, my shadow is a child again.

The Box

A day the color of night. Was it only this morning when I saw the day clear, the sky spread farther than all the camps? Was it only this morning . . . ? Where are we now? What has happened to time? Is there a place so black and we see it and we are still alive?

Yes, this morning. We were led through a gate to another camp, into a barracks with the windows boarded. A door closed and the morning ended.

We are women in boxes. My knees are pulled up to my chin. I feel in my back the knees of someone behind me. Someone in front of me sits on my feet. My elbows touch other elbows and I cannot straighten my arms.

It is quiet. We stopped talking some time ago. We sit in these cages and watch the darkness. We take the air and we give it back and each time there is less. The used air and no light, windows nailed shut, boxes of wood instead of bunks . . .

Pain creases in my belly. In my head a sound: the clatter of stones. I don't know anything any more. I don't know. I remember an angry surprise when they closed us in here. But now we are ready to accept the impossible. This is what it is. We are in boxes.

"They are going to kill us," says a voice behind me. I have heard it many times and each time I have understood it less. I find myself humming a child's singsong: "They're going to kill us, kill us, kill us; they're going to kill us, tra la la, la la." I hope they let us go to the latrines before they do it. . . .

I stop myself. I tell myself: Think. Remember the morning. The first light. The slow fog. Remember: Father standing in the middle of the road. His hands above my head. Large hands held there. They did not touch me. But I knew they were there. Waiting. Waiting with the words of blessing that I never heard before. Ancient words I could not understand, but I felt them, already protecting me. Nothing could happen to me. Then the kiss on my forehead. God bless you. . . . Father, wait. . . . You run along, now, my daughter. . . . Wait Father. . . . God bless you. . . . Wait. . . .

I remember the feeling of wanting to hold back. Not yet, wait—somebody make it happen—not yet . . . How many years have we known each other? I knew him before I knew about it—just wait a little. . . . But he turned and walked away. He did not show his face to me again. I stood on the road. And the same words coming into my head: Father, wait! It did not make any sense. He was not leaving—it was me. Why did I feel it was him?

Mother said last night, "You should not be afraid."

"I am not, Mama."

"There is nothing to be afraid of. You are going to work and we are going to stay here." Later she whispered to me, "I wish we'd had your tonsils taken out. If you catch cold, rinse your throat with salt water. Do you think you will have salt?"

"Maybe, Mama. Don't worry about it now."

"You always had a fragile throat. I wish now that we had."

"What, Mama?"

"Had them taken out."

She was lying on her back, her arms under her head. She did not look at me when she said, "Promise me to pray. If I knew you would pray, I would feel better. Promise?"

I felt then like telling her, We prayed all our lives. But I said, "I promise, Mama."

She slept with her back turned to me and I was holding her, feeling her against my belly, her knees bent; she fitted into me as if she were a child. She cried in the morning, her face red and the eyelids swelling from all the crying. . . .

"I wonder what time it is," says Ilse.

"It's too late." Eva's voice comes fast, as if she waited for that question.

"He said it was for work! I swear! The son of a . . ."

I remember when we walked through this camp—I saw no men. A squared world of women, a world with eight corners. All the barracks looked the same, even this one. We were led into it slowly, almost gently. But the door closed fast after the last girl entered.

Now it is only close-cornered darkness and no space for our bodies. But I was blessed. Why can't I bring back the feeling under Father's hands? All I feel is the sharp pain across my belly. I remember Eva's words when we entered this barracks. "We are much closer to it." The chimney, taller; thrusting to a far point in the sky.

Eva's hand is on my shoulder. I hear her whisper, "Don't worry, Tania."

"About what?" I do not worry. All I do now is: I remember. What was before? Our future is in our past and our past is here.

"About the chimney."

"Leave me alone."

"I have something. Look."

Eva takes my fingers and presses them into her palm. Under my fingers, the thin edge of metal; I slowly trace the shape back and forth, find a narrow opening in the middle, back again to the edge. A razor blade.

My hand pulls away, faster than the word: "No!"

She laughs. "I don't mean right now. But we might need it. . . . Don't you think so?"

Her voice is low; I can hardly hear her. I pull away. I twist my fingers to cover my wrists and lay my head, sideways, between my turned hands. Two bodies away I separate the form of Ilse from the dark. Her head rolls on her knees, as if she is saying No to someone inside her. Suddenly between heads the flash of light. From behind the light, one word:

"OUT!"

A fat woman in prisoner's clothes stands in the open door. I see her as the bodies in front of me slide forward and move to the door. The light swings across the bent women shoving out of boxes. The door is a slot of blue light. I push up from the box, splinters enter my fingers. I press my knees to straighten my legs. Kinked muscles pull tight in the back of my thighs.

Ilse walks with one hand on her back. "I told you," she says. "There will be kettles of soup outside. They forgot about us, that's all."

Through the open door I see the rounding air of night. We step out into that air. And there, in a strict line, the spaced shine of many buckets. The moon is a rim of light in the sky above the flames jutting from the chimney.

We sit on the buckets, watching the moon.

I wake up thirsty. My tongue dry and heavy to lift. What was the dream? Karel. He was under a waterfall. Slapping his chest, his mouth hollow to catch the white stream. I was above him and he did not see me, and somehow I could not go down to him.

The women sit with their eyes opened, without moving. Others are sleeping; some with heads on their knees, some with heads fallen back, mouths open, as if there might be rain to catch on their tongues.

"Tania," says Ilse. "I still have the feeling that we are going to get out of here. And the most important thing is . . ."

"Why don't you give up?" says Eva. "You and your most important things!"

Ilse does not even turn her head but continues looking at me. "This!" She holds the mess kit between her knees, her fingers beating the metal as a drum. "Because they did not take it. . . ."

We hear voices outside and the door opens to the fat woman. I don't like her. Under the shaven skull the shoulders thrust forward, as if ready to charge. Two other girls stand a pace behind her.

Again we move toward the door, toward the bright day. We are led behind the barracks. And there, in the open—faucets. My hand on the knob.

Water. Opening in a fold from the rusted pipe. I am pushed by the others, but I do not lift my face from under the water. The first gulp I swallow too fast and have the cool pain in my throat. Then, more slowly, I taste it. Water. I feel it filling my stomach. Water—all the meals in the world. I roll it around in my mouth, into the darkest corners, where I can never see, my cheeks swollen with it, spitting out my own warmth. And again and again, I drink.

I lift my head then and see the other women drinking: as if they never drank before. Surprise on their faces, the brows pulled up in creases. Like greedy children we go again, but more slowly back to the faucets. Water falls on my head, the world upside down from between my legs. I offer my face to the faucet and see through water, the sky. We fill the bottom part of our mess kits and are called back.

In front of the barracks is a barrel of soup. The soup tastes of rust and potatoes. I wish I had not drunk all that water.

"It must be some kind of a holiday," says Eva.

Ilse watches her, eyes above soup. "What do you mean by that?"

"Nothing. They are filling us up, that's all. We'll see what's coming next."

The fat woman stands, watching us. She gives an order and we form a square with the woman in the middle. She starts to count us, with the two unknown girls, her helpers. Their fingers point to each face, each becomes the next number, and they tell the numbers to the fat woman. She is our queen in prisoner's clothes. But the number is not right and we are counted again.

I hear then the laugh of Eva. It is not the laugh I know and I feel that she is not going to stop. Without speaking, the fat woman walks toward Eva. She walks slowly. In the sudden quiet I hear the sound of her thighs rubbing together as she walks along our line. Eva's laugh is a paced stutter. The thickened face of the woman has dents where the eyes are. Sweat in the armpit as she raises her hand, folding into a fist. I close my eyes, only to hear the flat meeting of flesh and flesh. It comes three times, the sound beside me, with the breath hissing like steam. My eyes are straight; the musk of her body is around me. Eva's laughter, higher and clearer—I feel her voice rising inside of me. The woman calls one of the helpers, speaks to her in their language. The girl runs and is back soon with two bricks.

I hear Ilse shifting her feet and I look at her face. There is a different face on Ilse. Her teeth press back her lower lip; she takes hold of my hand. We see Eva kneel in the center of the open square. Her arms stretch straight, high as the shoulders of the woman. The woman lays the two bricks flat on Eva's open palms.

Eva still laughs; the tears come now with the laughter. The bricks sway with the slow motion of her body. We are counted again and the sound slows, between sobs, then falls away. And Eva is still down on her knees, offering her bricks to the sky. Our shadows like wet shapes drying in front of us. Eva's hands come down, closer to her head—but the woman is there with her round fist sinking into Eva's face. Each time Eva lets the bricks slide from her hands, the woman raises her fist. The sweat is darker under her arm. From Eva's mouth the blood is bright. It is noon and the sun falls on our heads. There is no shadow to Eva.

Ilse carries Eva into the barracks, doubled over her shoulder, limp as a raincoat. We roll Eva into our box and sit her up straight. Ilse pushes her knees up to her chin and, held from all sides by the bodies of others, Eva looks like any of us, except for the head that hangs loose and sideways.

I watch her, clutching my mess kit full of water. It is warm now. Who knows when we will get water again, I tell myself, looking through the open door. This is my water. It is all her fault. I feel anger rising in me. They always hit people when they faint, to wake them up. But she was hit so many times. I feel the sweat coming down my back. I pull her face backward. And my hand is a cup that opens above her face. Eva's face is full of drops of water, as if she had come back from a slow walk in the rain. I keep my hand on her temples, moving in wet circles, and I see the eyelids move. I think of moths, grounded by rain. . . .

Her eyes open. "Where am I?"

"It's all right," I say. "We are back in the boxes."

The Shower

They come for us the next day. The air is the color of morning. There is this place with no contours where others have walked and now I am walking here. The more the column advances, the taller the chimney. For a house with such a tall chimney, the doors seem too small, in their color of mud. I imagined portals heavy with beams and thought often of the picture, *The Entrance to Hell.* The stone was black.

The column stops. I turn to see our old camp. I do not see anybody moving there. They must all be asleep. I see Ilse watching that quiet camp.

"They probably took them somewhere else." She answers my unasked question and I repeat after her, as a lesson, turning now to Eva, "They must have taken them somewhere else."

"Of course. And we are going to take a nice shower, that's what they said."

Her voice is pleasant and low. Since the bricks, she speaks in a lower voice, as if she knew a secret. I too have a lower voice, but it is inside me and I notice it only since we are here. It says the opposite of what I am thinking: We are going away from here. We will take a shower and get clean clothes and maybe some bread.

We are standing in front of the brick house. The brick house has two doors. There is nowhere else to go now. The line is straight to one of the doors. But I turn up my head and there is the sky. The blue as I always knew it and the islands of white. The same sky here as everywhere—but nobody sees it as I do at this instant. Like hope, it can change the colors of the mind.

"Look," says Eva. "They are here."

"Well . . ." says Ilse. "They . . . work here."

They stand in small groups—the special detachment of men. They did not know that one day they would be selected to be the "special" ones. I did not know that I would see them. Their faces are white but no bones show. They talk together; some even laugh. I remember the voice of Aram—it seems such a long time ago—

". . . Nobody knows much about them. Once they are selected for the 'special detachment,' they are put in separate quarters . . . so that they can't talk, you know. . . . Good food and no choice. . . . They load the ovens . . . three, six months . . . but they never come back. . . ."

I see Ilse running from the group of men—when did she leave?—and the laughter of the men follows her. It sounds so strange. Ilse's bosom is larger than I remember, her arms folded under it, as if to support a new weight.

"Here." The paper bag is dirty white and feels soft under my fingers, shifting the weight inside. The women around us don't seem to notice; they are looking in the one direction.

In my hand now the white powder; I carry to my mouth a palmful of sugar. "Let's save some for later," I say.

Ilse and Eva look at me. "Later?" Eva's tongue wipes grains of sugar off her upper lip; her eyebrows lift.

Ilse's free hand touches my elbow; her words are quick: "If they find it on us, they will take it away. So just eat, Tania, and don't worry about later right now. Right now we have sugar and we are eating it."

"Yes," says Eva, filling her palm again, "and don't worry about getting sick."

"Here. Eat." The round pink hand of Ilse in front of my mouth—I think of a horse I used to feed with sugar, his muzzle cool, and the sounds of Grandma's farmyard loud in the mornings, my parents still asleep and myself out there with the smell of manure and the feeling of life around me. Here, too, there is a smell—but it is not the same.

I have enough of sugar. The too sweet taste clogs the back of my mouth. I want water and there is no water. There was a pump in the middle of Grandma's yard and the sound of the bucket hitting the stone well. . . .

The sound of boots now—Ilse's hand drops the empty paper bag to her feet; it lies there crumpled; grains of sugar dot the dark earth.

I do not hear the order, but see raised arms pulling clothes over many heads and my own arms obeying. Naked, I cover my breasts with my crossed arms. But there are no men now. Except the green ones, far over there, at the beginning of the column.

Five hundred women are less than one. I look over the long line; a single, shifting animal, white, with many bosoms and many heads. Bosoms young and tilted, older and loose.

The sun is higher on my shoulders now. There is no wind; it will be a warm day. Over there our camp is empty. I know there is nobody in the barracks. Because this is happening to us, it has already happened to them. I do not think about where they are. I close my mind. Nothing. Nowhere.

The column starts to move. Already I see the first ones entering a door. Which door is it? They walk slowly and in order. The pile of clothes grows beside the mud-colored door. I walk so close to Eva that I can see, on her left side, the skin rising to the pulse of her heart. Our feet make the sound of brooms.

It is as if something has opened inside of me. The earth scatters at my feet. My head is filled with wind. Everything is swept out. I look down and see my foot on the first step, the wood cracked as if stepped upon many times. Mother said to pray. . . . *Shma yisroel* . . . the second step . . . What is the next word? I must not forget. . . . *Shma yisroel* . . . What is it? . . .

No sentences in my head, just loose words, words without meaning, no weight to my body, so light now; and my mind is a wide field.

Inside this naked body, at the top of the steps, the I, the weightless I, so still in the wind-swept world—the only thing I know—that exists.

I drop the bundle of clothes and feel more alone. After all, it is only the feeling of darkness in here. Where the hall ends, there is a hollow room of metal, gray, with small shower heads that jut from the walls. There are many showers. The shower heads are dry. I stand under one of them, next to Eva. I look at her and the beating in her skin has stopped. Her face is clean of expression as if she were holding her feeling inside, along with her breath. I see the soap container with its dry block of soap. I touch the soap. It does not feel like soap. There are no faucets.

"*Adonoy!*" I say aloud. That's it. The next word. My hand reaches for the gray soap and I wait, behind my closed eyes. For touch or smell. There is the hissing in the pipes. . . .

And the first touch of water. The room wakens to voices too young for the bodies arching under the spray. They turn and bend, legs spread apart, arms reaching through water, necks moving the heads around, circling the shoulders. I see, through falling water, arms lifting in the room. Eva stands still, head upward, eyes closed, hands open above her head. Then, slowly, on her toes she turns in a silent dance. Ilse, legs wide, her hands slapping all the sections of her body. And through wet lips words without meaning and from somewhere the almost forgotten sound of a song.

We leave that room, still naked. We stand in the long corridor, no longer in a straight line. With great hunger now in me, I turn to Ilse and say, "I told you. We should have saved some sugar."

The Place

We entered the train and almost at once it started to move. Our spines bent as the coupled cars bent. The train leaned on the first curve and in the corner the water rang in the pail. We held to each other and some started to sing and there was laughter, forgotten words coming back and smiles. We smiled at each other and could not see the smiles but felt them. Someone clacked wooden shoes together with the sound of castanets; the women sang and laughed above the grinding wheels. The splintered wood was soft to sit on. We had escaped.

A girl got up to drink, stumbled over my legs and said, "Excuse me."

We laughed and called "excuse me" to each other, the old words funny now. Ilse told everyone her recipe for mushrooms and eggs and explained how much rain there had to be before the mushrooms bulged under the trees. Some asked the question, "Where are we going this time? Where?" "Rome!" someone answered. "Paris!" another. It did not matter; there was no reason to go anywhere. We could not think of any city where the green ones would not be. . . .

The water knocks in the bucket and the smell presses down in the car; it is too warm now, and the others are too close. My skirt sticks to my legs and I wait only for the door to be opened again. The train stops. A crack in the dark and through that slot of light the package drops and the hands tear at the paper, splitting the rations. The hours go by and it is only that, finally, that matters. After the ration, the emptiness and our words slow and spaced, and winding finally into silence.

They are falling asleep around me. The bent heads roll to the sound of the train; the new gray uniforms are already old with dirt. I push my skirt between my legs, fit my face into my hands. It is strange, my face, to the press of my fingers. I have forgotten already: my face longer to the touch, no more the softness of hair. . . .

. . . I think of the lost hair. It lay there, spun upon itself, circles of yellow on the dark floor; that was my hair in the house of the showers. How difficult it used to be and Mother would use the metal brush in the mornings, her hand closed over the red handle, her other hand on my hair, following the strokes of the brush. It was on Fridays that I used to wash it and the shampoo smelled of camomile. . . .

I get up and walk across the straight legs to the bucket. The water tastes of coal and metal.

I sit down again, legs open. After the room where my hair lay, there was the other room—the white room where all the tables were. It did not hurt much. The woman had red hair; it was long under the white cap; in the opening of the white coat, the green skirt showed; the skin of her finger was red disappearing somewhere between my legs. I drew air in me as if to clean myself of that finger; the finger long again, coming out without finding anything—money or embryo. I wondered if I was still a virgin. To be deflowered by a woman with red fingers . . .

After that, hands without a face passing out uniforms, the endless blue-striped clothes. The walk was short to the train. And I turned, for the last time, to see the old camp. Already I was not sure I was looking in the right direction; we made turns—or did my head turn?—I was not sure any more of anything. The feeling of passing through fog, where close things become distant. The camp looked like a memory, already different in size.

Daylight remains in the cracks of the wood; sun bends on a beam. In the packed heat of the car I want to think about something else. The dog we had. I will think of the dog. The dog will lead me, wagging and with leaping barks, into the dining room. It will be winter. I do not know why I want to think of winter and the cold whiteness. But I do. . . . The dining room is wide. The voices speak to me and—sometimes—of me. I see the others already eating and my place waiting. I go to the window and push the curtains aside and see the white outside and think, Very cold; it is very cold and I am here. Snow falling in thick flocks. The houses round with it, but inside the known press of things to the fingers. Only the window panes between me and the white darkness outside. The double glass that shows the image of a girl standing on the falling air outside, looking in at me. . . .

The cracks in the wood are filling; the train turns away from the day. I cannot think of the dog's name. There are no voices from the dining room. The door does not open any more—I do not see my place. I would like to see the window again, with only the glass to separate me from the dark and the turning snow.

4

It was a great city. So wide that no one standing at its highest point—a fortress on a hill—could see the end of it. It met the sky on all sides. The canals, formed by damming two rivers, moved flat-roofed barges up from the harbor. Beyond the dammed basin there were the squares with markets and churches. There were many markets and many churches in that city and the churches had much gold in them because the warehouses had been full for a thousand years.

The warehouses stood above the canals, the iron doors high above the level water. When the rivers drained into the sea, the canals dropped and barges tilted on the sludge of the bottom. But with the pull of the moon at its fullest, the rivers backed up with the press of the sea and the canals flowed back into the land with the barges creaking against the stone ledges.

With the moon, the animals stirred under the warehouse floors, abandoned their tugging at the stacked bags; from between tea tins and starch sacks the animals scurried, following the stripes of light along the sagging floors. They dropped from bins, fell from bundled cloth, raising a dust of pepper and wool floating in lit spaces between the bulging shelves. And down aisles where the brown beans spilled, tracking through sago, bright sugar and tobacco, from stairwells to ramps, shoving and piling at the openings, then scattering through light, whisking over stones along parapets glittering from the canals. Along the ledges, round and bulging from their feeding, they moved their eyes among the others, and lifting with a quiver of the haunches, they mounted each other, bristling and squeaking as they coupled. As if these animals knew that the night would bring great bombs, they abandoned the dark floors and loaded stores to promenade by the water, meeting and mating under the moon.

From the air, the canals were guidelines, fingers bent and pointing to the harbor. On these summer nights, the planes moved, solid; some falling, but others crossing over all the sky. With a lift and shudder the lightened planes swung out above the spreading pods. Laddering down, as if unstrung, each filled container glided, steadied by fins, in slow, whistling arcs across the spread city.

The concussion blew air from the canals and the windows fell out, glass pushed into that sucked-dry space. With a rippling that twisted stones, snapping bricks and shooting rivets from beams, the steep walls of the warehouses heaved, lifted out and folded. And sound rolled down in a tide toward the harbor.

The stacked floors gave way, splintering. All gradings and levels scattered as the floors fell in. Sugar poured into herring, phosphate scarred tanning leather, milk burst from tins to mix with cement, frosted biscuits and cigars. Beer foamed in streams with soap and sulphur, manganese coloring the rising water. Floating now with clocks, oranges and mattresses, the rivers swelled against dikes and quays.... As smoke in balls rose above prongs of fire. As flame burst in the walls, bending steel. As hooded derricks swayed above blazing barges. As from windows jagged and flowing with oil, the fire in currents floated through the city.

It was a burning city each summer night.

At the end of a certain canal, one block of warehouses did not store merchandise but people. When the planes came, each night, the people went to the cellar. They sat, inches above the water, knees pushed deep into the damp slope of sand. Their faces were gray and none of them looked young. They did not know any more if they waited for the planes to come or to go. They thought about sleep: Though they were not going to sleep tonight or tomorrow or the night after, one day there would be a sleep without bombs or guards. They thought about peace and they knew that the planes had something to do with it. But still they were afraid they might die from the bombs. They thought about the ones in whose power they were and how they would be blamed for the destroyed city.

Nothing of this showed on their faces. But with each shake of the sand under them the muscles shifted under their skin. The eyes blinked away the dust and were ready to look again. And so they sat, with their thin bodies hunched forward, waiting for the lightened sky that marked for them the beginning of another dreamless sleep.

Animals washed up by the lapping water, hulked along their narrow beach. The planes went out of the air. The people mounted the steps; on the way to the sleep, they caught in their tired eyes the bright image of the burning city.

The Lost Days

It is dark except for that small bulb hanging from the ceiling, and after a while the light is more distant and the strange room stretches and becomes longer and nothing holds its shape. I sit up and try to hold on to something, anything—but everything slopes away into the corners. There is a hand that I see clearly for a moment but the hand fades just when I want to say, Bring things closer to me and stop turning them. I close my eyes, but the bulb is there, inside. . . . I don't want that burning in my head. . . .

I hear a voice—if I could only remember, I would know whose voice it is—but it is not worthwhile: The voice would only become something else and that other thing would go on in a far corner that I know is not there.

"Tania!" It reminds me of somebody. Mother? It can't be you. But if it is you, please, stay where you are and don't go away. If I look, will she be like that bulb?

My head falls in a large vacant space and my body follows. It is good, because it is dark. I have a thought, so clear that I could laugh, I am Tania, that's who I am and I will go to sleep now. I will ask them later where we are. . . .

There is a sound now that falls closer and closer. I open my eyes and no one is here. I sit straight, listening—the sound narrow. . . . It becomes wider and larger and it explodes. . . . I should be frightened. . . .

Everything comes back to its place. But clearer now. The bulb is without light, but there is the gleam of the outside. In that light I see it: the size of a bulb, not smaller and not bigger than it is. I am glad for that. I am less afraid of the sound than of that disappearing bulb. I remember very clearly. We are in a city. The city is bombed. They are all somewhere, hiding. They left me here. They left me here to watch that bulb—to see that it does not break. But that is foolish. Anyhow, they should not have left me here.

I close my eyes and remember: the train that stopped. The wide house. Steps. I remember the steps—how many there seemed to be. The doubled voices, repeating in the high room. I saw the dry fish being put in their hands and I knew then that I did not want fish or anything. The latrines smelled of yellow chlorine and it was there I saw the first blood. My blood. Meat red it was and it was only surprise that I felt, at something that should not be there. I stayed a long time, letting my blood go, slowly, knowing the fish would be gone.

I remember how I walked back, telling myself I must walk slowly, not to move the room too much or anything inside. I thought, Somebody should take care of me; I will tell them and they will put me in a white room with nurses with white sailboat hats. . . . Ilse, standing in front of a bunk, saying, "Well, where have you been? What a feast, wasn't it?" Her voice loud but already curving away . . . Ilse losing weight, looking less blond . . .

But how far away it is. Was it only this evening? It is night now. The planes are coming again. . . .

It is a strange feeling to be alone. I always wanted to be alone. Especially in that train. How many days was it? By the pieces of bread, three. One day without water—but there was the garlic sausage instead. They must have forgotten the water. How little we talked then. Even Ilse did not have anything to say. Eva looked like a boy with the skull showing through the dark dots of her hair. I vomited once and she was very interested. How did I feel? Ilse did not say anything, only looked at me. The other women were angry. That must have been yesterday. . . .

I put my feet slowly through the air; there is a floor underneath. Slowly, I unfold and push myself erect, hands clutching the wooden frame of the bunk. There is air coming from somewhere at the end of the room.

One foot in front of another, from one frame to another, I advance. There is a street between the bunks. I count two bunks and then sit down. Three bunks. I am walking slowly but more surely now. The room is very long.

I see now where the air is coming from. An opening at the end of the room. The sky comes into the room. An iron chain hangs between the portals of the door. The door is open. There is nothing outside, just open space.

I lean over the iron chain and see water far below: black, with a ray of light twisting in it. And in the distance, above the dark edges of housetops, the fingers of fire opening. Red light in the high windows.

I stand in the openness but I cannot move. It is too high. Nowhere to go. A canal below. I imagine on the shores the green uniforms marching in the night.

They must have stored something here. But what? Wheat? Yes. I like the idea of wheat. Wheat makes bread. I see ships unloading yellow wheat glistening in the sun. I lean over, to see more of the water, the black water that surrounds this house. How I used to like to swim. Jump and swim.

I stand breathing the wet air. And with the coming noise, I throw my head back and follow the dark shapes turning spokes of light on the revolving sky. I whisper, I am with you, up there, whoever you are. Throw down your bombs. Throw them straight. I see the shadows of the planes across the moon and in the distance another explosion. "Thank you," I say.

It is quiet now. I lean out over the chain. . . .

"Tania!"

I turn back to the room, catching hold of stone, seeing Ilse running from the door straight to me. Her hand is soft on my forehead.

"How . . . how do you feel?"

"Fine. You should not have left me here."

"Hell!" Ilse's hand is under my elbow, Eva's arm across my shoulders, helping me to walk. "In the shape you were . . . Anyway, in the cellar it's not much safer."

We are at my bunk. They lower me carefully. I push them away. "I am all right," I say.

"Listen." Ilse's voice sounds as if she is telling a secret. "If you could make it tomorrow for work . . . it would be better. They already know about you. . . ."

"Know what?"

"That you are sick. You know how they are."

"I know. . . ."

"This new commandant he . . . hell . . . you know . . . well, dammit he can send you back! You know that!"

Slowly, I lie down again. Carefully, as if to remember something, I say, "When was it we came here?"

Ilse's voice sounds angry. "Five days ago!"

"Five days. Yes, of course," I say, and close my eyes.

The Shovel

Days of earth and a shovel. The earth, gray on the surface and cracked. Deeper down, when the muscles pull heavy along the arms, the earth becomes darker. There is a worm sometimes, brown and twisting in the uncovered air.

I am a builder. In a wide field on the edge of the city, where nothing grows but bunched stalks of yellow grass—white flowers here and there—I am a builder of foundations. Someday houses will grow here.

The first day after the blood stopped, I went with the others out of the city and there in a field the shovels were stacked. I started to dig and earth came to meet my face. When I opened my eyes the yellow grass spread through my open fingers.

The days start at the edge of an unfinished night. With black coffee and a piece of bread. We take the steps down into the street. From other houses come other figures. The fair men in their torn uniforms, their feet wrapped in dirty cloth; they smile at us through faces of fitted bones and are led away. The other ones with blue berets have shoes and wink at us.

We walk along the canal, through the limits of this city. The shades drawn in the houses that stand. I wonder if there are people behind the closed doors, sleeping under the light white feather beds. Some houses are open. They stand, with their fronts cut out and their wallpaper showing—they have the sky for a roof. There are the red drapes over no windows, a picture hanging sideways on a nail, pink roses on a wall. Once there was a woman's hat, green with brown feathers, hanging on a sharp point of a broken wall and I wondered, Where is the head?

The sky is many-edged along the ridge of the houses. Nothing seems round in these mornings—except the small white ship that waits for us anchored in the canal. There I can sit, leaning on a warm pipe, and put my head in the coal dust. The stack is straight and white and the smoke comes out in round puffs and stays behind it for a long time.

Sometimes I sleep; sometimes I look at the passing villas above the canal, white in the middle of the green gardens, the stone steps leading to the water, the small boats tied to a ring. There are straw tables in the gardens, with colored umbrellas, a forgotten wooden horse or a white sheet hanging from an open window. Sometimes a figure appears in the distance—but it moves off without stopping to look at us. After an hour the ship stops and we get off. We walk toward the fields. Sometimes there are trees and high grass.

It is noon. Wind is the sound of water in the leaves; the air is white with sun. I walk through grass high as my ankles. The grass moves with the wind but the daisies are still. Open to the sun, the yellow circle of grains lifts the white petals, shape of my pointed finger.

"What are you looking for?" says a woman sitting on the grass.

"I'm not looking for anything." It is only a way of walking out of the cotton tiredness, out of the fog in the mind. To see things and know them again in their own shape and color. I want to think of big things that do not change. Oceans and mountains. But then I saw the ocean only once and then I was too small to know what it was. I remember only the white hotel and the balcony of the room and that I threw orange peelings down at the little walking people.

Noon is past. I pick up the shovel. It is a good shovel with a sharp edge. I am ready to shove the blade into the earth; I stop and walk over to Ilse.

"Give me your knife, will you?"

She reaches in the pocket of her dress. I take the knife. She watches me as I cut into the wood, carving in the handle of the shovel.

"What are you doing? Your number?"

"No. My initials." The *TA* is deep and clean in the gray handle. "It's a good shovel. I don't want to lose it."

I hand back the knife and start to dig. The sun is sharp in the sky as I bend down. My fingers part a three-pointed leaf and a berry is in the hollow of my hand. I separate it from the leaves and carry it slowly to my mouth. There is no taste to it. But the filling smell of earth.

The Single Sunday

I don't know how many weeks we are here. I used to count time by Sundays, but after so many Sundays I forget the count. The morning light is darker now; there is the sour smell of coal in the air. And Sunday brings only the man with the list.

Sunday: first the washing under the cold spray of water, then the coffee and bread, and the whistle. The man whom all the others salute arrives. He enters this room as he would a church. Instead of a prayer book, he carries a pool cue, sawed off. It must have been white once. We stand in a rectangle so that everyone can see.

A white piece of paper sticks out of his pocket, with numbers on it. I keep thinking that if I don't look at him, it will not be my number. Then I try looking him straight in the face, so that it will not be my number. It is quiet in here now and I can hear the sound of the canal from behind my back. The air is cool. If I wash my pants, they are not going to dry till tomorrow. . . .

He calls a number and a girl comes and stands in front of him, bending down now, her skirt pushed up, waiting. I wonder how many it will be today. Twenty-five is a long time to watch.

The sound of the cue pulls the air apart. The girl's face is tight, the eyes clenched shut. She stands, legs spread apart, her upper body supported by arms, hands on the knees. I watch the man. Under the officer's cap, his cheeks are pink and uneven teeth show in the parted mouth. I can't help counting. Ten times the arm rising with that short weapon and the saliva starts running from the corners of his mouth. By fifteen, there is the foam under the lower lip. They say he is insane. From a wound in his head. I don't know. . . . It is all over now. The girl pulls back her skirt and walks to her place. As she walks by, I see the colorless drops on her forehead.

He will leave now. But he stands there and his right hand pushes his cap back from the smooth forehead. He looks almost gay, as if drunk, with that crooked cap on his head. His hand reaches into his pocket and he pulls out another piece of paper. His eyes circling us, they move round and round, as if he wanted to guess the face behind the known number. He reads off the number, the sounds rolling from his throat like small stones. He waits. There is a movement from the last row as they make room for a girl. She is short, her body full, and there is color on her cheeks. It is a familiar face; her name is Sonia. It was while she was digging one day next to me that she told me about the man she knew in the old camp and how they will be married as soon as . . .

The man is looking at her. She is small, her head lifted up to him, the fingers of her hands spread apart on her thighs. Her face is without expression.

"On your last visit to the infirmary it was discovered that you are pregnant. An unfortunate thing, as you know. This is not a proper place for a child. You will be sent back. Tomorrow morning. Be ready at six o'clock!"

The man is gone. Sonia stands still in the same place. Then she turns and is facing us. Nobody moves in the silent room. Somebody coughs and all at once we start to talk and to move toward her. The girls are all around her. They say, "You will come back. . . ." "It's nothing. . . ." "You will be all right. . . ."

"I don't know," says Sonia. "It's just that . . . all alone . . . I am afraid. . . ."

"Sure," say the girls, "but they won't do anything to you." "It's just that you can't have the baby here." "You will be much better off."

The whole afternoon they bring gifts to Sonia. Ilse offers a piece of broken mirror and my gift is a length of yellow string.

Eva unwraps the gray underwear and opens it to Sonia. In the middle of the crotch lies a slice of bread. There are other gifts on Sonia's bunk: one green apple, a comb, a patch of blue cloth, half of a candle. There is a festive air about her bunk. The girls talk of childbirth.

When evening comes they go to wait for the Sunday soup. Now there are only Sonia and I and the scattered gifts on the green cover. I watch a flea jump from the green wool, when Sonia says, "If I knew there would be others . . . I know . . . what they will do, but . . ."

I smooth the thin wool under my hand. "There will be others, Sonia. . . . You don't have to be afraid. Hundreds of others."

"I never liked to be alone," says Sonia.

The Chocolate

The sound is low first, broad, then lifting on an opening cry it narrows—sharpens to a bright point in the center of sleep. Three times it jabs, slackens—until the one word is a light in my head: RAID.

My eyes open. My mouth is cool, round as if with an expected kiss or candy. I reach over the edge of the bunk and touch out my shoes. I hear Eva's cough among the squealing bunk boards, the scuffling of feet. Everywhere the bent bodies straighten, the sound of feet; the line thickens and a slot of gray opens in the door.

I press my hand on the wall of the stairwell and start the descent. With each lowering step, Eva's cough, above and behind me. Down, following each footfall. Faster, down. The teeth are foreign in my mouth—I shake. But not from the cold spiral of the stairwell. The raid is on schedule; the shove of the guard is known to me. The feet stepped upon, the press of bodies—all this is only a repetition of all the nights in this place.

This inner cold comes punctually with the first sound of siren, with the first shake of powdered mortar from the rafters. It settles on my skin where it leaves a hundred grains, sifting and sinking, through muscles into bones. This feeling is inside of me, beyond my will. This fear is a dust that I cannot shake free.

Each footfall lower. To the bottom. Where the steps end and the middle part of night begins. In the cellar, where the walls are damp and the floor made of wet sand.

The guards leave, locking the heavy door behind them. The rats, big as rabbits, run low; their brown fur quivers in the yellow light of candles. There is the sound of water down the slope, where between pilings the angled cellar opens on black water. Beyond the canal the *dum* sound of bombs falling in the city.

Eva is sitting with her back to the wall. She is coughing into her hand. I wish she would stop. I do not know why, but her cough makes me angry. She stops for a while, closing her eyes, coughs three more times and then, her head rolling on her shoulders, Eva is asleep.

I sit close to Ilse, feeling her warmth. With the whistling sound above us, the fall and the walls shaking, Ilse sits, her knees drawn high to her chin, frowning. She is watching Eva. She stands up, her long body stretching, takes a few steps, her hands locked behind her back. She comes back and squats in front of me.

"I never have a cold!" she says.

"No, you don't." I watch the round hollow beside me, the imprint of where she sat. I wish she would sit down again.

"Now, let's see . . . what was it that I used to . . . Honey! Because the sweet soothes the throat . . . I wonder what happens to the bees during a war?"

"They have a queen that takes care of them," I say.

"Yeah. Listen," she whispers, "I have a plan. You know the men prisoners. . . . They are right next to us. Their cellar, I mean. I am going to see them."

"How?"

"I didn't tell you, but I saw them last night. I did not talk to them, I just watched them. They talk in a funny language."

"But there is water . . ."

"By this bend here, it only goes to your knees. I just waded around the corner of the wall and there they were. . . ."

The planes must be right above us now. The sound of their engines throbbing in the sand. But the sound slackens and the released bomb falls somewhere else again.

"It's very dangerous, Ilse, don't . . ."

"The only thing I am afraid of is water snakes. Isn't it funny? I am sure there are none here. It's full of rats, though. God, the big bellies they have when they drown! Anyway, they did not see me. The men, I mean. Some of them were chewing on bread. I figure they must have Red Cross packages." Ilse stands up, waving toward the wall. "They are prisoners of war, you know? That's *much* better than us!"

She slaps me on the shoulder and takes off her shoes. "Good idea, isn't it?"

I nod. "Yes. Be careful, Ilse."

Ilse fades from the circle of light. Stepping over the spaced bodies, she walks down the slope of the cellar, moving between pilings to the supporting wall. She enters the water and her hand drops from the edge of the wall. I cannot see her any more.

The flickering light of the candle makes Eva's nostrils bright. But the cheeks and eyes are hollows of dark. I am holding my hands together to stop them from shaking. It is good that they come, the planes. Without them it would never end. It has to be. Maybe they even know that we are here and they would laugh if they knew about my fear. All they are doing is for us. This is the way the war will end.

Voices behind me sputter and hiss: "Right across from the movie house. You take the tramway . . . number ten . . ."

". . . We will plan it very, very carefully. . . ."

". . . It's bound to fall on us one day. . . ."

". . . You let the butter brown and then slowly you add . . ."

". . . The first time? I don't remember the first time. . . ."

I sit, waiting. Sometimes it seems to me that I am watching all of us from the outside. As if I was not here, but was observing from some safe distance. But that is even worse. Because I feel more helpless than when I am part of them.

The siren blows the end of the raid, and looking up, I see the sand-marked knees of Ilse in front of me. There is water dripping from the hem of her skirt. Her right eye closes in a wink.

I move to Eva and touch her arm and whisper to her, "I think that Ilse has something for us."

"How come you are so wet?" says Eva.

"I went for a midnight swim," says Ilse.

Upstairs, we are starting to undress when Ilse whispers from her bunk, "All right! Hold out your hands!"

Into the darkness, Eva and I stretch out a hand.

"I have three pieces of chocolate," says Ilse.

Eva coughs and I pound her back.

"One . . ." says Ilse. I hear the rustle of foil paper and Eva's mouth full with the hollow cracking of chocolate.

"Two . . ." says Ilse. I feel Ilse's hand flat on my fingers.

"And one for me," says Ilse.

I press the empty hand to my mouth and my lips make a sound. As if there was a piece of chocolate.

The Old Man

From a sky heavy and gray, the first snow comes. The known touch in this foreign land. There is the cold in my body and I tear off pieces of blanket to roll over my feet and tuck into the wooden shoes.

Our shoes slide on the tumbled bricks, splinter against stones, are caught and pulled loose under the bent beams. We climb hills of stones where the houses were and pass the stones down, hand to hand, lowering the hills on which we stand. Above the mounds, in the streets leading out from the city, the walls are bright with squares of paper where the rooms were. The floors are gone, leaving the scenes on the charred paper of gardens and hunting. There is that slight difference on the walls but the fireplaces are alike, one on top of the other, each black gap holding chars of wood that warmed the houses that are ashes. We clear the streets and bring the wide holes to a level again. We stack timbers and sort, from shards, molten pots, piling the metal to be used again. The snow helps to fill the holes in the streets and on the few streets where there are no holes the snow is scraped away.

I push snow away with a shovel from the broad sidewalk. The white is everywhere. Blank faces without sight or voice pass covered in furs. Sometimes the children look at us under their knitted hoods, until a gloved hand pulls them away. Their shoes are made of felt and leather; sometimes I see black boots, sometimes a high heel—all have warm stockings.

The snow falls silently. It falls on my head wrapped in a piece of cloth and freezes in the small hair above my forehead. Sometimes it is like a crown that crackles under my fingers. It falls into the wide gap around my ankles. When I pull off the shoes to wrap my feet tighter in the pieces of blanket, my toes are without color and I can't feel them when I pinch them. The cold makes my eyes run and I see the sidewalk close through the tears, as once I saw the print swell on a page through glasses.

The metal shine of my shovel strikes the pavement. The pavement dark, with white lines where the squares join. I move further. There is a house in front of me and a sign: RING THE BELL, PLEASE. I push the snow and say, "Ring the bell, please." It does not make any sense. In front of the house is a garbage can. How many have I looked into? They never put anything in them but what I would throw away. The guard is on the other side of the street. I push up the metal cover. The brown leaves of cabbage, peelings of potatoes. A glass jar and a torn letter scattered in the white shells of eggs. Ring the bell, please.

The whistle blows. It is noon. Ilse stands beside me, hands under her armpits, her feet stamping the snow. Some of the women sit across the street in a cavity of a house without a roof. They have a small fire between the stones. There is only one guard; the others have gone to eat.

"Let's go," whispers Eva, pulling at my sleeve as I am ready to cross the street to join the group at the fire.

"Where?"

"Look around."

"All right with me," says Ilse, jumping from one foot to the other.

When the guard turns his back to us, we go around the corner. I walk behind Eva. She has a brown coat with one black sleeve. On her back is painted a big yellow cross. The yellow crosses come with the winter coats. The winter coats have one sleeve that does not belong to them. I have a gray coat with one blue sleeve. Only the crosses on our coats are the same. We walk down a slope. At the bottom, there are no houses any more, but craters filled with snow. Farther away, across a small plain, a few shacks, with wood nailed over the windows.

"Nothing here, let's go," says Ilse.

"Wait, isn't that smoke over there?" Eva points to one of the shacks, where a thin twist of smoke comes out of a tin chimney.

"All right, who wants to try?"

We look at each other, thinking of the reports that come to the commandant. The people in this city, they tell. They have to report. Order.

I see old papers blown by the wind—the headlines tell of another victory—turning on the snow.

"Let's all go together," I say.

We move toward the shack. There is no light inside, but the smoke is there. Eva crosses two fingers in the air, for luck, and with her face turned to us, her hand closed in a fist comes down three times on the wooden door. Something moves behind the door. Eva smooths the cloth on her head; she has the face of someone going for a visit.

The door opens. We look at each other. An old man stands there, dressed in black, his head covered with a small black cap such as I used to see on the heads of the praying men. Is it possible? . . . He looks at us without saying a word. His face is creased.

"We wondered, if you could . . ." Eva clears her throat, her hand motioning toward us. "My friends and I thought . . ."

The door is wide open now. Eva walks inside first and we follow her. The old man closes the door and turns a key. It is dark inside and warm. A wooden bench and a table, a stove in one corner.

In the other corner a bed with covers on it. A cat sits there, licking its paws.

The old man speaks; and what I am hearing is the almost-forgotten tongue. He is pointing to the puddle of water spreading from our shoes. I close my eyes and listen to the old man. His voice rises and his lament has anger behind it; somehow it is like a prayer even though the words complain: We dirty his floor and we will bring death to him. We have no consideration and they are going to find him. He has no responsibility for us and it is not his fault.

He walks to the stove, his voice muffled as he bends above a pot. We are beside him without speaking. The deep wooden bowl in my hands—I carry it to my mouth, drinking that familiar smell, that cooking made at home on a stove; the ingredients I know, the taste so often dreamed about: a thick pea soup. The bowl is torn from my hand—he pushes a spoon at me. We have to eat with a spoon. He returns my bowl, filled. We each eat three bowls with the spoon.

The old man turns his back to us and talks to the window, "What did they teach you at home? Eat like dogs . . . the children of Israel . . ."

I look at his back and see him straightening; the voice is saying: ". . . the only one! I must be the only one in the whole city. . . . Me, Jacob Samuel, against this whole, great city . . . Ha! Ha!" The chuckle is so surprising that I stop eating. But he starts to murmur again and I hear only: ". . . Our God is hungry . . . the children of God . . ."

We finish with the soup. There is nothing left in the pot. He looks at us. We stand each on an island of water where the ice has melted from our shoes. The cat jumps from the cot and stretches, the two front paws spread out, the rump higher than its head. It walks to Ilse and leans against her leg.

"Hello," says Ilse, bending down to it.

"Just forget you saw me," says the old man. "As they have forgotten me. I am only one and too small for them to see."

The cat purrs at Ilse's ankle. She is squatting down to it, her fingers dipped in its fur.

"Yes," says Eva. "And thank you very much."

"And don't come back. I never give twice."

"That's a fine cat you have here," says Ilse.

The old man leads us to the door, and before opening it, says, "I give you soup because I must. You do not know why and you leave only water on the floor of my house."

He nods his head. "God will be with you." The door is open.

Walking across the empty plain, we turn to see the footprints leading to that door, but already they are being filled. There is no smoke now from the shack. It looks like all the other shacks. The snow falls faster now and we are running up the slope with the single flakes entering our eyes. We forget for a moment the frozen hardness under our feet.

"Tomorrow, we are not going to believe it," says Eva catching her breath. "It's . . . impossible."

"He was strange. Like a saint or something," says Ilse.

I look at her. "We don't have saints, don't you know that? We have only prophets."

The Moving Days

There is a bundle beside me not much bigger than my hand. A piece of broken comb and a flat oval of gray soap, rolled in the old summer uniform. I look at the dress, the cloth thin, the known shade of gray; I brush the dust from the dress I wear. . . .

I remember the moving days. The smell of dust and moth balls and Mother's head covered in a red bandanna. The rugs rolled in the hallway, tied with rope, the straw cases with their smell of summer vacations. The moving men would come with their large shoulders. They tipped their caps back on their heads and stood in the middle of the room, their legs spread apart and hands on hips, the brown straps hanging around their necks.

I would watch them then, going down the steps. Their backs were chairs and armoires and I would listen to their descending voices. Mother would lean out of the window and watch the truck. Looking down at the men, their legs were shorter, the caps flattened. In the sun the furniture looked older. The last walk through the empty house: the windows without curtains larger, the stains on walls that were not there before, the walls without pictures— the lighter squares hanging under single nails. The hollow sound of the rooms. For the last time I rang the doorbell, listening to its own sound, and wondering about the next doorbell.

Before jumping into the truck, the moving men dusted their hands, pulled down their caps and spat in thin arcs on to the sidewalk. . . .

I smooth the green cover and look at the cot. How small it seems and my body never filled it. I do not leave any marks behind me. It looks as it looked when I first slept in it. The cover seems thinner now that it is winter. I know the notches of wood, the wax in the cracks where I sealed in the bugs. The dark grain above my head, the bottom of the cot above.

At the sound of the trucks from below, I stand up. Once more I am ready to move.

The Pines

Beyond the city, the pines bend hollow branches under the snow; their points white against the sky, the hidden moss a white mound around the bark.

In the clearing between the trees the barracks are yellow in their new wood, their smell filling the square of the yard. The wide country surrounds the wire, the young trees on the west side grow into a forest. On the other side, past the river, where the slope of trees opens into a field, the metal lines of a railroad shine black in the uncovered whiteness. The rails run straight and join at the edge of the land with the city beyond, its smoke flung back across the land by winds from the sea.

The air clear and cold under the gray sky, the fields spread in that winter light the color of quiet. I turn toward the young trees. After that time in the city, the trees are like something lost and found again and I would like to touch all that grows outside the wire. I try to imagine how it will be in spring. There will be mushrooms growing under the green shade of the pines and above them the birds will fly again in that free air. They will pull the wind in their wings and move in patterns known only to them. My feet will unfreeze and the river will let go the captured ice. The pines will drop their needles over the wire and their smell will come through the open windows. . . .

The room is large and in the corner the stove is red with heat. Already the smell of bodies fills this room. The green blankets stretch straight across the bunks, the gray metal kits lie upturned, the wooden shoes stand under the bunks with pieces of paper stuck into them.

"What do you think about it?" says Ilse. "Like a resort, isn't it? Like I always say, just give me the country."

Eva sits scratching her head. "I don't know," she says. "It's the wrong time. It reminds me of how we went once to the mountains, to some resort place, I forget the name. There was nobody in the hotel but us—it was too early in the season. My parents played cards and I took cans of sardines with me and sat on a stump and watched the mountains."

"What kind?" I say.

"What, mountains?"

"What kind of sardines?"

"There are only one kind. Portuguese."

"That's true," says Ilse. "It's the oil I like."

A new girl sits on a bench opposite us. She has been with us several weeks, but I can't think of her name. She smiles and says, "Do you ski?"

"No," says Ilse. "But I f____." The three of us laugh. The girl stops smiling.

I climb to a top bunk and stretch out, hands folded under my head. From here I can see the pines through the window. "I think we are going to be all right here. It's so different."

"Maybe there will be fewer air raids," says Eva. "Unless they want to hit the railroad."

Ilse stands up, beating her chest with her fist. "Country air. That's good for you. Of course, I was practically born in a field."

Outside it is dark. Our first day is ended. The pines look narrow now and the snow is blue under the tilted moon.

It is still dark when we set out for work. I shiver, hands in the pockets of my coat, and as I walk through the open gate, I turn to see the trees through the sifting snow. Sleep still fills my head, but my body is alive with the cold. I think of the lukewarm coffee and the voice of the commandant, shrill with numbers.

The column starts to move and there is only the sound of soft snow under the wooden shoes. We follow roads cut through the trees and our ranks split—going to different jobs. I watch the swaying yellow cross on the back of Ilse and sometimes I reach to touch squared layers of flaking bark. It is a long walk. I start to count the trees.

We come out of the trees on a road between two fields. The road is covered—the snow sticking now to my shoes, so that I have a second frozen sole. I stop to kick it off. Soon I drag my feet again, with the new weight pulling me down. There is the sound of sticks cracking against shoes. Behind me I hear Eva, stopping, kicking away the snow, then the soft cursing of her voice, and the snow keeps falling. I walk on high heels of ice.

There are houses now, white in their gardens of dry bushes. There is a factory that I enter: a building filled with gray dust. I have a sack of cement on my back and I carry it to a man in prisoner's clothes. His feet stand in water and he is mixing concrete. The girls stand by machines, the blocks coming out of them. I walk beside the dark racks, where the blocks are drying, back to the smaller room of stacked sacks. As the day advances, each sack becomes heavier. I know the weight of it now. I learn how to shift it from one side to the other, to lean on a rack, to carry the next one in the circle of my arms, supporting it with my belly. At noon I sit on the wet floor and the men with their prisoners' faces sit, looking into their gray hands. Some start to sing a foreign song, but soon they also stop and drop their heads on their folded arms.

The day is long and the muscles stretched too far. I think of the country outside—dust clogs my lungs. I think of the pines—I cough to spit out the fine particles of cement.

The walk home. A time that will end with the white hands handing me back my filled bowl. I walk with my head down. I do not touch the trees any more. I do not look up where each one ends. I see only their trunks, squat in the hollows of snow, and the branches are sticks in my way.

The new girl walks beside me. I lift my head and see her walking straight, a twig in her hand, slapping the trees. The snow falls off in bunched whiteness. She is young. I close my fingers on a small piece of blanket that I keep wrapped around my hands. I see her gloved fingers: black wool, with small dots of red.

"What's your name?"

"Dasha."

"Where did you get the gloves?" My eyes move to her feet. Again, real wool, blue this time, turned over the ridge of her shoes.

"They are mine," she says. "The socks also. They took everything away from me but these. Nobody here has anything of their own any more, do they?"

"No," I say. "We don't have anything any more. How long is it since you left home?"

"Three months."

I try to remember how it was for me, when it was only three months. I see the gate now, and looking at the camp, there is only the old pattern of barracks locked in the frame of barbed wire.

"Look at the pines, aren't they beautiful?" says Dasha as we enter the gate.

"What?" I measure the distance to the door of my barracks.

"The pines. I like pines, don't you?"

"Sure," I say. "Sure I like pines."

I enter the room and look toward the corner; the stove is hot. I move toward the smell of burning pines. The room is small enough to hold the warmth.

The Snow

It is quiet in the yard but for the measured steps of the green one outside the wire, his figure caught in the sweeping light of the watchtower.

The washhouse, set apart in that far corner, seems further to me and there is the floor of snow to cross. I start to run, my feet loose in the open shoes, the cold meeting my face. I find the single freedom of a minute, and I see myself running through an infinite space, with no doors at the end. My shoes leave holes in the snow and I remember how I once stopped and with a stick wrote my name and it was still there after I came back from the washroom, and I erased it with the same stick.

The door of the washroom is hard to open and I lean with my shoulder and push myself into the cold, damp air. The room is empty. The gray metal tubs, above them the small faucets holding that water, to which I run each night. I throw the clothes on a stool and open a faucet. The water comes slowly out of the pipe. My fingers seem bent in the water, my body narrower and longer. The water makes my eyes ache; at the wrists, the blood is close. Where I am the warmest, I feel the cold most. I catch the air inside me, filling my lungs with it, and have a head full of air. With the soap in my palm, I move my hands fast over my body and my single voice comes back to me, new in this empty room. The skin is thin under my fingers; as I dry with a small cloth I find the heartbeat, the small bones of my shoulders. I dress fast, not feeling the cold any more, but my teeth still click in my mouth.

Walking back, the distance seems shorter. One more barracks to pass and I am home again. It is then that I hear the voice of the green one. I turn, without stopping, thinking he *has* to be calling somebody else, but see his outstretched hand pointing to me. I did not do anything. . . . What does he want? But there is no answer in my cold head. What did I do? The yard suddenly seems smaller.

I walk slowly to the wire and stop, my hand closed over the gray soap, the other hand holding my coat tight together. It is the only protection I have, standing there, the soap and the coat. What does he want? I did not do anything. I dig my nail into the wet soap. He is still looking at me, his boots working the snow, his face not young or old. He has warm pads over his ears and the point of the rifle shines white in the light of the moon.

"I like girls that wash themselves. You come out later and we can talk. I will give you some food. I will be at the other side, by the entrance to the shelter."

The light is coming and I step out from its beam. How much of my face did he see? I back away from the wire and hear him say, "How about it?"

"Yes, sir," I say and start to run toward my barracks.

I close the door behind me and feel the beating of my heart, as if I had been running through the snow for a long time. The room is as when I left it. Except it is even warmer and smaller. Ilse is sitting on the lower bunk, Eva's head in her lap, her fingers parting the short hair. Looking for lice.

"None today, Eva," she says with some regret. Eva sits up, stretching her arms, yawning.

"There will be some tomorrow," she says. "It's the eggs, you see. The eggs are the most important. And you can't get rid of the eggs!"

Dasha is sitting beside them watching. They make room for me and even before I sit down, I say, "Ilse, the one outside, on the watch . . . he . . ."

Ilse looks at me, then closes her eyes. Her voice sounds tired. "I told you. You and your late washing yourself! What did he say?"

I repeat each word, and say, "Maybe there will be an air raid, so . . ."

Ilse dusts off her hands. "He can't do anything. He will not recognize you. We all look alike to them."

Eva is sitting with her hands in her lap, as if she was visiting. "It's the same with us, you know? They all look alike to us."

It is true. The man in the watchtower, the guard behind the wire, the commandant in the house standing on the small hill overlooking the camp. They are all one. I climb to my upper bunk and hear Eva's voice saying, "I always scratch myself when they look at me." And Dasha's voice: "What did he offer you?"

I cannot sleep. The room is dark and through the window I see the snow falling, no sound to it. A flake slides across the windowpane. I feel safe under the cover, protected from the snow and the yard and the man walking back and forth under the white moon. I make a home of my bed. And as I close the door on everything outside, I see the house and its known lock, the small chain and the brown carpet in the hall of my childhood. The house where home was and the door to it a passage to safety from the street and lost games and the sudden darkness of winter afternoons. I hear the sound of voices known beyond the remembered. I would like to hear the voices of a future home, but that house is silent, as if the people had not moved in yet.

Last Sunday, I heard the commandant make a speech. It had to do with the future: ". . . rumors, you hear rumors. . . . Yes, even if we did lose, which we will not . . . yes, even if we should . . . not one of you is going to get out of here. . . . I have a bullet for each of you. . . . Kindly remember that. Don't have any dreams. . . . In work is freedom. . . ."

I hear somebody getting up. I lean over the edge and see Dasha putting on her shoes. She stands in the middle of the silent room, looking at the window. I remember how she said, "I like the pines, don't you?" The light of the snow and the moon is in the room. She hesitates, then covers her shoulders with a coat, all the time watching the falling snow. She turns and walks fast out of the room. I wait for her return. Maybe she went only to the latrines. But it is late and nobody comes through the closed door.

It is the first time for her—I am sure it is the first time from the way her face looked. She made the step from one side to the other. In my mind there is a row of green ones: the commandant and his bullets, the guard and his rifle and, shining as if wet, the man without a face in the watchtower. They are all there, on the other side, waiting for her. *They are all alike,* Eva said.

Before turning into sleep, I see the yard and the snow falling, covering all footsteps. I know how the snow works and I accept it.

The House

"We are going to the house," says Eva. "I am sure of that."

"Which house?" I fill my lungs with the unexpected air. The cement factory is already behind us, with its single pine dusted with gray.

"The owner's house. He was bombed two days ago."

There are four of us walking behind the one guard. Ilse stayed behind in the factory. I slap my hands together to bring warmth into them and pull up the collar of my coat. Eva is in front of me; Dasha walks behind the guard.

"Good," I say. "A house. Imagine a real house."

We cross a narrow road and take a path twisting up a low hill. The sky is flat and the snow falls, each flake turning in air.

"It's been years since I was in a house," I say. "Do you think their houses are different from ours inside?"

Eva picks up a stick and swings it against the air. "A house is a house," she says after a while. Behind the trees now, the house. Eva points with her stick and says, "There it is. There's still something left."

The house stands in a garden, behind a white fence. There is a small statue of a boy playing a flute. The flute is thick with snow. The boy is naked. There is a white wooden swan squatting in a corner of the lawn with brown earth on its wings. Behind the swan the earth is upturned and dark.

We are in front of the house. The front wall is not there and the roof hangs in green shingles on one side. Through the open front I see white curtains flapping through red shutters, open upon no windows. From the garden we step into the living room. The guard tells us that the stones are to be carried away and the rugs, curtains and smaller furniture to be brought downstairs. There is a tumbling sound from inside the house and the guard leaves us. I see him sitting in the garden on the head of the swan.

There is a fireplace filled with earth and snow and a great mirror in a golden frame standing on the marble top of the fireplace. It must have slid down from the wall and it leans now—unbroken. On the piano a black shawl, red roses sewn across it.

"Let's see upstairs," says Eva.

A stairway leads up from the living room. The railing of the stairway is marble and cold to my touch. I mount steps covered with snow, the snow sifting down on to a rug the color of red wine. It is like climbing toward the sky with rugs below.

There are other rooms, the same heavy furniture, with fireplaces and rugs. One room is smaller and I stop there by the wall. I see a painting of ancient galleys and ships with their prows bent above the blue water. They face a city of stone, with its yellow houses in sunset and the sky over it the color of water. There are towers in the city and I see a small bell, shaped like a grape. I touch the frame, my fingers finding the cracks, and the dust solid in the carved hollows. The cloth is smooth with old paint. I feel the thickness of it and slide my hand back and forth. I feel the snow falling on my head and see some flakes stuck to the painting. I wipe them away with my sleeve.

Eva comes into the room. "There are some pickled eggs in the pantry downstairs. The other girl told me. That's all there is. Just pickled eggs! Can you imagine?" She walks to the frame of windows and touches the draperies. They are heavy gold brocade, and I hear the sound of ripping cloth and see Eva sticking a piece of it into her dress. We walk to the open side of the room. A carpet is hanging where the floor has gone; the fringes lift to the small wind. The guard is pacing back and forth in the garden, smoking.

We pick up a small sofa and carry it downstairs, the steps swaying under our feet. In the pantry, I raise the cover of the barrel and my eyes open to the round surface of transparent liquid. The eggs glow white, like oval fish. I pull out an egg, the water dripping from my elbow. Eva hands me a rusted knife from a shelf and with its point I pierce the shell and sip the raw yolk. We drink three eggs in silence and then we go and carry chairs and tables. The guard is lying on the sofa now, covered with blankets. I hear his snoring. Back in the pantry, we sit down on newspapers and eat more eggs.

Dasha comes in, closing the door behind her. Her face is drawn with disgust when she sees Eva, head thrown backwards, sipping from the white shell. "Raw? You eat them raw?" She sits down and pulls a cigarette from her pocket, striking a match.

"No," says Eva, waving the shell. "They are scrambled."

"All right, I don't care. Is it lunchtime now?"

She pulls a piece of bread from her pocket and leans on the wall. "One day, I am going to have a house like this. Go in and out when I want."

I watch her eating the bread; suddenly I think about what she said. Maybe a house does mean that—a place to close the world out or let it in if you want to. But, no, that is not it. "You don't need walls and doors," I say aloud. "You want to be free, don't you? Well, freedom is not a place you can own, it's . . . it's a home inside yourself."

Dasha does not answer. Eva looks at me in surprise. She scratches her head. "I don't know. We used to have a house. It was different from this one, smaller and well . . . different. After the war, I won't need a house. What would I do with it? Just somewhere where it is warm."

"You don't know what I mean," I say.

In that ruined house we talk about freedom. "I remember," I say. "I remember in that town where they would not let us on the streets. I wanted to go out so much and the streets were so close: below my window. Later, we were allowed on the streets, but not after eight o'clock at night. And I wanted the feeling of nights outside in the town. And now . . ." I look up through the split wall and see the sky edged by the torn stones. "It always seems so close. Just on the other side of what you can do."

Dasha pulls another cigarette. "I still would want a house."

"You probably will have it. You get everything, don't you?" Eva motions to the cigarette.

"It's funny when you think about it," I say. "No matter what you exchange with those who have more, they will always have more, and soon you will have nothing."

Dasha smokes in silence.

"You listen to us, young child." Eva is mocking. "We have years of experience. Maybe you will survive because of that." She motions toward the crumpled paper where the bread has been. "With us—if we survive—it's from habit."

"I don't know why you are all after me. I want to eat, that's all. I don't want to become like those others. Did you see the one with the swollen head? Did you? Water, that's all there is in her. I don't want that!" She holds her head between her hands.

"They are funny, the new ones," says Eva scratching her head. "Because their blood is still warm, they think they have some special knowledge." And standing up, she says, "And let me give you some advice: Keep the lice out of your hair! It doesn't matter how much you eat—if they eat you."

The voice of the guard calls us back to work. I walk up the stairs again and into the small room. I take the picture off the wall and carry it downstairs. I lay it across the piano. The snow is melting on the black shawl. I take a newspaper and cover the painting. At my feet lies an old grandfather clock in a frame of brown wood. I see it lying there, that clock that is part of the house. I pick it up and lean it against the wall. Just then the brass pendulum moves and the sound of the false hour rings through the ruined house.

The Men

There is a new camp being built next to ours. We share the wire on the east side and one watchtower. How fast a camp is built. The builders are never seen; they are not there yet when we leave in the morning and they are gone when we come back in the evening. It is as if the barracks grew by themselves.

It is one Sunday morning that the men arrive. I stand in the yard watching them. The striped clothes, the shaven heads. They walk by twos or threes, around their yard, hands joined in the sleeves, an arm raised in an unknown question. Their heads bend over the distant faces. The moving spareness of their bodies, the cloth flapping loose on their backs.

The women stand in the doors of the barracks watching them. Some are standing on their toes, as if they are looking for somebody. Not finding a familiar face, they turn back into the darkness of a barracks. These are not our men. The tongue familiar but not known.

I walk back into the room, past girls saying the Sunday words, past bickering and whispers, hands moving, past the smell of women, past the rope hanging across the room with the drying underwear, a gray that cannot be washed out. I climb to my bunk and lie there, my eyes fixed to the ceiling.

Men. What do I know of them? Even when we speak the same language. Perhaps one day I will understand them. One day, I will have my man. I try to see his face but there is only the body, dressed in prisoner's clothes. I remember Ivan, but now Ivan is only a name, lost in the past of other names. If there was no war, I would have known men. I would have walked with them, hands joined, through streets and parks, sat with them in theaters, shoulders touching, met them in rooms and through words I would have known their minds. That would have been. If there had been peace. It is war that takes men away from women.

The men outside—who are fighting this war—they are so unreal. . . . I see them dressed in iron, as in a history book, riding horses, holding flags, and the enemy emerging from the opposite page. There is a lot of red in the picture. I know that they are not on horses any more. They are in planes that come over the city each night. Some of them die and it must seem to them like a mistake. I think there is always a mistake in dying. . . . Someday I will meet the men from the outside and they will tell me about the war.

The men of the other camp will have nothing to tell. I think that people will pity them, if they come back. They will pity all of us. Pity I do not like. It hangs like a bad smell and it is hard to get rid of. What could the men tell? About their stomachs? How it felt? I think of the word "hunger." I am hungry, Mama. What a small word, as if made for children. There should be new words made. Maybe we do not have enough words. No word of the time of peace can fit a time of war. Like "captivity." The men are "captive." The yellow bird of my aunt. Fluttering of wings and pattering of seeds falling on the newspaper spread below. Singing when its cage is uncovered, swinging on a perch, sticking a yellow beak into the white bone . . . I wonder if the men feel about time the way we do: time going by and around the four corners of the camp, not moving inside, not changing anything. I can only tell time by the color of the sky or by my body.

Do the men believe they have enough strength to wait? Is their hope coiled in their stomachs? In the creases of their hands? How strange that the hands of these men do only peaceful things in the time of war. They build roads, work the earth, twist the metal caps that stop the ticktack of a timed bomb. I wonder if they fight among themselves.

The men on the other side. They are very close to me. There is a warmth in me, as if the love I feel was made of wool, like a blanket. I would like to spread it over them and make a new sky for them.

"Six for Special!" shouts the Elder in the open door. I raise my hand and climb down. Eva and Ilse are already putting on their shoes. I glance at the window and see the rain behind it, the sky dark. I have an agreement with Ilse and Eva; we always go for "Special Duty," hoping each time to find some food. But usually it is only to gather branches in the woods for the commandant's stove or to sweep their barracks. One Sunday, in the green barracks, a guard came into the room and without a word threw a piece of bread on the table. We looked at it and I remember Eva saying, "I do not think this will engage us in further activities, considering we are three." And it was after all a very small piece of bread and we ate it, the brooms resting under our chins.

Today we push carts in the rain and take a different road. Out of the portal, down a slope, following the hooded figure in front of us. We walk beside the railway and take a narrow path on the left, where the poplars stand, their branches squeaking in the wind. The road is muddy with puddles of yellow water, the tracks of a wagon filled with water. We walk with heads down, our shoes sinking into the wet softness.

"We must have been crazy," whispers Ilse. "In this weather!"

"You will see," says Eva. "Tomorrow it will stop raining and we will have to go to work."

"It's clearing already," says Ilse. "If it rained for a week! We could sleep . . . let's see . . . about a hundred and thirty hours . . . with time out for air raids."

Our words are the background for rain. I watch my shoes sink with a splashing sound, remembering how I used to walk barefoot in the summer rains, the mud coming through the thin space between my toes. The special smell of the earth after rain, the leaves glistening in the white air . . .

Beyond the bend in the road, we see a small farmhouse. We walk faster now, the mud lifting behind our heels. Eva closes two fingers in the shape of an egg. "Of course not," I say. "Those things never happen twice." Ilse moans every time we speak about the eggs. "Just when I am not around . . . It has to be when I am not around."

The other three girls in front of us talk of chickens and whether chickens are as stupid as they pretend to be.

"There will be something today," says Eva. "I can feel it."

"All I can feel is water in my shoes. But we can always pluck a goose and make ourselves quilts," says Ilse.

We stop in a yard: smell of manure, straw and cattle. The farmer comes out of the house. Throwing a black raincoat over his shoulders, he greets the guard. He has a long pipe hanging from his mouth, the stem bent, ending in a white porcelain bowl. He spits brown juice and slaps his hands; he motions toward a shack with an open door, where the sacks of provisions are stacked.

The farmer is asking the guard now to come inside and have a drink. The guard looks at us and then says something to the farmer, who nods his head. The old man looks at us. With a motion of his pipe, he leads us behind the house. Down the steps, the old wooden door with an iron latch is open and closed behind us and we are left in the dark, hearing the bolt catching. There is a sour smell in the cold cellar and the sound of the rain as if from far away.

"He winked," says Eva.

"Who winked?"

"The farmer. Like a sign."

Ilse laughs. "Maybe he thinks it's funny to be locked in this goddamn cellar."

"I smell something," says Eva, her voice trailing from the darkness. "You three take this side of the wall and we'll take this one. Stretch your hands in front of you."

Half-bent, hands forward, we search. We cannot say for what. There is only the sour smell in the air, but that could be just the way the cellar smells with nothing in it. It is Eva who bumps into it.

"It's a barrel," says Eva.

"Again? This is a nation of barrels," says Ilse.

We lift the heavy wooden lid. Twelve hands drop inside the barrel. It is soft and cold, the curds flatten when pressed between fingers. "Cheese. White cheese!"

It is a high barrel. We hang over the ridge of it. The wood presses into my belly, my hands down, coming up to push the soft cheese into my mouth. We do not talk and there is no sound to the eating. In the dark, not even our shapes are seen. The cheese melts away in our mouths, more and more cheese. The whole black world and a barrel of white cheese at the bottom of it. We hang there for a long time.

My stomach new to me, full of weight, I say, "Let's take some with us."

"How about the guard, if he searches us?" says one of the other girls.

"He won't. He will be drunk. Besides, he would not think there was anything in this cellar."

We start to search on our bodies for a piece of cloth to put the cheese in. The bandannas from our heads, a half-torn sock, one girl takes off her pants. We fill what we can and hide it in our clothes. The farmer's voice is loud on the stairs, talking to the guard.

The door unlocked, we load the provisions on the carts and push them back to the camp. We unload in front of the green barracks.

In the camp, the distribution has already started. We hurry for our mess kits and stand in line. Back in our room, we eat the soup. There is a smell of rotten leaves that I hadn't noticed before. For the first time, the unknown feeling of eating without being hungry.

"Let's save the bread for tomorrow," whispers Ilse. "If we figure everything, from now on we can be all right. We can *always* be ahead with one ration. Now when you think that tomorrow we will have the bread from today and the day after tomorrow we will . . ."

"One day, I will find a barrel of alcohol and pour it over my head," says Eva. "Then I will be really living."

"On the other side," says Ilse, "they get even less than we do."

"How do you know they get less?" I ask.

"Oh, I don't really know. But it looks like that. What kind of a language have they, anyway?"

"You wonder what work they can do," says Eva.

"I heard that it has something to do with the bombs on the ground that didn't go off," says Ilse.

"It's a wonder they don't blow up."

"They do."

"My brother one day did some experiments in the bathroom. Chemicals, you know," says Eva. "The thing exploded. You should have seen the ceiling."

"I didn't know you had a brother," says Ilse, tucking the cheese under her mattress.

I am putting my shoes on, the cheese still lying cold between my breasts.

"Sure. And we had just painted the ceiling."

I close the door behind me. The rain has stopped. On the other side they are going for their soup. The men are all out there, some walking back into the barracks, others shuffling in a long line.

The guard is in the far corner of the yard. Ilse said they have even less than we do. But she really does not know. I am closer to the wire now, where the small opening is. I stop and say, "Pst . . . Hey . . ."

But nobody hears me on the other side. They walk back and forth; some stand, drinking the soup without carrying it into the barracks. There is one now, passing close to the wire.

"You . . ." I say.

He turns at the sound of my voice. His face is tight and his eyes black. He turns his head away from me, but stands still, his back to the wire.

I smile to myself, proud of him, that he knows what to do. I look around and bend down fast. Through a broken square of wire I push the soft package of cloth. I have to squeeze it to the shape of the opening. It rolls a little way, like a white ball. The man scoops it from the ground. He drops it in his jacket and walks quickly, not turning. I walk toward the washroom.

How large his eyes were in the white face. The cheese will be good for him. In the washroom I find around my breasts small clots of white. I lick them off my finger and start to wash myself.

I wonder what it is made from. Sour milk? It will make him stronger, not much maybe, but sometimes even a small thing like that . . . Dairy products, they used to call it. A man needs dairy products.

I start to sing under the cold water.

The Gift

It is the time before Christmas. The first dead are driven out on a peasant wagon and buried under the snow in the field by the railroad. We do not assist in the burials; we only watch the wagon and its gray cloth, filled with wind, shaken by the high wheels, go down the slope.

But Christmas is coming and there will be more food and maybe more wood for the stove. I remember that one year—I don't know any more where it was—we had jelly for Christmas. The spoon turned on my mess kit and left it there. I remember how red it was against the gray metal and how sweet in my mouth, the forgotten taste of summer. . . . Now, in the evenings we gather memories of Christmas. A few still talk about the times at home, but not many, and I listen to them as to the old stories.

It is Sunday. In the empty dining-room barracks that we never use, we get ready for Christmas Eve. The decision of the commandant to have a celebration is accepted like any other order and obeying is our trade. Eva has written a play. When I ask her how it is going, she says, "I wrote a first draft, that's all. Then somebody stole my pencil." The play is about Mary, a woman in a camp, and her son. I am in a group reciting poems; we learn by repeating in loud voices after the one who knows them. Ilse is going to dance her own improvisation, and Eva will tell jokes about food and overeating. After we finish, girls from the other barracks come to rehearse their programs.

Back in the room, I pull a bench to the stove and have my Sunday. Eva sits on her bunk, needle and thread in her hands, sewing.

"Where did you get the needle?" asks Ilse, peeling a moldy potato.

"From the repair barracks. I told them it's for a costume," says Eva, biting off a thread.

I recognize the golden cloth of the stolen draperies. "What are you doing?"

"It's a surprise. Don't look! I am almost finished."

I turn my face again to the stove, watching the pot. I do not want to think about what is in the pot, but if it is cooked, I will eat anything. The girls pass by, throwing in the pot whatever they found during the week and cannot eat as it is. I know it is all rotten, but it will be cooked. I have learned many things. Not to touch the raw cabbage leaves that are like oiled parchment, not to drink the unknown water, yellow from a pipe. Through seeing others, their mouths open to a flow, the hands spread over a belly of pain, I learn. Will power, I could call it. But "will" is only a word for obeying my own orders.

The snow has stopped. Through the window I see a piece of gray sky and the quiet land beyond the trees. The warmth from the stove comes up my legs. Just to sit close to the stove, the buzzing voices around me, looking through the window or watching the pot, to close my eyes or open them to see Eva up there sewing—that is my Sunday. Cup in hand, waiting to dip into the soup, I shut my mind away from "tomorrow" and the waiting sacks of cement. There is only this room and the known faces and Christmas coming. . . .

Sometimes on Sunday I think of the future. I see it only as another, better camp, with more food and two blankets. The past is almost gone now. It is as if there has been no distant past. I think of the near past, the past of camps. But even that does not hold together; events unravel, and places and times pull apart. On Sundays I repeat my name, so as not to forget. I say it to myself: Tania Andresova, born . . . age . . . Each Sunday I regain my identity before becoming again a blank face among other blank faces, a pair of feet sinking in snow, a mouth gulping down a bowl of soup. Eva calls the soup "ambitious" because we put everything we have into it. Sometimes on Sundays I look at my hands, when they are clean, and try to recall if they were different before. But I cannot remember. I do not remember anything of my body from before. It is as if my eyes were always too big for the tight face, the neck too long to the touch, the shoulders ending in these sharp bones, the breasts always as flat as my back.

There will be another year, maybe another bunk. But I think that one day it must end. I think about it—shy with the thought—as if not to destroy the chance that is not yet there, but will be. That is why I keep getting up in the morning. That is why I run each night through the snow to find only the clear, cold water at the other end. To be clean is to wait. And I am waiting, all the time I keep waiting, not doubting—on Sunday—that this will end.

. . . I think about the world outside: a world of real kitchens, tables, plates, knives and forks. But would I know how to use a fork? In which hand did I hold it? There is only a spoon that brings to my mouth all there is. I see them—the heaped table—laughing, talking, and in between they pause and put something on the fork and say something else and swallow. ". . . You want some more? . . ." ". . . I could not possibly. . . ." ". . . Just a little more . . ." And they carry away the rest and bring the dessert, because there is always some room left for dessert in that world. I close my eyes and see the whole world eating. . . .

"Tania, Ilse!" The voice of Eva brings me back. She is waving a hand at us.

"All right, we are coming," shouts Ilse. "What's the matter with you, taking a train or what?"

We climb the ladder to Eva. She sits there, waiting. Her hands drop into her lap, then come up into the air. From each hand, the straps around a finger, hangs a golden brassière, the light shifting on the old brocade.

"Here."

Ilse takes the brassière; her mouth falls open. "Well . . . I'll be . . . I missed that thing more than . . . than anything!" And over the shapeless gray dress, she holds that golden frame on her bosom.

I am still holding my brassière in my hands, smiling at Ilse, my fingers caressing the shimmering cloth.

"Look, everybody," shouts Ilse, climbing down to the waiting women, the brassière still over her dress. "Look, you can see a real woman now!"

"You will fill it up . . . one day," Eva says to me. "I thought you should have something . . . something like before."

"Yes," I say. I nod my head and look down into the empty gold cups.

We come home early on Christmas Eve. My thoughts are only of the food that we might get. Two portions of soup maybe and a double ration of bread with . . . with jelly? The girls talk of sugar; somebody from the kitchen said . . .

It is a double portion of bread and a piece of margarine. I advance then in the other line, from where the girls carry away something dark and solid. Meat!

"It's meat, Ilse, really!" My heart beats fast. This feeling is something forgotten, this impatience for the things ahead.

The dark pile is hard from outside and soft inside. I eat it, rolling it on my tongue.

"It's fried," says Eva. "Blood."

"You are right," says Ilse, waving a spoon. "It's goose blood. All these geese killed and what do you do with the blood? It's Christmas, isn't it?"

The coagulated blood leaves a sweet taste in my mouth, the smell of poultry. I would like to hold it longer, but it dissolves too soon, slipping down my throat.

"This is the best meal since . . . I don't know, since the war," I say, watching Ilse licking the sides of her mess kit.

In the light of the bulb, with the stomach filled for a while, the room is a home. Christmas Eve.

"It was like a liquid steak," says Ilse.

I think of the Christmas Eve before Grandma died. How she made a soup out of the dehydrated vegetables she had saved. And Mother took the last jar of mixed butter and flour and put the last of the cocoa and saccharine in it, and turned it till it became soft and smooth. Then we rolled it into small round balls in our palms. That was our candy. She told us then that each time should be cherished because the times could always get worse.

"Somehow, it does not seem proper," says Eva, holding her empty kit, turning it around between her knees. "I mean blood, really! And there will be no seconds."

From the yard I hear the radio from the green barracks blaring out "Silent Night." On a small mound, outside the camp, where their barracks stand overlooking the camp, they have built a snowman with a branch of holly in his head and a broom in his plump white arm.

We walk into the dining-room barracks and some green ones are already there, sitting with their backs against the wall, swinging their lidded steins. The girls sit on the new wooden benches, row after row. They sit politely and quietly, with their hands folded in their laps, watching the still, empty stage. Their faces are clean below the bandannas and for a moment there is almost the air of a real theater. Instead of this ordered performance, I would rather sit on the bunk in the familiar air and not think about Christmas.

An order is shouted. We start with the poem. We are six voices in a monotonous string of words, then one, three, then six, our voices rise and fall together. I look at the green ones and they look bored, some with their mouths opening in a yawn. The poems are in our language and they do not understand. The girls give us the sound of their hands and we leave the stage for the play.

I sit down on the corner of a bench. I lean on the girl beside me and close my eyes. I feel tired after the work and the meal, and I doze off in the middle of faraway voices. . . .

It is the cough of "Mary" that wakes me. The girl who plays Mary is wrapped in a brown blanket that comes down over her head. That cough does not belong in the play. I look at the guards and they seem impatient, but Mary has a fit of coughing. I think how strange it is that they have to wait until she finishes. She is for that instant the distant figure, out of their reach, doing her individual act of coughing.

Mary parts the standing group at the front of the stage; tears from the cough catch light in her eyes. Behind Mary there is a red board with painted black lines crossing each other, to suggest the wire. The lament of Mary has the accent of my country, the words come, sounding foreign in her mouth: ". . . *He was born when the star shone large and bright. He always liked the stars. I went with him across the country, into a foreign land, and the stars were always there. Later, he had a star on his chest and a cross painted on his back. My child . . .*"

It took Eva two Sundays to do this. Maybe with three Sundays, it would have been better.

"But why did he kill himself? He did not have to do it." The figures around Mary speak.

"He did not do it. He was picking small white flowers. They grew close to the electric wire. And he was pushed. Nobody knows who pushed him. He fell across the wire, arms spread wide. There I found him—what was left of him—black, and the coat calcinated, but for that yellow cross on his back. On that wire . . ."

What are they saying? The soldiers will be angry. I hear a sound from the back where they sit and my head drops lower between my shoulders. In the silent air, where no hands come together, I slowly turn my head.

And with my eyes widening, I see the green men. I see them pull white handkerchiefs from their pockets and wipe away the tears, embarrassed. They try not to look at each other. Then they clap their hands together in a loud applause, swallowing the last tears. . . .

There is Ilse now doing her dance and I hear their laugh. I walk silently out of the room.

The sky is very dark and I am glad for the darkness. I hear the whistle of a train from below the slope. I lean on the side of a barracks. Such a wide night! I hear faintly a song from the other side of the wire. I wonder what they had for dinner. With that far song and the laughter of the green ones from the dining-room barracks, I feel so alone. I pull the coat closer around me. I should think of other Christmases. I knock the snow off my shoes. I should do something, try to explain to the others how I feel. But I cannot . . . even to myself. I should go inside, talk to somebody. This is Christmas Eve. I repeat it to myself. Maybe next year . . . I feel that I should say something.

"Thank you for the blood. It was very good. Keep me well, and Ilse and Eva too. Don't let my toes get any more blue than they are. That is all." There should be something else. But I do not have many wishes. I look up in the sky. . . .

There is only the single beam of the watchtower light, crossing slowly back and forth.

The Women

It is a long winter. I imagine sometimes that all seasons have faded away and that winter will be upon earth forever. All colors will be hidden and the earth will not emerge. The sun will be heavy with the cold and it will not rise to the top of the sky. With the weight of snow the world will tilt and the sun will no more lift to its bright angle. I am white and cold—perhaps I will myself turn into snow and become part of the endless season.

The women quarrel less now and steal more. Ilse and Eva are more quiet. Ilse often lies on her cot in the evenings, not talking to anyone. Once I find her with eyes swollen with tears. "What's the matter?" "Nothing." Her face is more yellow and the golden brassière that she wears every day is too loose.

Eva finds a pencil and sketches. On a piece of crumpled paper she makes lines without apparent design, the dark circles upon white spaces. "What is it, Eva?" She holds the pencil to her mouth, wetting the tip. "Abstract. That's our room." She promises a ration of bread to whoever can bring her more pencils. She quarrels less with Ilse and talks to me about Greek mythology.

And then the snow upon earth becomes thinner, darker. I watch the sky for more snow, but it does not come. Finally the snow begins to melt away. There is a slow change in the air; it is a kinder, softer wind and around the wire the flattened stalks of frozen grass start to lift. . . .

One day in the early spring five green women arrive. They walk beside the guards, their skirts the only difference. Black boots to the knees, caps balanced like narrow boats on their flat hair. They walk through the morning fog with long strides, striking their boots with peeled branches.

Now each morning they follow the columns going out to work. They wait for the ones who cannot catch up and swing their sticks against the bent backs. They use sticks instead of their hands, poking, hitting—there is always the distance of a stick between them and us. It is since they came that I know how we look. It is suddenly as if in the world there are three sexes: men, women—and us. I think of us as something that the world has not seen before.

We work outside now on a large plain. We dig again, the square, large holes into the wet earth, the size of a house. The feel of the shovel is familiar to my hand, my horizon again the brown earth dotted with pebbles and upturned roots of grass. As we dig deeper, we make three high steps for the shovelfuls to be dumped on and lifted up to ground level. From my place at the bottom of the hole I can see only the ridge of ground with no landscape but the sky above. It is a private world and we build our own walls to it. Each morning, holding the same shovel, I go back to where I stopped the night before. I recognize my heap of earth, its color lighter where it dried during the night; my footsteps, still printed there, mark my existence.

We have a foreman, a quiet, short man, who shouts at us only when the guards approach. The women like to stand there, looking down at us, with sticks motioning us to keep moving, to stop talking. Sometimes I look up and I can see the legs, shining in black leather, and the stick disappearing in the twist of a skirt blown by wind. One day the foreman tells us about a son killed in the war. We listen to him and when he finishes Eva says, "Do you have a piece of bread?" "You do not eat enough?" he asks. "They do not give you enough to eat?" The next day at noon there is a barrel of soup from a nearby factory and from then on we have our midday meal.

Each day the bodies bend lower; down goes the shovel, up comes the earth. I throw shovelfuls up to Eva. She passes the dirt to Ilse. Ilse spills it out on the ground.

"A little faster, you bunch of lazy pig-dogs!" says a woman standing above us. Her stick moves, twitching against the square sky. The woman walks away. Eva is wiping her forehead with her sleeve and Ilse motions to us. I put down the shovel, its metal almost blue with the light of the sun. I stretch my hands above my head, feeling the muscles shifting. We climb up and join Ilse, who is now pointing upward. We grip the edge and pull ourselves up, heads above the rim of earth.

In the distance there is Dasha near a wild berry bush under a bare tree. Next to her is the green woman, the one they call Carl. I see the shadow of Carl's hand across the face of Dasha. I cannot see Dasha's eyes, but I imagine that they are closed and that she is smiling.

I let myself down again. I watch Eva's feet dangling in her too big shoes. There are holes in the stockings that end under the angular knee. The knee is black and there is a red scratch.

"Did you see?" says Ilse.

Eva jumps down, carefully brushing the dirt away from her skirt. She brushes herself for a long time.

"Yes," I say.

"I know what Carl is," says Eva. She pronounces it "less-bien." "I knew it when I first looked at her, but they all look like that."

"I did not know that Dasha would . . ." I say.

"Pfui!" Ilse spits on the ground.

"They all lived on an island and wrote poetry," says Eva.

"Pfui," says Ilse from above.

It does not really matter, I say to myself, picking up my shovel. I dig into the earth and throw the dirt. Down again the shovel. My foot on the metal edge, I push my weight on it and it sinks deep, and with a lift I raise the mound of earth and toss it above. "Work is freedom," it says above the gate of the camp, the letters twisted in iron, and when the snow was heavy I could not read the inscription. There was only the white twist of snow like a frozen snake.

"You know," says Eva, "it's not as if she was a whore. It's something else. She keeps on running like . . . like there was something to catch." There are deep lines on Eva's face, alongside her nose down to the corners of her mouth. Her face is white and the eyes like black stones.

"Maybe she will get out faster if she runs. When this thing is over . . ." I sweep my hand across our dug-up square, as if that was the war and the peace was just above, where the grass begins. ". . . She'll have to keep running."

"She will never think of it," says Ilse. "She will settle down and have flowers in her room and do push-ups on a polar-bear rug."

Eva laughs, her teeth white, some blood running across the gums.

"What happened to your mouth?"

She wipes the blood away with her thumb. "It's nothing; it's the gums get loose or something."

"You have such good teeth."

"It's not the teeth, it's the gums."

"I lost one yesterday," shouts Ilse from above us.

"What?"

"A tooth. It's the first one. It just fell out like a nut."

"Probably was rotten," says Eva.

Ilse leans down toward us. Her face is angry. "It was not! It was perfectly healthy."

There is the noon whistle. I climb up, Ilse and Eva still arguing about teeth. There is a long line in front of the barrel. We pick up our mess kits at the side of a shack and wait in line. I see Dasha already by the barrel. Carl walks along the column. Her body is flat, her hair short and straight. The eyes are searching. I watch her, the gloved hand, the white points of a collar over the brown sweater held together with an ivory brooch. She stands now in front of the barrel, holding her stick across the chest of a girl, then lifting the stick and letting her pass, and again the stick presses against another chest. After a while she starts to walk again, back and forth. I look at her: The eyes are gray, turning in that head of a hunter. She stops suddenly and we look at each other. I see the known look; I stand still, my eyes straight across from her round face.

She plucks a glove from her right hand. I see her lips narrow—the point of a red tongue sliding—then the teeth show and the sting across my eyes, the button of the glove cutting my cheek. She hits me three times and walks away with fast steps toward the shack and I hear the door slammed shut.

Ilse pulls a cloth from her pocket and wipes my face. She stands there with feet wide apart, not saying anything, wiping my face. She puts the cloth back in her pocket and blows away a stalk of weed from her mess kit. Eva is whistling between her teeth, looking up into the sky. She says then, still looking up, "Can you imagine? There come the birds. Look!"

There are many of them, circling in a tight pattern. Some dropping out and flying on their own, then lost again in the moving denseness. Their narrow wings open small against the cold blue of the sky.

The Loud Sky

The column moves faster at the first sight of the camp. There is a shift, the heads lifting and backs straightening, legs that barely lifted above the ground now fall into a step. The barracks waiting, the watchtower green in the orange light of sundown.

"I got a book today from the foreman," says a girl next to me. Her eyes are large and blue and there is a straight smile on her face. I do not know this girl. She is working somewhere else and lives in another room.

"What is it about?"

"It's about trout fishing. But that's all right; it's a book."

"Can I borrow it when you finish?" I ask with not much hope.

"Of course," she says, and turns her face fully to me.

We should know the girls from other rooms better; this one is nice. As we enter the gate of the camp, the sound of sirens tears through the quiet air. Another air raid. I look up and see the artificial fog spreading from the direction of the city. Feet running now, heads bent low between the shoulders, hands moving fast along the bodies.

"All in the shelter, all in the shelter," shout the guards.

The women run toward that higher ground that covers the dark square, four walls of earth in the ground. Louder than the voice of the guards, the noise of the sky spreads over the camp.

"They are starting early," I say to the girl with the blue eyes.

"I am not going in the shelter," she says.

I see Ilse and Eva running by, shouting something, Ilse's hand in the air. The circle of women widens away—they blur—dip down their heads and shove into the dugouts.

"Come on, everybody is going in the shelter today!"

The girl and I are tall and alone in the center of the yard. The sky widens with the coming sound. The air throbs with engines. I am ripping the sleeve of the girl.

"Come on . . . We can't be caught . . . alone. . . . Come on!"

"No." She leans away. "I want to read," and she starts to walk toward the barracks.

"You can't," I shout after her. The planes spread above the hill—a darkness rising.

She runs now, then turns, both hands over her mouth. "Make up your mind! Don't stand there!" A barracks door closes after her and I stand still.

I stand alone stranded somewhere between earth and sky. And from the sky it comes, the descending noise, and all my body listens to its growing roundness. The sound of its striking, before that second sound, the sound of wind through tunnels. The mountain comes up, made in the sky, the black earth at its point. Falling back, slow as water. And smoke rising from that place where men slept last night.

My feet moving under me. To go where? The nearest barracks . . . the dining room . . . I am in. I run between the benches toward the back door. Before I reach the door, the sound again, closer—the sound running after me, larger. I remember I should open my mouth. . . . Who said that? And with the mouth hanging wide open, I fall down under a table and in the explosion I hear a scream.

Only when my lips come together does the scream stop. The world upside down from under a table—two walls to the room. And my table a solid shelter against the war. I lie there, waiting. I feel the warmth of my body. I hear my breathing. I have to touch something: the wood above me. It is solid. Good. But my fingers slip and pull away sticky with sap. Sap, the blood of a tree. I listen to the quiet outside and roll from under the table. I smell the smoke; there is a burnt taste in my mouth.

The quietness makes me move uncertainly—I do not want to disturb the quiet. I open the back door. The shelter is close, a dark mound. The quiet ends. The edge of the sound closing in again. Why don't they wait? A little while—enough to get to the shelter. I stumble down steps cut from the earth and bend my head under a beam into that body-warm air. Touching bricks with both hands, I step into a light of candles. From outside I hear the sky full of engines again, its mile-wide sound. The women shake in my eyes and bricks come loose under my hands. I fall with the press of dark and earth behind me. I turn in earth made fresh and the blood is a wet cloth struck across my eyes.

But the women are here, pulling me toward them into their smell and their warm hands and shoulders, and I sit, breathing as if after a long run. Ilse comes crawling on her knees. "Where have you been, Tania? You're a mess. You hurt?"

"No. A scratch. I think they got the railway finally."

There are some women at the entrance, trying to push the bricks and earth away. It is quiet outside. We wait and it is not broken. There are voices now and the sound of a shovel. Through the uncovered entrance I see the sky, color of flame.

The night is over what has been our camp. The barracks have been shattered; they lie in mounds of wood. The only one still standing with two walls to it is the dining room. There is a big crater in front of the hospital barracks.

We bring the wounded and the dead into the dining room, laying them on the tables. I am covering a girl with a blanket: a girl with blue eyes. She looks as if she were reading.

With the eyes half open.

The Silence

The open gate swings on the shattered pole, the squeak of the wood regular as breathing; the three walls of wire lean close to the ground.

The red light of fire from the next camp is gone now. Only a trace of smoke sifts through the night air. I sit on the ground and watch the men being led out. They move quietly in a dark line, two by two. I hear only the voice of a guard: "Seventy-four, seventy-six, seventy-eight . . ." and then the trucks carrying the men away. I see the dark outline of a single barracks, standing untouched and alone, among the fallen ones.

The moon is hanging in the sky, widened at the bottom through the level of smoke, like a last coal in a charred sky. The air is warm and some girls are sleeping on pieces of wood. There is the sound of whining from the dining room. I hear a car pulling away. Maybe they have the body in there of the guard who was killed at his post. *Dead for the country.* The car disappears into the night. All is silent again but for the calls of the wounded. . . .

I wish I knew what they are going to do with us. How fast they decided what to do with the men! There is a big hole in the center of the yard where one bomb fell and I think about the man, the one arm that made the decision of that exact moment, *now!* He made a mistake and he may never know where it really went. I wonder if it is cold in an airplane. I am hungry. We missed the soup with all that. I wish I could sleep like the others. There is nothing to do now but wait. Dasha walks by. I recognize the sound of her shoes even though I do not see her face. Her shoes make a different sound; they are of leather. Carl came running in after the sirens sounded off to be sure she was not hurt. I remember Dasha saying that Carl loves her. Love. I love you. A world of lovers giving each other leather shoes. I follow with my eyes two dark figures, bent, running silently. To the east side of the camp. They are over the leaning wire. Where are the guards? I don't see anything now. My head is heavy. I repeat to myself, They escaped. I saw two girls escape! I sit still. No whistle blows, no rifle shoots. How easy. I always thought there was so much to prepare, to calculate. Why don't I go? Over the wire and out into freedom. I continue sitting here. I wonder if Ilse thought about that.

I stretch my hands above my head and yawn. I am hungry. I would like sweet-and-sour cabbage. They will stay in the woods during the day and walk at night. With their striped clothes. I wonder if they know the direction. Direction to what? There is no place out there. In which country are there no green ones? I can't remember. The lands over the ocean. I see myself asking passers-by, "Please, which way to the ocean?"

"Tania?"

"Sit down, Ilse. Tell me, would you like to escape, Ilse?"

Ilse sits down, stretching out her legs. "Escape?" I see her head turning toward the gate hanging loose on its hinges. There is the shadow of a guard walking back and forth. Then her eyes move toward the leaning wire and across the empty camp over there. "No. They catch you. And I don't know where I would go if I were out. Besides we would have to separate. I read somewhere once that you have to be alone. I don't know why."

"I saw two of them get away. Just a while ago. They crossed the wire over there. It was easy."

"Who was it?"

"I don't know, I couldn't see."

"Well, I wish them luck. But they are going to get them."

"Maybe not. Oh, I hope they don't!"

"I was thinking," says Ilse, "that the pantry is still standing. You wait here. I will find Eva."

I close my eyes after she leaves. What time is it now? The morning will come and their decision about us. They must have called the . . . Who is it that they would call? Some main commandant or maybe the Big Leader? No, not The Leader but some smaller leader. And he tells them over the telephone. The wires of a telephone, they carry everything. All messages. I never understood how a telephone works. That a voice is carried in a wire . . . I do not understand about a radio either. Maybe it is not important to know. It is not important to me that the message gets through. I wish it never could. I would like to cut all the wires over this country. What I really would like is to be somewhere else, without having to go there.

I hear Eva and Ilse. I stand up and follow them without speaking. The pantry is a small wooden house; its door is shut. Eva stops, pointing to the door. "I told you. It's no use."

"Let's try it. Maybe they forgot to lock it."

Before walking farther, we turn to see where the guard is. On the other side, two figures with rifles across their shoulders talk together under the light of the moon. I run fast to the door. My hand on the knob; I turn. The door opens easily. I step forward and stumble over something soft. A loaf of bread where the girl from the kitchen dropped it when the planes came. We close the door behind us. I pick up the bread from the floor and Ilse pulls it out of my hand.

"Why, that's dirty, Tania. Have a clean one."

On the shelf, the loaves are stacked in line, like soldiers. I hold a loaf in my hand, caressing the long surface. Then my teeth sink in. We sit on the floor, eating bread. There is no time in here. The world could end now but I would continue eating this loaf through eternity. It is surprising how long it takes to eat a whole loaf of bread. Then each of us breaks a loaf and sticks it into her coat.

Outside, nothing has changed. The guards are still talking. Only the moon has shifted its position. We lie down on the ground.

"They will never know. What's six loaves?" says Eva.

"We have to eat the rest before morning."

From the dining room again the sound of whining.

I lay my face close to the earth, feeling warm inside. I touch the rest of the bread, to be sure it is there. The earth smells of smoke. Eva's voice is muffled by her sleeve. "They are not going to send us back. . . ." Her voice trails off; it is not a question nor is it a statement. It is a thought she tries in words. In front of my eyes, the chimney stands orange, as if in bright sunlight. I sit up to shake the image out of my eyes.

"Of course not," I say.

There is a scream from the wounded.

"Why don't they do something about them? When I think we were stealing all this bread, while in there . . ."

"We were hungry, weren't we?" Eva's voice is angry. "Besides, we can't help them if we don't eat. . . . They will be all right. At least half of them should pull out."

There are voices now at the gate. We watch a group of green ones walking through the light of the dawn. They walk toward the dining room.

"They are going to help them," says Ilse sitting up.

There is the door, although the wall is gone and the doorframe stands unsupported under the sagging roof. The first one, with black-leather case, opens the door and goes in. The rest follow him. They bend now above the tables. An arm rises, a head lifts, moving from left to right as if saying no; and the wounded fall back, straighten. The officers move forward, bend again above the next table. Behind them on all the tables the wounded lie still. Their voices drop off one by one until everything is quiet.

The green ones come out. The first one is buttoning the black-leather case. They walk past us and I see the wrinkling shine of their boots. The case has a square brass catch.

After they are gone, we reach into our pockets. Without a word we eat the rest of the bread. We eat it now with the urgency of someone in a hurry.

5

It was spring in that country. For many years the people of that country ate the seeds of others and spring was only a season when the weather turned and the sun spread over the green land. But now the cities went down like dominoes toppling; and still the people believed. They believed, because they had been told that their souls weighed more than the souls of others.

But that year, it was a different spring. Black crosses sprouted in the fields of blond wheat and in the clover grass the peasants found green helmets that held the rain. (They shook their heads and did not understand.) A different spring: The soldiers marched back through the land and sometimes the planted mines took their shiny-soft boots away. The roads moved with the click of their feet, the dust lifting in round clouds. In woods green faces were swelling like melons in gardens. Across rivers where the bridges folded in, the running army crossed like insects on leaves. Phosphorous bursts bloomed above the hills and the red deer came down to the plains where the fireweed grew.

On other roads, the others were walking. Without boots and helmets, they walked slowly below the stone castles, along fields where the horses stood with drooping heads. They did not believe or refuse to believe in the importance of their souls. It was one of many questions they had long since forgotten to ask. They were tired walkers and they did not see the landscape. They did not know about the running army. Sometimes they walked close to the shiny-soft boots, lying crooked beside the road. They did not look to one side or the other but followed only where the road led them. They were glad it was spring. But only because it was a kind season to their bodies. They did not know where they were going, but they did not question that either. They walked as sleepwalkers, without seeing and knowing. One, two. One, two. For a long time. There was nothing left in their minds now but roads and feet. If there was death for the ones that made them walk, they did not know it. (It came low along the ground, with a sputtering of dust. It floated slowly downward, swinging from silk.) They did not know that flags switched color on the poles and were folded away under the wedding dresses. They did not know that the fear, so familiar as to become part of their bodies, had started to turn behind the wide belts of the nation that made them walk. The same ones that threshed cities and ground villages to a fine white powder—it was their turn now to listen to the whistling that filled the air above the growing mound of stones.

They kept on walking. If they had been told about the cloth blossoming and the soldiers dropping, they would not have believed it. And so they kept walking through the spring, with an ancient patience, on roads that nobody else took.

And yet on other roads, soldiers the color of earth pushed forward. The sun rolled in the sky, indifferent to all that went on, on all the roads.

The Long Walk

If I keep watching the feet in front of me, I will do the same. One, two. One, two. I close my eyes for a while and listen to the footsteps. It gives my eyes a rest. My whole body wants a rest. The feet in front of me now are lost in yellow dust. The road must have changed. I lift my head. There are hills now and white cows with black spots. One cow is lying down. Why don't all the cows lie down? I want to lie down. I feel the push from Ilse. She won't let me slow down. Always that push and I do not have the strength to turn and tell her to let me be. I am not so stupid as to stay behind the column. I just want to slow down. But I am not that stupid. After what I have seen done to them. When was it, the third day maybe . . . The shot was as if muffled, but I heard it and I turned around. The girl, far back behind the column. Her feet turned in dust and she spun upon herself, her arms waving at us. There was one more shot and then the soft sound of her body hitting the ditch. I remember that we walked faster after that. The ones that stay behind, they never cry out when they see them coming. They do not try to catch up once the soldier walks back toward them. There was one who sat down in the middle of the road and sat there waiting. . . .

The trucks stop sometimes and wait until some of the guards climb up. One, two. Soon there will be a stop. Every time Eva gets up in the row in front of us, I know there will be a stop. Eva is funny. The more tired she is, the faster she walks. Once she made three rows ahead. When I look at Eva, her neck is always stretched and the cords stand out. She looks so fierce. Angry. Ilse's eyes are bigger, but she walks always the same, not slow or fast, her feet grinding the earth. If I knew that somewhere there was a place where we were going. If I just knew that. But last night, in that forest, when we lay down, I could not even sleep and could not get the shoes off my feet. They are so big, my feet. I keep thinking that we are going nowhere. We just walk and there are not so many of us now, and when there is nobody left, they will all get into the trucks and ride away. Lying under that tree last night, my mind was clear and I could see that. I laughed. There will always be somebody left and they will not be able to get up into their trucks. They cannot shoot us; they must have orders. Just the ones that stay behind. Where do the trucks get the bread? They ride away and come back with bread and water. Sometimes we pass through a town and are given soup or turnips. I wonder where our commandant went. And the green women. One, two. Down the hill. There is a river and a bridge. The column stops. The guards pull out their cigarettes and sit down in the grass.

I walk down the small slope to the river. There are some trees with their branches bending into the river. I sit down where I can touch the water. The coolness is on my face and I lick my palms. Ilse is taking off her shoes and sits with her feet dangling in water. Eva is throwing water on her head.

"What do you think, is it all right?" Ilse turns to Eva, who somewhere along the road has become the judge of water.

Eva holds the water in the hollow of her hand, looking into it. "Go ahead. It's running fast here."

I lean over the river, my face wider in the current. The water is cool in my throat. I am glad that Eva knows about water. Maybe she does not know much, but we have not been sick yet. The water has a distant smell of mud and fish. But it is transparent and glistens in the sunlight. We lie down. The grass is soft and there is the breeze from the river.

"You have to get your shoes off." Ilse is kneeling by my feet.

"If you get them off, I can't put them back on."

"The water will do them good. Here we go . . . there . . . I know it hurts . . . Now stop kicking me."

The smell of sweat with that of dried blood. But I feel the air on my feet, the cooling air, and slowly I move my toes. Without getting up, I push myself down to the river. I let my feet hang there, feeling the water coming up my legs, my body knowing the healing coolness. My toes move more easily. I pull them out and the flakes of blood are loose under my fingers.

"How are they?" Ilse's voice comes from the grass.

"Fine. I think the swelling is going down."

"We will be there soon."

I do not turn to her; I watch the river and my feet in it. "Where?"

"Where we are going."

"I don't care. If we stopped more often . . . Maybe we will be walking next year and the year after. You see," I say, watching a bird settling on a branch, "we might get used to it. Now, it is so . . . I don't know; it's this being without any place; it's that we still think we belong somewhere."

"I sure would like to see the wire now. It is somewhere; we have to make it to there."

"Sure." The bird is flying away. I watch him against the blue and then he disappears behind a hill.

"Anyway," says Ilse, "it's the end. Everybody must know that. And they must have a reason for making us walk like this."

I pull my feet out of the river and let them dry in the sun. "So they have a reason. . . . Will that make us feel any better? All right, tell me. . . . I'll listen. . . . Tell me." I lie down and fold my hands under my head.

"Trains," says Ilse, a stalk of grass between her lips. "They don't have trains. And that's true because that's what Dasha told me. And you know Dasha knows it from them."

"She is always at the head of the column. It must be the shoes."

"Did you hear what I said?"

"Yes. They don't have trains. Because they don't have trains, we walk. Of course! They don't have trains so we walk." I start to laugh. I laugh and when I can stop for a while, I hear my voice, so high it sounds like a child's. "So we walk. . . . So we walk. . . ." I roll over and tap Eva's shoulder. She opens her eyes and I am laughing so hard now that I feel the tears rolling down my face. "Did you hear, Eva? Did you hear?" The laughter is coming up in me like nausea. "It's because . . ."

The slap on my face is so sudden that I stop laughing. It is Ilse who slapped me. That's all right. I was getting tired of that laughing. But it is funny. I lie down again in the grass.

"Well," says Eva, scratching her head, "it *is* funny, Ilse. Don't you think so?"

"Yes, very," says Ilse.

There are the trucks coming back from somewhere. I see Ilse's hand under her dress, tearing a piece of her shirt off. She hands me the gray cloth.

"Wrap your feet in that and throw that other one away; it's filthy."

I wrap my feet in the new cloth. It feels warm from Ilse's body. It is easy to put my shoes back; my feet are cool. We line up in front of the truck. There is a piece of bread and a kettle of soup. I untie the mess kit from the string around my waist; it is filled to the rim. We go back to the river, and after we have eaten, stretch out again in the grass.

"You know," I say to them, "there *is* a camp somewhere for us. All we have to do is walk a little more."

One day we come to a village. There is a pond and black ducks with their heads hidden in the rippled water. There is a dog that runs along the column, barking at us, his teeth yellow in the half-open muzzle, sniffing our odor, the skin wrinkled alongside his nostrils. The peasant women with their colored bandannas on their heads and aprons around their bellies; they stand in front of their houses, watching, their arms folded, a finger pointed, the heads turning. One woman leans out of an open window and spits three times. The windows of a church, blue, green and red, made into the figure of a saint. The old men sit on the steps, smoking the long pipes; holding the porcelain bowls in one hand, with the other hand shielding their eyes against the sun. They watch the column pass through their village. Their faces are brown from weather; only the eyes, sharp, see, watch; up and down the eyes go, row after row. They tip their fingers to their foreheads in salute to the guards. There is the jug of beer offered or a glass of wine. The green ones push their caps back and stand with their booted legs wide apart, drinking. They exchange words of weather and crops.

In the yards, the manure stacked high, and the white, moving heads of chickens, pecking in circles. There is the sound of water being pumped out of a well. Over the village the smell of smoked meat, manure and baked apples.

A woman standing alone on a corner. Soon we are going to be out of the village. . . . Something hitting my feet; I look down. The girl in front of me stops also and our two hands meet above the ground. I push her hand away fast and close my fingers on the red apple. "It's mine. Let go!" She turns and continues walking. Nobody has seen it. . . . Eva is looking now into my hand, surprise in her face. The village behind us, Eva turns to Ilse.

"Knife."

Ilse pulls from her pocket the old knife. I don't remember when she found it. It was always there, the knife: rusted, the handle gone.

"What have you got?" She steps into our row. Eva makes three lines on the apple with her nail; with her finger and thumb measures the distance between lines. The apple divided, she hands the knife back to Ilse. They bite into the apple at the same time. Eva eats slowly, rolling it in her mouth. Ilse makes sounds deep down in her throat. I still hold my piece of apple, the skin red, shining. No flaw, no mark on it. I carry it to my mouth, the smell of forgotten times near my face. I bite into it: the sound like no other sound. The shape of my mouth dented there. The skin breaking in my teeth, the meat filling my mouth, the juice running off my chin. I swallow, watching the back of the girl in front of me. I bite again—I spit into my palm the fresh bite and touch the girl.

"Here."

She takes it fast, pushing it into her mouth. "Thanks."

"That's all right," I say. Eva motions with her finger to her forehead. "You insane?"

I shrug my shoulders. At the end of the apple I eat the part where the seeds are. They have the bitter taste of green almonds.

The sun is hot now in the quiet midday. I walk with the coat over my shoulder and the wind brings to me the smell of Ilse. How quiet the column is. Noon: the time when the day divided is longer than a day, when hills shift in the glimmer of the sun and horses stand with manes loose over a fence. Brown, green and yellow is the country. The small white clouds hang without design or purpose.

"Eva, how long is it since we started?"

She walks with her eyes closed and there is no answer. It was a long time ago. We were singing and marching in step, as if we knew where we were going and wanted to get there. I hear Eva stumble.

"Talk to me," she says.

"Yes." I have to talk. There are many things we can talk about. What are they?

"Go ahead. Say something, anything!"

I wonder what time it is. The sun is still up there. I look at her and her eyes are closed again, the lashes dark and long on the white face.

"It's time for tea," I say.

"More."

"My tailor is better than your tailor. . . . The sun is the color of an unripe orange. If you would bite it, there would be yellow, hot juice. The sun is very old. The sun has a place in the sky and will not give it up, not for the moon."

"That's funny." Her eyes are open now.

"Is the sun a he or a she?" She does not answer. "Is it a he or a she, I ask you?"

"Son of a bitch. It's a he."

"All right. We should have some kind of an order on earth. Stop shuffling."

"I don't shuffle."

"You don't?" I turn to Ilse. I see the sweat on her forehead. "She shuffles, doesn't she?"

Ilse lifts her eyes. "Shh . . ." she says.

"You see? It's that I can't walk when you shuffle. I need your sound."

There is a muffled shot. "In the amusement park we ate hot chestnuts in winter," I say. "In summer candied apples and ice cream. We shot into the colored bulbs. Once I won a plaster lamb and once a stuffed mouse."

"I can't imagine why a stuffed mouse," says Eva.

"They are all right. Plush gray." I see Dasha coming down to us; she has stopped and is waiting.

"How are you doing?" she says.

"What do you mean, how are we doing? Just what do you mean by that?" Eva's eyes are fixed on her face.

"What's the matter with you? I just ask . . ."

"What's new? Did you hear anything?" says Ilse.

"Even if she knew, she wouldn't tell you," says Eva.

"I don't know anything. They said only that it won't be long now." She walks ahead, outside the column.

The sun is wider going down. A dark forest on one side of the road; the air is cooler. Suddenly there is the sound of airplanes in the distance. We jump into the ditch and lie flat in the smell of damp leaves. The ditch that is always with us. The grave or the safety into which we jump. Sometimes there is a creek running and the earth is wet and the frogs, four-legged and green, jump high as the grass. Lying there, I think of the world locked into a circle of ditches, ditches everywhere, ending only at the sea. The planes leave and we walk again.

The road goes down a slope now. There is another village on the plain. It hurts my feet more to go down. They slide in the shoes, my toes hitting the wooden tip at each step.

"I used to like to run," says Eva suddenly. "On a field with the lines marked in white and, at the end, the ribbon. All the time while I was running I would think about the ribbon."

It makes me sad. I would like to have a ribbon for Eva at the end somewhere. I feel the tears running down; it must be that feeling in my feet of hot needles. We cross the silent village and stop at the end, in a field under a roof made for stacking wheat. They give us bread and water. We lie close together to keep the heat of our bodies. Ilse is rubbing my feet.

Eva's voice comes as if from far away. "How did you get that apple?"

Ilse is lying down now on the other side of me. I feel my face getting hot. "Yes, how did you?"

I would like to be somewhere else. "She was standing at the corner of a house, alone. She had a black and white faded cotton dress with one missing button." I swallow the air and continue. "She had a straw basket on her arm. When we came to her, I saw that the basket was full of these apples."

"So?" I see Eva leaning on her elbow.

The country around is silent. Nothing moves in the dark air. There are the clustered shapes of houses, where no light comes through the locked shutters. There is only the distant sound of cats with their repetitious demands for love.

"I stretched out my hand. To beg, you know?"

I feel the strong hand of Ilse slapping my back. "Good! I was always telling you, we have to plan things. Get organized. Now, in the next village . . ."

Eva's voice is low but clear in the quiet night. "It was a fine apple. In fact, it was the finest apple I can remember."

The early-morning air, cool, and the mist rising above the meadows like white smoke. The coat held tight, the ring of the mess kit swinging on the cord. The body moving but not ready for the new day. The feet heavy as if sleep had settled there; the voice inside me, repeating again, No, I can't any more, I can't.

Something must happen. And deep down knowing, it will go on—in an unchanged world. The meadows, still, the morning cows steaming, the air warmer and yellow at noon and cooler blue when the sun sets; the road paved sometimes, potted with holes, rutted earth; a village, a ruin, a castle, a bridge, stations and orchards, meadows and cows, hill, stop, night, sun, get up and walk, always get up and walk. Words, but fewer now, the feeling of lightness in my head, how light, as if swimming through air. Sometimes the land turns in a circle and settles again into solid ground. But I know it turned.

Eva moves her head to the side and quietly vomits, still walking, the liquid flowing from her mouth like green water.

"You sick?" I don't know why I whisper.

"It's nothing," she says, wiping her mouth with her sleeve. Her face is gray, her eyes deep in their sockets.

"It's morning sickness only," says Ilse from behind. "She will be all right, won't you?" I hear a threat in her voice.

"Sure," says Eva.

"You know," says Ilse, who suddenly walks between us, "you know what I dreamt about last night?" She slides her arm into Eva's and mine. "I dreamt of some kind of a factory where there were big machines, and out of them were coming all kinds of food and there were not enough pots to catch it all, and then mashed potatoes were spilling out and growing and I was running. I don't remember eating the potatoes. . . . Then I was walking on an old square with a blue umbrella against the sun and there was the old dog I had when I was six years old. Funny, isn't it?"

"I guess," says Eva.

"Let's sing something," says Ilse after a while. "Now, what shall we sing, Tania?"

There is a change in the trees. There are no pines anywhere any more but low and wind-flattened oaks; the air is drier and the sun almost above our heads.

"I said, what shall we sing, Tania? Tania!"

"Yes. What shall we sing? Maybe we can ask somebody."

"I don't know, you are so . . . so stupid both of you. Is it so hard to think of a song? There are millions of songs. You don't want to sing!"

"Oh, but we do, don't we, Eva? Let's see. . . . We will sing, 'Little red scarf, turn round, round, round.'"

Ilse takes a large breath. "All right, one, two, three: Tralala, lalala, lalaaa . . ."

Our voices thin, we sing, off key, "The Little Red Scarf." It leaves me tired and without breath. "That's enough for today. We can sing again tomorrow," I say.

I hear the trucks moving off. I turn to Eva, wanting to tell her. My mouth already opened for the coming words, I see Eva's knees bending forward, Ilse's arm pulling and Eva's head rolling on her chest. I am on the other side of her. I see the knees giving in as if struck from behind and her body twisting forward. I look at Ilse, a cold sweat breaking out on my body. Her eyes—I don't remember ever seeing them as they are now—no light in them. Her head turns to the fields as if help might come from there. Eva's feet drag far back behind her body, a swell of dust from the tips of her shoes, the scraping sound following us. She is heavy. I am surprised how heavy she is.

"She will be all right," says Ilse.

"Yes . . . she is heavy." I feel my heart thudding against my ribs and we bend to drag the loose body. We hold her, one hand in an armpit, one hand forward, reaching for balance, stumbling with each step.

"It's . . ." Ilse's free hand has the uncertain motion, palm turned, then up again. "It's nothing . . . something she ate."

The sweat is spreading down my back now; there is a thought I cannot hold. Ilse's eyes are fixed at the head of the column. I will not look there. Eva's armpit is sliding from under my hand. I take a better hold of her.

"I heard the trucks just before. . . ."

"They should have been back long ago, the sons of bitches."

"When they come we will stop," I say.

The line of girls moves farther down behind us to leave space for Eva's legs. . . . There are calls telling us to move aside.

"What takes them so long? All she needs is a little water; that's all she needs," says Ilse.

"She is heavy."

"Shut up!" says Ilse.

Is it ten minutes, an hour? Her mess kit hanging above the road, the end of the string swinging with our steps. A button off her coat rolls in the dust. Suddenly I have the thought that she might be dead. How do we know she is not dead? I put my other hand on the hanging forehead. Her face is heavy in my palm. It is warm and wet. . . . I think of Eva back in the city, a long time ago, playing the harmonica and her mother bringing ice cream into the blue room where we were sitting. I remember how Eva jumped up, throwing the harmonica on the couch, running to her mother, turning her around the room in a waltz. She was like that, Eva, then. She belongs to that time. She is the only proof for me of the existence of those times. And hanging on to her now, on this road,

I cannot let go. I grip harder. It is as if I am hanging and she is the one who pulls me. . . .

And with a roaring the trucks arrive. The column stops. We drag Eva to the ditch and prop her up. She looks as if she is sleeping. We walk forward then to get the rations.

"What about her food?" I say. "Can we take it for her?"

"No. We should not bring any attention to her. She will have to make it."

"How can she make it? Didn't you see . . ."

"I'll make her. That's how!" There is such anger in her voice, as if she is insulted.

There is boiled barley and hot black coffee; but still no water. We start to eat while walking back. Eva is in the ditch, her body shifted to one side above the straight legs. Ilse kneels in front of her. She loosens her dress and pushes her head. There is Dasha sitting quietly above the ditch, watching.

"Get some water," says Ilse, without looking at Dasha. "Get it, they have it!" Dasha walks away and we eat the barley. She comes back with a mess kit full of water. Ilse drops a handful on Eva's face. A trembling rising along the legs, the chest heaving, the movement ending in a jolt of the head. Ilse holds the water to her white lips and Eva's eyes open. She does not say anything. Her eyes, dark, suddenly looking so wise. She shakes her head twice, as if to clear it of sleep.

"You have to get your ration," says Ilse. "Get up!"

We help Eva up. She looks around in surprise, as if she expected another landscape. Once out of the ditch, she starts to move on the road. We watch her walking, her body swaying, stumbling, but she straightens, shoulders back, arms stiff at her sides. She looks suddenly tall on that road. She walks slowly, her head up. I know that her eyes are fixed as always, forward, where the trucks are.

We drink the coffee, eat the remaining barley, and she is standing above us. There is a small smile shaking on her mouth. "Barley! What do you know!" She sits down in the ditch and eats slowly. We both watch Eva eat. I see Ilse watching her so intently that her mouth opens each time Eva brings a spoon to her mouth. She sips, then gulps the coffee. She looks up at us and, smiling, lifts the mess kit and clinks it first against Ilse's and then mine.

We stretch out in the grass. "I was thinking," says Ilse. "I was thinking that all this time we have been walking south; only I don't know what it means."

"I would say, if you see no objection to it, that we are not far from the mountains," says Eva slowly. "That's north."

"You think you are smart, don't you?"

I smile, then close my eyes and listen. How good it is to hear them argue again.

"I did not want to say anything, but yesterday I already noticed a difference in the trees. And the air . . ."

"So, all right," says Ilse, "if you are so smart, what do you do in the mountains?"

"You don't ski, do you, Ilse?" Eva chuckles.

"We can go north and still find no mountains. But even if we do, we sure as hell won't ski. Anyway, who wants to break a leg?"

The grass is soft under my head. I lie in the shade and I can see the wide, high, level land. There is no horizon to it. At the end it bends with the faded sky.

"But the mountains," says Eva, "everything ends at the mountains. Roads and . . . and borders."

The order comes down the line. Slowly we get up; we push away the ground, straighten our bodies, knees popping. Ilse offers Eva a hand to get out of the ditch. But Eva shakes her head and makes her own way. Again we walk. Ilse between the two of us now.

"And then, after the war," she says, as if continuing a conversation, "I am going to take a bath every day. Every single day. Let my hair grow down to here." She motions to her knees. "Wash it every week; that's not too much, is it? No, that's just right! And clean underwear every day! Then I will get married."

"Like that," says Eva. "You won't know anybody. They will all be . . . strangers . . . the other ones, the ones that stayed."

"There will be men. They are never strangers for long, you know. Besides, I can always go somewhere else. It's like a cafeteria, a whole world to choose from. You know, men are really superior. They don't even have cold feet in bed. And a man is all in one line, straight and hard. We are all in and out and soft. I think that God created a man *after* he made a woman. Because he was not satisfied."

There is the sound of a wagon, creaking on high wheels, coming closer. The man on the seat, in a blue jacket; the bones of the horse jutting in the brown skin. The hoofs beat the road with a sound of empty shells dropping. The wagon is open. The wagon is full of bodies, heads mingled with dangling feet, the toes white under the light of the sun.

"I think we are not far now," I say.

The horizon does not lift. Eva is walking with her head stretched out as if to see sooner. At an intersection we take a narrow road.

"Look," says Ilse pointing into a ditch.

There is a man lying there, in striped clothes, face down. His arms under his face, he is lying there as if he were crying. We walk in silence. The ditches are not empty now; the bodies of men there, crooked. Why did we think we were the only ones? There were others on the road before us. They started from somewhere; they took a different road. But there is a center somewhere into which all roads drain.

And then it is there: the camp. In a field, the barbed wire stretching long as the horizon and only the watchtowers rising and pointed roofs, barracks taking shape, becoming more real. My head turning, searching . . . It is not there. No chimney there. The column moves faster now, the voices raised, heads turning with a smile, fingers pointing. . . . The guards and the opening gate. Papers held out, the voices of our guards, salutes and click of boots. The sound of numbers, *three hundred and two, three hundred and three . . .* Passing through the gate, I see our green ones standing outside—not entering the camp.

Once again in a space that has corners, Ilse turns her face to us and says, "Home again."

"I wish we could have at least seen the mountains," says Eva. "We did not walk far enough."

The Sound

They are broken, the windows in the barracks. Between the sharp edges of the glass, the morning sky as if torn. I lie still, listening to the breathing of the room. The bodies stretched out without blankets and no cots to mark where one ends and another begins. I sit up slowly, my hands locked about my knees. I shiver in the morning air. From outside, the smell sweet and insistent, brought by an edged wind . . . I lie down again and close my eyes. It is not hard to remember. Only the line of time is not clear. The camp as I first saw it . . . There was the square yard and barracks like everywhere else. Only the women showed the difference. They pulled themselves flat along the barracks, fingers reaching to find a hold, a notch, a space between boards and the arms, a slow lever, pulling the sliding bodies along.

When the gate was locked behind us, I noticed that the green ones did not come in with us. I turned and saw them walking away. We went into barracks and waited. I remember how we waited. Ilse said, "They have to come and count us again," and Eva said, "Sure they will come and count us." They did not come. Finally we shouted a question from the window. But the sliding ones, holding themselves up, did not answer. The language of the camp is silence.

I shiver. I should not be cold because it is spring. I know it is spring because I remember the road and how everything was green by the river. I wonder if it was so bad on the road. But how we wanted to get here. I wish it was like the other places. I think I have fever. I wish they would come in and count us and tell us some of their rules. How many days is it since we came here? They should know how many we are now. There is no order here. When we are thirsty we go to the wide space where our camp ends and there are the faucets and there are the cabins where we can wash. It is the only thing that is here, the water. No bread since we came here. One cup of soup in the evening. We lie on the floor the whole day. We just lie and wait.

I feel Eva awake now. Her eyes are wide open; she has been watching me. "Hello," I say. Her eyes stay on my face for a long time. She sits up and pats my arm.

"You don't look so bad. All you need is air; we will go out today."

The room turns. In the mornings it always turns and there are the bright dots swaying like tin dust inside my eyes.

"It is because of the cups," I say aloud. "A cup of soup is not enough. I wish there was some Elder or somebody." I reach out to touch my cup. And the soup will not be there till evening.

"Come on," says Eva, reaching across me to touch Ilse. "Time for a walk."

"Oh, why don't you shut up."

"You go ahead, Eva. Ilse and I are going to wait right here for you, aren't we, Ilse?" I push Ilse and settle against her back.

"I wish you two would let me alone," she says, sitting up. "What's the matter with you anyway? I am busy right now. Can't you see I am thinking?" She looks at Eva and says, "All right, all right. I've got it. We will walk if that's what you want."

They both stand up and suddenly look very tall. I stretch in the new space. "You go. . . . I'll wait here."

"You are going to get up!" shouts Eva, the color rising over her face.

"Don't shout. Of course, I will get up. But not right now . . . later."

Ilse kneels down. Her tongue makes the clicking sound as if I were a bad child. "You are going to get up because you know that's best for you and . . ."

Eva pushes Ilse away. "All right. You know what will happen to you! You know it! And I don't care, you hear me, I just don't care!" She walks across the room, stepping across the others. Then, with her hand on the latch, she turns. I see her dark eyes. She looks so thin and distant and she is only by the door. She closes the door behind her.

"Listen," says Ilse sitting beside me, "I have some good news. I will tell you outside."

"Oh, yes? You got a letter?" But slowly I push myself up. Maybe from habit. It costs so much to stand up. What news can there be? One lie is like another and I have no news to trade and nothing to make a story from.

Out in the yard I close my eyes. I cannot get used to this yard and its smell. Eva is waiting around a corner. We walk alongside the barracks. I see my hand sliding over the splintered grain of wood, the wall solid against my hip. I lift my hand to screen my eyes.

"Where do you want to go? There is nowhere to go." The five-fingered shadow fades from the side of the building as I lift my hand. I quickly grip the rough wood again.

"We go to the water," says Ilse. "Water is good for you, especially in the morning."

Eva turns around. "We should have gotten away when we could. The night of the bombing. It would have been easy."

"It doesn't matter now," says Ilse.

"What do you mean?"

"I will tell you as soon as we sit down."

I do not want to think about an escape that we did not make. This is not the time to think about it. I cannot accept even the idea, as I cannot accept any more the thought that one day this will end. I live through days of dimmed light—there is no edge to hours and nothing is sure any more. Only the wood and hurt of splinters. A slow light that goes away, not far, only behind the flat line of land and sky. A tin cup filled. Day returning.

We do not look at each other as we walk now, close to the buildings. Where the last corner of the last barracks ends, the gray grass begins. The tufts are spare and flattened. The sun is blank, as if drained, the light spread through white levels of haze. I look across the blurred land and follow Ilse, touching her shoulder once for support. From the outside land no tree comes to my eyes. Within the wire a crouched figure moves, tugging at the grass, slow as smoke and close to the ground.

We sit down to rest. I reach out one hand through the tines of grass and lie on my side. Seeing it this way, one eye above the other, the colors are stacked squares and the edge of the land goes up and down like the side of a barracks. Squared patches of gray sand like dirty windows, spots of brush rustier than nail holes. It is all part of the same thing. My knees shake against the stiff grass with a life of their own. I sit up and fold my legs, hunched forward. The slope goes down from yellow to gray, and in that motionless space only a drift of dust rises a few inches in a windless air.

"Now I will tell you the news," says Ilse.

"Yes," says Eva. "Tell us something."

"I heard last night . . . a sound. I sat up. . . . It came again. Boom. Then again . . . boom, boom . . ."

"That's good," says Eva. "Thunder. There will be rain then. . . ."

"It will take the smell away," I say.

"Listen to me, you two! This is what I figured out this morning. Don't you know what that is? Coming closer, growing . . . the noise . . . all night . . ."

"It should rain today," says Eva.

"That would be nice," I say.

"Idiots! It was them! They are coming! Cannons, I tell you!"

"We can't know. Someone would tell us. Thunder . . ."

"Yes," I say, "and then rain. To clean the air."

"You don't see . . . it's got to be them! Guns . . . big guns . . ."

"Yes!" I am surprised at the shout. It is me. As if a large splinter entered my mind. *"That's it! Ilse . . ."* I feel the warmth coming up out of the earth and covering me like water.

"Sure. I told you. We'll hear it. Tonight we'll stay awake."

"We can't lose sleep," says Eva. "Sleep at night. Walk by day."

"I know it was cannons. . . ."

"I know too, Ilse. Eva, Ilse heard cannons."

"Dreaming. She always has loud dreams. Guns? You know what that means. . . ."

"Shut up, Eva. She wasn't dreaming. We will listen tonight."

"Who knows, maybe next week . . . tomorrow night . . ." Ilse laughs, something like her old laugh, but drier.

Across the dividing wire I see the flat land and wonder how anyone could cross it in a day or a week. I look where the haze fits the land and try to imagine there could be something beyond that. But it is too flat. Maybe the world *is* square; and that is the edge of it.

"But *how* can you know?" says Eva. "How can you tell guns from thunder? No one has told us anything. . . ."

"No!" I push the ground away with my hands, straightening my knees. I stand up. The white edge and the black wire shake once; the wire continues swaying. I can see more now that I am not on my knees. More of the same but more. "No! She is right. . . . Ilse . . . you are right! You have good ears. She has good ears, Eva! I always said she had better ears than we have. . . ."

"Of course, Tania. Don't fall down!"

I am steady. I will not fall. My legs are wide and will hold me.

The Tent

In the early afternoon, the room is larger with the light filling all corners and the bodies on the floor are too long in sleep and no sound from outside. I lie with the others, the heaviness long as my body using only the thin space that is me. I look at Eva beside me. Her eyes opened dark in that white face, she moves a smile toward me.

"How do you feel?" she says.

"Fine."

"Maybe we'll get some bread today."

"Sure."

Already the feeling that it does not matter. There is such a loneliness in being hungry and with the loneliness a feeling of wanting to go even farther back into myself. Into private rooms where the windows are unbroken, steps silenced, and dreams come without the faded color.

I do not think about the ones that have been carried out. They are gone and if they should ever return, I would not recognize them. I listen to my breathing: quiet, slow and steady, as if it did not belong to me; in and out it goes, and I do not know one breath from another.

"Did you see that big tent, way back in the field?" says Ilse turning to Eva.

"Yes. Like a circus."

"I wonder what's in there." Ilse leans on her elbow, watching us. "Let's go and look."

"I never liked the circus," I say. "But I never told them. I would pretend how glad I was and I would close my eyes whenever I could, so that I did not have to watch the animals."

"I like the trapeze. You never know if they are going to fall or not," says Eva.

"They have nets," says Ilse.

"Maybe we will get some bread today," says Eva.

"What month do you think this is?" I ask.

"April. Why?"

"Nothing." April! I will have a birthday. Or maybe I had a birthday already. I would like to know if I am twenty or not. Twenty is a nice round figure. It almost finishes something. I don't know what. I used to think that was old. Twenty is married and powder, high heels and headaches, a certain smell and lips painted red. I don't feel twenty but maybe I am. The birthdays . . . The first watch and first silk stockings, the books. The watch I lost the same year in the electric-car races. That was the game. To bump the others off the track. I stayed on the track but lost the watch. The stockings never lasted long. There were only the books to count the past birthdays by.

"How old are you?" I ask.

"I will be twenty-two in December," says Ilse.

"Really?" I envy Ilse for having more years than I do.

"Let's go out. What does it matter, twenty or twenty-two. It doesn't make any difference at all, if you want to know," says Ilse.

"Let's see what's in the tent," says Eva. "Maybe . . ."

We go out. We move as always close to the barracks, but we must step away where they are too clustered. The sun is over the far field and over the wooden roofs. If I touched that white palm on the ground, that hand opened like a beggar's, maybe it would be warm from the sun. But I don't feel like touching it.

"How sweet they smell," says Eva, turning to me as she steps over a young girl, lying face up. In the wide space of the outstretched legs the grass is yellow.

". . . It's sweet . . . like a kind of icing," continues Eva.

"All right, you said it once!" shouts Ilse. "That's enough!"

"I don't know why they don't bury them," I say. "There is no order here. Look at that!" I sweep my hand over the yard. There are many. Each day there are more.

"It's terribly unhealthy," says Eva.

I step over a woman, arms folded above the dark hair; a fly walks along the blue vein of her neck. From behind a barracks Dasha comes out, walking with another girl. The girl runs to a door with her head bent down.

"Hello," says Eva. "You always know everything; maybe you can tell us what's going on here."

"You mean this?" She points to the ground. "That's a very good sign."

We lean on the wall of a barracks and she says, "Most of the guards are gone. There are only a few left. It's practically the end. You heard the cannon?"

"You see?" shouts Ilse, slapping my back. I hold to the wall, not to fall down. "Sure we heard the cannons!"

"How come you know about the green ones?" says Eva.

There is a smile on Dasha's face, half pout, half pleasure. She looks at the ground, kicking the grass with her leather shoe. She lifts her head and, still smiling, says, "You want to know? You really want to know? I will tell you, because I don't care to keep it a secret. This way, you will be in on it."

"All right," says Eva quickly, "go ahead, tell us!"

"Carl is here."

"Carl!" We say that name, the three of us together. "There are none of the old guards here; what are you talking about?"

"I didn't say she is here in uniform. No. She is smart. She is here as one of us. Prisoner clothes and all. She smuggled herself in here and burned the uniform. There are plenty of striped clothes in here."

"But why?" I ask, although I already know.

"That was her, the one that went in the barracks. She is with a bunch that don't know her. She thinks I am going to save her. You know: when the army comes, that she will be like one of us and I will protect her. Love, you know." Dasha laughs, head thrown back, her white, large teeth glistening wet in the sun.

We are so stunned that we don't say anything. After a while, Eva says, "And what do you plan to do?"

"Me? Nothing. Now *you* know about it. Others might find out too. Who knows what will happen?" The smile is all pleasure now.

"By God, you are the worst!" Ilse spits on the ground. "It's not that she should be protected . . . but the way *you* do things . . . why . . . you're worse than she is." There is a surprised look on Ilse's face, as if she did not know she was going to say it.

"Well," says Eva, "we have to go somewhere now, so if you don't mind . . ." Her tone is formal, as if we were on some important business.

"I will see you around," says Dasha.

We continue walking. "You and your questions, Eva! What did you have to ask her for?" I say.

"Well, at least we know. It's the end," says Ilse. "Now we know for sure."

"Do you know," shouts Eva, "do you know how long it can still take? They advance, take a piece of a hill, next day the others take the hill. Didn't you ever read about the Thirty Years' War? And there is always nothing on a lousy hill, except it's on a map."

"Sure, but they are getting closer every day," says Ilse. "Listen, I tell you it won't take them long. They are coming. Thousands of them. Thousands of men! It will be wonderful. . . ."

"Listen to her! Already she wants to put on a party dress and have her hair done. Let me tell you what *I* heard!" Eva is slapping her chest. "I heard that they will mine the camp. And we will all be blown to pieces. That's why they don't bury!"

Ilse laughs. "Mine the camp? You're crazy!" Then she looks at me to see if I think it is crazy too. I don't say anything. There are equal chances for everything. That is why there are wars and why they take such a long time.

The tent is not far now. The peaked cloth staked to four corners, the sloped top white with sun, the light stretched between two poles. Suddenly the top lifts, the creases bend out as if with a wind. But the wind is in the ground—a rumble shaking under our shoes—the sound like growling in the earth. The cannon, somewhere beyond the flat edge of the land. Listening, we stop. The ripple of guns spreads across the air.

"Shall we go on?"

"Sure. That's why we came here."

There is that smell again. No sound of animals, no band playing under that big tent. My forehead wet and my hands dry as we move forward. Eva is ahead of us and reaches it first.

"What is it?" says Ilse.

But Eva is already ducking under the slanting ropes, lifting a flap, and the cloth wall falls behind her.

"What is it?" Ilse shouts.

And the laugh comes from inside. It is a large laugh. It is Eva's laugh but it is not Eva's laugh. It is the laugh of no one and it is the laugh of thousands. The laugh repeats; it is not going to end—and then it stops.

I run and pull the tent open. I stop. The cloth scrapes through my nails and the tent falls shut behind me. I am inside. In that close air. With the light threaded yellow, there are all those faces in stacked levels above me. I don't know that I have moved, but I am in the center, with all those faces which are one face—not flat and not round—ringed above me. I close my eyes.

My name shouted. I look. Eva. "Tania . . ." My sleeve in her fingers.

"What is it?" Ilse.

"Stay out . . . stay out. . . ."

Eva throws back the cloth and the light opens. Ilse backs away. Eva is crouched where a rope coils about a stake pounded into the earth. Eva is sick by the stake.

Ilse shakes me. "What was there?"

"Dead . . . they are all dead."

Eva stumbles away from us. She starts to run across the deserted field. The long sleeves flap as if empty. The figure of Eva is smaller now, moving toward the washhouse. Ilse and I, saying nothing to each other, walk slowly.

Under the cold water, washing ourselves, Eva says, "Do you know what I heard?" We stare at her. "Did you see that girl that just went through the door? She said that we will get bread today."

The Bread

With the rumor of bread, we wait. Some pacing back and forth, some sitting, some standing at the window, waiting. The rumor is solid as bread itself.

Rocking myself, head on my knees, the word "bread" becomes a single picture on the walls of my memory where a white space has been: *The making of bread. Mother. Wrists deep in the dough, palms stretched out, fingers closing, the dough squeezing through the space between them. The bubbles of air, stretching, pop and form again that yellow softness. Into the oven. The smell of yeast and flour becoming one smell. Later: the round loaf out of the oven, struck with flour and cracked, darker on the edge of the cracks. My teeth come down deep in the crust, sound of crust against teeth. . . . Brown marks on my fingers. I lick away the dots of flour, caught in the fuzz above the upper lip. . . .*

I shift on the hard floor. "Give us this day our daily bread, and forgive us our debts as we forgive those who sin against us." If I eat it fast, I will not have the taste to remember in my mouth. If I eat it slow, holding it in my hand, it will fall into crumbs. It is hard to find crumbs. It is a loss. But I will not eat it before soup. I think I will wait.

"You can do so many things with bread," I say. "It always tastes different; it depends what you put on it."

"I wonder who discovered bread," says Eva. "I mean who ever thought of making it? It's like it was always here, but of course it wasn't . . . in the beginning . . . no wheat."

"Those guys," says Ilse, "the first guys, you wonder what they ate, except animals that they hunted. Without bread, it couldn't have been much of a life. But maybe not . . . What you don't know, you don't miss. Before I ever made love, I didn't miss it, and now, I don't miss it either, because I forget how it was." She thinks it over, then continues, "I think with bread, it's different. You never forget it."

"There are potatoes, of course," says Eva.

"Yes, but that's not the same. You can't put jam on them and you don't hold them in your hand. It's like a slice of bread was made for your hand. Isn't it funny?"

"Did you notice how you never know when it's the last time? The last time eating bread or the last time walking over a rug. Maybe if you knew . . ."

"I wonder what they are doing with that bread," says Eva. "It's getting dark."

From outside now, the voices and the sound of a wagon. The bread is here. All moving toward the door, the shouting and pushing. Outside, the line moves toward the barrel and that stack of loaves. Already I see the girls with the bread in their hands. Their mouths are covered. But the hands come down, I see the lips now, the tongue pushed between them. I see a girl spit.

"What's going on?" I hear a voice.

"Oh, nothing. She found something in it."

"It's bread, isn't it?"

I am holding my piece of bread. It is larger than we used to get. I carry it to my nose, closing my eyes. It smells like bread. It is mine. Real. Before I enter the barracks, I bite deep into the crust—a grating under my teeth. The grinding of sand. I touch one finger to my mouth and pull away a bright point of glass. I carry that grating sound with me, to the space on the floor. The white is soft, with spaces of air suspended in a pattern of lace. Sitting down, still holding to my mouth the piece of bread, I spit out a larger chunk of glass and try to swallow.

They want us to eat this bread. Apart from the glass, it is good. But as I raise the piece to my mouth, my fingers close to crumble the bread. It sifts in crumbs through the space between my fingers. I drink the soup. I lie down on the floor. I feel tired. Eva and Ilse come and sit down silently.

"So," says Eva, "we had our bread day."

Ilse doesn't say anything. All around us, the words . . . *After all, what can happen . . . ? It was a joke. . . . I just ate the crust. . . . Did you eat the whole thing? . . .*

"You can never say you know everything," says Eva. "You would think you would die *without* bread. They want us to die *from* bread. . . . The green ones—they are funny."

"Very funny. Well, they will have to think of something else to get *me*," says Ilse. She is bitter, as I have never seen her. "We are smarter than they are. Someday, we will feed *them*, what do you think?"

"I don't know. I really don't know," says Eva.

The sound of cannons, suddenly, far off, spaced regularly, the feel of it in the floor and walls.

"What a bunch of great guys!" shouts Ilse. "They are coming!"

"I wonder if they know that we are here," I say.

"Of course they know. That's why they are coming!"

"I wish they would hurry," says Eva quietly. "I wish they would."

We lie down, waiting for the night. Later, I hear the women going out and through the window I hear them outside, the ripping sound of their retching and the low, rocking sound of their crying. I turn and, falling asleep, I think, You shouldn't have eaten their joke. It is enough if the mind has bread.

The Earth

"All right, keep moving, get going, pick them up, pick them up!" The almost forgotten voices of a few green ones.

We are all outside in the yard. I bend down, my hands behind me. At the touch of cold, I close my eyes and the hand slips out of mine. I see a guard coming closer. I bend down again, reach behind me and get hold of her with both my hands. I straighten up. At my feet the grass is flattened.

I walk, keeping my head up, looking into the dull sky. I do not want to look behind me at her; I do not want to look in front. I would have to see them, all of them. Right now, I don't see and I don't think. She keeps slipping from my hands. It is different from cold. It is not like the snow of the winter or ice on a wagon in summer. It is like nothing else. As if this were the root of cold.

Through the gate of the camp, on the yellow road, the long string of figures ahead of me, turning in the bend of the road; two by two we walk. One figure taking step after step, the other dragged, we are locked together by hands, the warm and the cold. The bodies leave an imprint in the road like many wheels. The dust drifting, the land blurred with the dull light of sun over it. On one side the wire of the camps, on the other the plain. Soon the camps are left behind us. On a sandy path the column stops. I do not let go of the hand behind me. I got used to her during this silent walk. I do not mind her much now, except that she makes me tired. I do not know how she looks. She is my body. I think of how dusty she must be. She is something inane and cold, but something I am taking care of. She is indifferent as the earth I am dragging her across. The earth will take her, as it takes the rain and the sun.

I hear the sound of thumping as the column slowly advances. I see now the large pit. It is wide as a lake—without water. The ground goes down to it on a slight slope. I bring my girl, rolling her on the slope. I see her short hair, color of dust. Down in the grave, I put her beside the others. I straighten her hands and her legs. I look at her face now, but she is so dirty and bruised that I cannot see much. Another body is landing on top of my girl and I do not see her any more. I climb out of the grave and it seems to take a long time; the bodies are rolling down from all sides. I brush my hands on my skirt. There are only the crumbs of earth on them, from the ground I gripped to climb out. The girl did not leave any mark on me.

Back in the camp the yard is clean and half of the tent is empty. Another group starts to walk out of the camp with the remaining bodies. I hear the shouting of the green ones. I run fast, in the shadow of the barracks, through the open door, closing it after me. I lie down on the floor, my heart beating. I cannot go again. I feel the sickness and nothing to give back. I don't know where Eva or Ilse are.

The armies will come. But if they don't hurry I will not be able to wait any longer. There is just that short time more, but how short? It is like somebody is coming after a long, long time—and they are late and after all this time I may be too tired to go to the door to greet them—I may go to sleep. They are so late.

Ilse gave me two gulps from her soup yesterday. She watched me swallow twice and then tore it from my fingers. Sometimes the room becomes larger and I cannot see the corners. The window is sometimes far back in the field. I drink a lot of water. It is a new thirst in me and I think of all the water that is still in the pipes.

Eva and Ilse talk about the end all the time. The end is not enough. There must be a place to start. But where to begin? Where in a city that may wait for me as I wait for the armed men—where in the past is a place to begin?

My fingers twist the cloth of my skirt, thin and rough; the dirt has become the color. I think of a blue velvet dress I once had. I remember the woman, Miki, who came to sew on Wednesdays. She sat in the kitchen, the sewing machine under the window. There were threads and pieces of material around Miki, her heavy legs going up and down on the pedal of the machine. When she finished that blue dress, she said, "Now you're a real young lady, I say, if you're not the nicest young lady that I ever made a dress for. . . ." She ate all the time and Wednesdays were the days of special cooking. I wonder how she is. She has other Wednesdays somewhere else. . . .

I hear them coming back; they drop to the floor.

"They are all gone now," says Ilse. "You would never believe there were bodies all over here."

"I saw some green women," says Eva.

"You did?"

"Just a few."

"How about Carl?"

"Carl?" says Ilse with surprise. "You don't know? Carl is dead. How come you didn't tell her, Eva?"

"I forgot," says Eva.

"How? Who did it?"

Eva is silent. "She was strangled," says Ilse. "The women of her barracks found her in the morning and they don't know who did it. There was still a piece of cloth around her neck; they couldn't understand. . . ."

"She must have gone in the pit with the rest of them," says Eva. "I wonder who carried her. . . ."

"Do you know what this cleaning up means?" says Ilse. "It means that they know the army is coming and they don't want them to see. . . . It's very simple, it's the end."

"You said it a long time ago. Remember when you first heard the cannon?" I turn to Ilse.

"It can be only a few days now. I was thinking about sleeping outside tonight. This barracks is infected; it's unhealthy," says Eva. "From now on, we should take all the precautions."

"That's true. If we wrap ourselves in the coats, we will be all right," says Ilse. "And when they come, we will see them sooner."

We sleep outside this night. Close together, on the earth empty of bodies now, we sleep a cold sleep. I wake up in the middle of the night, not knowing where I am. I open my eyes to the dark sky, the stars clustered in their far light. The sound I hear is the sound of trucks, the motors throbbing low in the night. Then the shift of speed and the steady, slipping sound of wheels.

I wake them. "Listen! They are taking off. They are leaving!"

"This might be our last night here," whispers Ilse. We clutch our knees to keep warm, and sit, listening. More trucks are moving off.

"I can't believe it." I too whisper, as if not to disturb anything. "Maybe it's a trick. Maybe they are going to blow us up."

"Oh, no. That was just a crazy story," says Eva. "This time, that's it. Now that I think of it, I always knew I would see the end. I mean, I never thought I would *die,* did you?"

She says the word "die" as a foreign word, new and unused. I think of how already we discard death as something that is only for others.

"We should get ready," says Ilse. "Let's go wash ourselves." She is standing up and Eva laughs, pulling her down. "Wait a minute, they are not here yet."

"I am ready," I say, lying down on the earth, under the wide, dark sky.

The Gate

I dream of walking through a field. *There is mist everywhere and I stretch out my hands and lift my feet off the ground and with easy strokes I swim above the earth. There is a constant drumming and when I put my feet down to rest, I feel the earth rocking. I swim through air again. Close to the ground I swim, and the noise is greater. The earth below me is swelling and opening and I try to fly higher. All the time the noise of thunder and smaller sounds of wind against rocks . . .*

I awake. The noise of the dream still around me, the distance humming. I sit up. I hear the sound of roaring engines, the heavier sound of iron rolling over the ground. It is early morning, the gray fog rising from the yard. The light feeling in me and maybe if I tried, I *could* lift my feet from the ground and swim through air.

I shake them awake, shouting, the urge to laugh so great, as if something comical is happening. "*It's them! They are coming!*"

Ilse and Eva sit up, listening. We roll on the grass, pulling at each other's clothes, slapping backs, laughing into each other's faces.

"You see!" says Eva, as if her own personal prophecy has come true.

Suddenly I am in the center of motion. The doors of barracks flung open, the figures running, some wavering, hesitant and the voices now from all sides: calling, praying, crying, a high pitch of laughter and spaced sobbing. We are caught in the stream, turned as in a current and carried in the flow of figures. Hands raised in front of my face, feet stepped upon, the movement faster now, I keep running with them, the press from behind greater, wanting to stop but there is no room left for a single body. We are all one. The stream takes the direction of the gate, fists pounding, voices shouting:

"Out! Out! Let us out!" Across the main road of the camp, other figures are clinging to the wire, pounding at their gate, waving their hands at us.

I bend down and on my knees crawl out; they are spreading now alongside the wire, facing the road. I make my way farther to the side, seeing the moving head of Eva above others. I push my way through to her; Ilse is making room for me at the wire. "Here," she says. "Hold on!"

My hands holding the rusted wires, I feel the push from behind and the sharp angles of the barbed wire pressing into my body. But already I see Ilse, braced on legs wide apart, her arms holding the wire above my shoulders; I start to breathe. In my shoes I feel the familiar wetness of blood. I have the sudden thought that, very soon, somebody will take care of my feet. This . . . this army. I turn to Eva next to me, and shout to her, above all voices, "Who are they?"

She looks at me as if she does not understand. "Oh! I don't know, I have no idea. They are . . . the liberators."

The word sounds strange and not right. I want very much to know who they are. I turn to Ilse, shouting over my shoulder, "Do you know who they are?"

"Shut up! Shut up!" screams a woman on the other side of me. "Why don't you shut up?"

I feel tears in my eyes. It is a long time since I cried. Why won't she let me ask who they are? It is important to me. I feel my lips shaking.

"There are three possibilities," says Ilse, not paying any attention to the woman.

Her voice is lost in a sudden clamor. The sound from the right, at the main entrance to the camps. Those, who already see, their thousand voices rise, rush on the air. A wind of sound turns our heads, the roll-over clang of metal ringing along the wire. Yellow dust lifts now—the road darkens with their coming.

No thoughts in my head, but the feeling like tasting water after years of thirst, gratitude beyond knowing for what, gratitude to be, in this instant, here, to live it; and it is as if there was nothing before. Filled with voices and the feeling of light. I am only eyes fixed on this yellow road.

And I see the tank. The dip and rise of that growing metal, the hard mud flaking from the studded iron. And higher than the bulge of dust through which it rides, the white flag tosses, light as white water. The flag on a pole, above the round lid, and there, erect, stands a boy with eyes the color of somewhere else. Eyes that follow the road and do not look at me—I lift my hand and my fingers flap, slowly as the cloth of that flag. The tank lengthens and goes past. The trucks follow and more tanks. Our voice is one wind rising, above the hum of engines. On the trucks, the soldiers with the bright points of bayonets beside the tilted berets make a sign of a V with two fingers above their heads. I do not know what they mean; perhaps it is the Roman numeral—five, for the number of years. Some, as if they did not want to see us, hold their heads bent above their knees.

A new sound now, the sound of feet. The soldiers march, one hand holding the sling of the rifle, the other hand raised to their brows in a salute. I cry silently at the sight of these soldiers, marching and looking so straight ahead, never turning their heads, and giving us their salute. I feel we do not deserve it and I look around and see how we must look to them. We are in rags and not clean and they salute us. I shout now with the others, clinging to the wire, tears rolling down my face; I laugh and wave my hand and they march, the dust lifting behind their heels, saluting, saluting. . . .

They pass our camp and I see the receding column, as they walk forward in front of the other camps. Somewhere the sound of engines stops and is replaced by voices of command.

In the yard now, the women turn in a dance, their legs spinning bones, rags lifting above swollen knees, the faces white, the smiles too wide under the sunken sockets. Sitting in a circle, the older ones pray, bowing their heads in an ancient rhythm. I look upon the twelve barracks, the yard, the field beyond. . . .

. . . I imagine myself beyond the wire. Walking through a country between brown and yellow fields, roads and paths that twist, and I can take any one of them, walk as far as I wish, no frontiers and no end to anything. Cities with lit-up streets, cobblestones under my feet, neon light. A room with shelves and warmth from somewhere, always warmth; in the center of the room, a table, a bowl, blue grapes with drops of water hanging on the finger-shaped fruit. To close behind me, a door. The pull of the knob and the solid sound that shuts all others out. No other hands, no other bodies to touch and smell. No witness to thoughts, no voice and eye . . .

I sit close to the gate. There is a woman beside me, stretched out in the grass. I watch her, thinking of other things. Her face is white. After a while I notice that she is saying something in a low voice. I bend above her.

"I saw them. I saw them. . . . Now I can die."

I laugh. "What an idea! You crazy? Nobody is going to die now! They will give us food and take care of us."

She turns her eyes to me and looks at me for a long time. Her arms are those of a child. I shift in the grass.

"You sick?"

She nods her head, looking up into the sky. "We are all sick," she whispers. She fumbles with her clothes and opens two buttons of her dress. On the white skin of her belly the spots are many, the color pink.

"Listen, there will be a doctor. It's some kind of a rash you have, that's nothing."

"Water . . ."

"I'll bring you some, you wait." And kneeling in front of her, careful not to touch her, I say, "Don't die; it's too late to die now."

I get up and run into the barracks to get a mess kit. In the washroom I fill it with water and run back.

"Here," I say.

Her mouth is open, the eyes fixed toward the sky. I drink some of the water and throw the rest away. I sit down farther away from her. From time to time I turn to see her long body resting in the dry grass. I am angry. She shouldn't have done that. Now that they are here. I don't know where Ilse and Eva are; I am glad I am alone. I have to prepare myself for the future; arrange and sort my thoughts. I wonder where the pink spots came from.

There is a motion in front of our gate. Figures in their light-brown uniforms.

Hands go toward the lock.

They lean against the gate and it swings.

So easily, it opens.

The Doctor

By a window, looking out on a square. In the middle of the square is a large patch of flowers, red, yellow and white. The sidewalks made of asphalt, the buildings white as if freshly washed. The women walk about, some talking to soldiers. I watch them in their print dresses, their shoes made of leather. The legs look too thin above the heels and some of the shoes are too big.

The room is bright and the air warm, coming through the open window. The white, clean room. The door of the closet is half-open, showing the empty hooks. Four cots stand along the two walls, a large table in the middle. I sit down on my cot; white plates are stacked upon a shelf, the cups turned over beside the new toothbrushes, a ball-point pen, a chocolate bar, a glass with a single sweetbrier, its pink flower bent above the hooked prickles. A whole week of brightness and food.

I remember the first food in the camp: the rice and meat, the sweet coffee, the chocolate. Then there was a tent pitched at the end of the road where the main gate was, a spray of white covering all; the smell of disinfectant and the heap of new civilian clothes, the creases still sharp in the sleeves. Trucks waited in front of the gate. The road was different from the one we walked and it led to a project of white stone houses, three stories high. There they explained to us: These were the officer's quarters and farther across a meadow the hospitals for the green army. In the stone houses the rooms and in this room I sit.

Dasha walks in. I do not like to live in the same room with her. She is pale and I notice how her feet do not lift enough from the floor.

"What's the matter?"

"I don't know," she says in a tired voice. She lies down in her blue polka-dot dress, too long for her.

I get up and stand by the table. There is perspiration on her forehead. She closes her eyes and I watch the window. Maybe I will go out and lie in the grass. There is a large meadow, not too far, the grass high and the trees bordering it. I look at Dasha again, the sweat rolling on her face. Maybe she is too warm.

"Why don't you undress?"

She opens her eyes; they have a glassy look, like on a doll I once had. "Do you want to undress? You will feel better."

Her head rolls on the pillow. I bend above her and start to push the pearl buttons through the holes; I hold her up and pull the dress over her head. She falls on the pillow again. She has white cotton pants on, very clean. Otherwise, she is naked. Above the elastic band of her pants I see the pink dots. I roll the pants down a little. There are more spots across her belly, some darker than the others. I cover her up and walk out of the room. I hurry through the hall. Two soldiers are carrying a stretcher and I step to the wall, letting them pass. Two more stretchers are carried down the steps. At the end of the hall, the back door is opened upon a square of blue sky. In that squared light more stretchers are lifted into a white truck.

A man is coming toward me. Not a soldier. What is he doing here? The men are on the other side of the town. White T-shirt, beige cotton trousers. His head is cropped. Suddenly I think of the men's camp next to us; he might have been there. I am looking down at the yellow linoleum and see the canvas-topped shoes stopping. I lift my head. He is lighting a cigarette, waving away the flame of the match.

"Hello," I hear myself saying. I just want to know if he was in the camp next to ours.

"Morning. What number?"

I look at him. "What number?"

"Of the room."

"I don't think that's any of your business." I start to walk away. Men! I have to tell Ilse about it. I hear him running after me. His hand grips my shoulder. He lowers his face to me. It is a thin face, the eyes almost black.

"What *is* the matter with you? Do you need me or don't you? I don't have much time, you know!"

"Need you? Why should I need *you*?"

He leans on the wall, crossing his arms. They are thin, but there is a shift of moving muscles beneath his skin.

"I am the doctor," he says, bowing his head above his crossed arms.

"You . . . a doctor." I am laughing. "I . . . did not know. It's funny, I thought . . ."

We look at each other and join in a laugh that hurts my chest, but I cannot stop.

"Cigarette?"

I take one as if I have always smoked. We turn and walk toward the back door. The ambulance is not there any more.

"Where have you been?" I say.

He looks at me without understanding. He goes out the back door and sits down on the steps. He motions with his hand to me. I sit down next to him.

"What do you mean?"

Suddenly we laugh again. "We have great difficulties . . . understanding each other," I say.

"I am not much used to talking. The ones that call for me, they don't talk. And when I am not on duty, I sleep."

"I meant . . . where have you been before? You know, there was once a camp of men next to ours and I always . . ."

"No. I was not next to anything! We were under the ground. In a tunnel, building secret weapons. Way down." He points to the ground. "Came up only to sleep. Well, I have to go."

I stand up with him. "Listen, Doctor . . ."

"I am really not a doctor yet. Almost. Vito is my name." He holds the door open.

"I am Tania. Listen, there is a girl in my room; could you look at her?"

"Sure. What number?" And our laugh sounds strange in the quiet hall. We stop in front of my door and he says, his voice low, "I can tell you already what she has and that I cannot do anything for her."

"What is it? I saw the stretchers. . . ."

"Typhus."

Dasha is lying there as when I left her. Her eyes are open, but she does not seem to see us. He bends above Dasha and pulls the cover off. "Yes," he says.

"Where does it come from?"

"Lice carry it."

"But there are almost none now."

"The lice are gone, yes. But they have left the sickness in our blood. It doesn't show right away. Some will not get it. Some will recover. They are lucky—or strong—or—we don't know. . . . Yes, the lice are gone, but the sickness is here, still, in these neat rooms."

He takes from his pocket a small bottle and shakes two pills into his hand. "Give these to her with some water. I will send the stretchers."

"Will this help her?"

"This? It's aspirin. It won't help her but it's all I have."

His large hands smooth the cover; gently he tucks her in and turns away.

The Louse

I close the door behind me, in the cool white shower room. The water is warm; the soap smells of flowers. I wonder why I am still so tired. Soon the war will be over. This is a good soap; I can see the pressed letters in it, but they start to melt away. I rinse the soap suds off. I wonder what is happening to the three of us. Maybe we don't need each other any more. What was it that held us together? Was it only fear? Fear makes friends, needs witnesses. But that is all gone now. Left behind with the weight of hunger. Towel. I press the softness to my face, smelling the distant disinfectant. I step out on the tile floor. Eva is translating for them, copying documents. I do not see her during the day. She calls it her "career." She knows everybody. The steam lowers, pushing through the half-open window. The sky is blue; it will be another warm, sunny day. I wade through the damp air, where my clothes hang. I wish there was somebody I could talk to. Sometimes I wait for Eva late in the evening and she tells me the military news. Comb. Clean brown comb with the trademark stamped into it. My hair has started to grow. It almost reaches my ears. I wonder how I look to Vito.

Through the hall I walk slowly to my room. Ilse is gone already. I don't know where she spends all her time. Outside. Laughing and talking. Sometimes she comes running into the room, always in a hurry—ruffles my hair, pats my shoulder, throws a package of cigarettes on my bed, runs to the bathroom to wash her face and is gone. "I will tell you later. Take a nap, you don't look so good. Bye, bye."

I put the soap on the shelf. On the empty cot that belonged to Dasha is thrown a terry-cloth robe, dark blue. I pick it up and hang it on one of the hooks. It is a man's robe, Ilse's newest possession. I sit down at the table and drink the rest of a lukewarm cup of coffee. I look to the empty bed, the covers stretched tight. I should try to find out where she is. "*. . . impossible to find anyone there . . . nurses? Yes, green nurses . . . no personnel . . . the halls are full. . . . They come back or they don't but you certainly can't find them. . . .*" Maybe Vito? No, he does not know either.

I should go for a walk. I should start to think more about the return. It will not be long now. As soon as the war is over. I never hear any cannons or bombs. Strange, how I waited for that sound, the first days. Quiet. That is peace maybe. I feel very safe here. Safe and warm and tired. I turn to my bed and roll a blanket under my arm and walk out of the door.

The streets are full of girls. Sitting on the benches under the trees, walking, leaning out of white windows. Further, on a corner, Ilse is standing with a soldier, laughing, with her head thrown backwards. We wave at each other and I walk by without talking to her. There are nights when she does not come until early in the morning. If I am awake, I pretend to sleep. I wonder why she is doing everything with such speed. There is time, plenty of time now for everything. I am not ready for anything. I have to prepare myself slowly first, for . . . for life.

Out of the complex of buildings I walk and soon I am on a road. On the other side of the road is a meadow. There are trucks driving by, ambulances, cars. Some soldiers wave at me. I wave back, smiling at them. How much I like them! They are kind. One day I sat on a bench next to a soldier. We talked about his country. "Is there anything you need?" he asked then. "No, I have everything now, really." How he insisted. But there was nothing I could think of that I needed.

I cross the road and walk in the spotted shade of trees. It is very quiet here. I pick up a large pine cone and carry it in my hand. There are wild flowers and, lower by the ground, the small, clustered leaves of blueberries. The round, tight fruit not ripe yet. Down in the meadow, I stretch the blanket over the knee-high grass. My blanket is as if suspended, before my body flattens the stalks.

. . . Underneath my closed lids I feel the orange light. Hot. Quiet. I remember the first time I walked around the buildings, crossed the road, waiting for somebody to stop me. Nobody did. There is a limit to where we can go in the woods, but it is many miles. I saw Vito last night sitting on the steps. Why does he always sit on steps? I sit up, thinking of the quarrel we had. It seems to me that the few times we meet, we either don't understand each other or we don't agree. I asked him about the tunnel. He was angry. "Please, isn't there anything else you can think about? Don't you have enough of your own without my tunnel? It's over, finished." I tried to explain to him that we have to find a right attitude toward the past. "Bury it!" he said.

I straighten my skirt. Blue cotton and a red shirt. Colors of the flag. I take off my sandals. Vito puts some paste on my toes. I have a jar of that grease now on my shelf. It is cooling and smells of camphor. I remember Uncle . . . What *was* his name? That uncle who came to spend a few days with us one summer and by the river I saw his foot. It had no toes. . . . It was round as a fist, his foot. I could not take my eyes away . . . smooth round . . . no mark on it, the foot as if folded over something that had been there before. "War," he said, "you don't know what it is, little girl. A war in snow." I hope I do not have a fist for a foot. No, I will be all right. Everything will be all right. I am getting too warm. Under my arm is a dark patch of wet. I will have to wash the shirt tonight. It does not matter. I look over the meadow, the trees spread above the levels of shade.

I am in no hurry to be sent back. I like it here. There is food and I am left alone. I like it. I do not have to decide anything. That is fine. I will have to move under the trees, into those islands of shade. I sit, running my finger over the dark brown blanket. In the air the distant humming of insects.

I feel a bite and stiffen. It is as if everything around me has stopped. The branches are still on the trees; the humming moves far back in the meadow. I see a small louse twitching across my forearm. I feel the prickles of heat under my skin. I smash the louse. It leaves a yellow liquid on my arm. I stand up slowly, knowing: This louse did it. I do not think of other lice; I do not think of time. There is only me and the dead louse and the smear on my arm. I bend down for the blanket, so distant, small below me. It is a heavy blanket; I sit down again. I close my eyes.

. . . When I open them, the sun is going down. There is a meadow flooded with a single shadow. The trees are black. I am afraid of the distances. I have to go somewhere. I stand up and walk. I turn and see a brown blanket crumpled behind me. I continue walking. There is a road that I cross. On the other side I sit down on the stiff tufts of grass. I am sitting in a ditch. I get up. There are white buildings; I will find someone in there. . . . Uncle Emil was his name and he had no toes. Poor Uncle Emil. I have to sleep. There is a square and flowers in the middle. Men's voices, singing, "Roll out the barrel . . ." The white houses all look alike. "Roll out the barrel . . . Roll out . . ." I belong here, I know that. I would like to know which house it is. How can I know? "Roll out the barrel . . . roll out . . . roll out . . ."

Soldiers sitting on the steps to a door and one girl with yellow hair. She shouts something; I am too tired to turn. "Tania, Tania." That's me. I walk on, to the next house. There is nobody on these steps. Somebody running behind me. I lost one sandal. "What's the matter?" My lips are dry, they stick together. I continue walking. One sandal. A girl hangs on my arm, saying, "Whatsamatter, whatsamatteritsme. Itsme." I look at her and she floats against the white building. She is a splotch of yellow against the white wall. "Ilse! Don't you know?" Ilse . . . Roll out the barrel . . . Who is Ilse . . . ? Go away. . . . No time . . . have to sleep . . . find Uncle Emil. . . .

I am lifted above the ground and see the flowers below, the colors smudged, held together in a square of chicken wire. Let them out, the flowers . . . There is a pink arm in front of me, another arm with hair on it. White wall. Where did the bed come from? I stretch my legs but cannot reach the end of this bed . . . rocking . . . floating in a deep room. I will not listen to voices that sound like insects humming somewhere in a meadow. . . .

The First Steps

In the white room I raise my head and listen to the clump of steps outside, the hush of doors, the hiss of showers. Sounds that each day tell me the time.

I do not remember anything about the days I have been lying here; I do not know anything of that time. Beyond the range of my knowing there was the time when I lived without thought or feeling. No recognition of darkness or light. I lived in a colorless space, where heat or cold could penetrate the body but not the mind. I bypassed death with an indifference, not recognizing it in its new form.

The room becomes what it has been, walls and corners, the cots, the shelves. Only the table grows older. I can see, when I sit up, the brown stains. This was my sickroom; the hospital was full. I am glad they did not move me. . . .

I do not want to move. Only to wait for the ones that will tell me about the outside—that is enough now. I turn my head to Ilse's bed. A picture of a soldier on the wall, with two red thumbtacks. The soldier of the week. There are lavender silk panties thrown across her bed. I hear steps in the hall and the door opens.

"How do you feel today?" Vito stands in front of my bed, arms crossed over his chest.

"Fine."

He sits down, taking my hand, his fingers on my wrist. In a while he will ask me if I want to try and get up. Eva asks me every day; Ilse too, but she always sounds as if it is something that just occurred to her.

"Do you want to try today?"

"No, Vito."

He does not insist. He pulls out a cigarette, leans back against the footboard and stretches his long legs. He clicks a match with his thumbnail and opens his mouth to a lopsided ring of smoke.

"What are you going to do . . . when you go back?"

"I don't know, Vito. Maybe finish school . . . It's funny, they always used to ask us, What do you want to be when you grow up? When I was very little I wanted to be an usher in a movie house so that I could see all the movies; then I wanted to sell candies. Later, I wanted to be a poet. Your mind full of words that you think are precious, words that nobody ever put down in just the same way. And now . . ." I sit up and look at him, thinking hard—and where are the words now? "Right now, Vito, I don't want anything. I have to learn. . . . Whatever I do, only I can answer for it. Only I can make my choices. That's why it's so difficult. I really don't know what the choices are."

Vito reaches behind me to straighten the pillow. "Freedom . . . We can take only a bit at a time. It reminds me of that canned stuff the captain first distributed. I don't know if you got some or not. I persuaded him *that* was not for us. It was too good and there was too much. It killed some. What was I saying? Yes, a bit at a time. You can't gorge yourself."

His hair has grown since my illness and his chest is larger in the white T-shirt. That T-shirt suddenly I remember, like a sail floating above the space I was falling into—during the days of not knowing.

"I think I remember you bending over me; you had no face then, but I remember the white shirt."

He laughs. "Not that I did much for you. You want to know a secret? The revolution in all modern medicine: black coffee and aspirin. That's all I had to keep you going. I had the coffee made in the kitchen especially for you. It was so strong, you could chew it. But it keeps the heart working."

He puts his hand to where my heart is, bending down to me. The face is becoming larger, closer, the eyes . . . His lips are lightly on mine. . . . His back straightens; he is walking to the window.

"This is a big day, you know," he says, his back turned to me. "A beautiful, big day!"

"Yes . . . it is . . . beautiful. . . ."

"Well, I have to go now, Tania. By the way, I found out from Ilse that you are from the big city, same one as I. How is it possible that we never talked about it?"

There are hurried steps in the hall and the fumbling with the doorknob; Vito opens the door to Ilse.

"Chicken bouillon, chicken bouillon, steaming hot, served direct to your door from our modern kitchens. Hello, Doc. What a day!" She puts a red bowl and a covered plate on the table.

"I can see you are in good hands; I will see you later, Tania. So long, Ilse."

Ilse's eyes follow Vito to the door. She looks at me, but says nothing, and smiling, brings me the soup. I do not eat with hunger, but I can eat forever without having the feeling of having eaten. Ilse sits on my bed, smoking, getting up, picking up a bar of chocolate. She cracks it between her teeth, throwing the other half on the table.

"Hmm . . ." she says, with her mouth full. "Good! You know, I might go straight over the Channel. I might not even go back."

"You have time to think it over," I say, knowing that each week for Ilse brings a different plan.

"It's unbelievable the amount of tea they drink," she says after a while. "I am getting used to it now. Maybe it purifies or something. I certainly feel more ladylike. But I have to go pee all the time."

I hand her the empty bowl. "Wait," she says, "there is a rice pudding for you. Cooked in powdered milk. Did you ever see powdered milk? Looks like DDT. Exactly."

I eat the rice pudding. "Oh, I almost forgot," she says, slapping my shoulder. "I knew there was something I wanted to tell you. We can write a letter now. The mail will go tomorrow morning, so you should write, right now." She stops, looks at me. "I don't have anybody . . . do you?"

"I have . . ."

"That's right . . . an aunt. . . . Write her, Baby."

I am glad to hear that old name again. She leaves on my bed a small sheet of paper, an envelope and a pencil, and carries away the dishes.

"I will come for it later," she says in the open door.

Alone again, I think of the letter I will have to write. "Dear Magda . . ." I remember her face, the round foreign face. She always knew she did not belong among us. She did not have the required features of our tribe. She was like a stalk of corn among the black iris. Hugo and Magda. I wonder what happened to him. . . . No, I don't have to wonder. . . . They were married secretly. The two names were said many times. First in anger, then in wonder. Finally as one would say salt and pepper. Hugo and Magda. Linked together, one could not be said without the other. During the big family meetings, Magda would sit, her face flushed above the white Damascus cloth, as if she had been running to get there. Mother was her first friend and they laughed together in the Sunday air of the dining room, drinking coffee and whispering sometimes behind the closed door, until the laughter broke through the walls.

Magda will be there. For the thing she was guilty of was what kept her alive, while all the uncles and aunts and their sons and daughters, the cousins and half cousins, were spread over the land in drifting smoke. Magda is sitting at a table alone, flushed as if in embarrassment.

I turn my face toward the wall, holding the paper flat on it, and start to write: "Dear Magda." I stop, licking the pencil, thinking of what to say. "It was a long time ago . . ." (There lived a princess beyond the seven hills . . .) "I am fine and will be coming back soon. I hope all is well with you. I will ask for your hospitality. When you will open your door to me, maybe you will not recognize me. But only because it has been such a long time. It will be me. With love, Tania Andresova." Although I write only a few lines, the sheet of paper is filled with the big letters, as if an old woman wrote, or a child. My body is at peace; only my hands are not. On the envelope I write the address that I have never forgotten.

I lie down again, tired from the effort. I think of that thing inside me that makes me live. I feel apart from it, as if I was following a pattern decided a long time ago. Like a river that flows always through the same bend. Dying would be taking another route.

Eva comes into the room, lighting a cigarette. She stretches out on her bed and smiles at me.

"Did you eat?"

"Yes. Tell me, I've been wondering . . . how was it with Dasha?"

"Why do you ask?"

"I was just thinking . . . that I am still here. You did find her finally, didn't you?"

"I ran into a stretcher-bearer that I know and he said he knew where she was. I went there the same day. She had just died.

Remember that polka-dot dress? That's what she had on; it was much too big for her. Somebody put a red flower between her hands."

"That was . . . nice of them."

"I think it's rather funny. . . . Horrible! She was a traitor! That's what she was!"

I don't say anything. I think of Dasha, saying, "I like the snow, don't you . . . ? I like the trees. . . . I will have a house like this one day. . . ." Going that first night to meet a guard in the snow. Dasha, the lonely one.

"How do you feel about going back?" says Eva.

I think, This is the second time today I have been asked that question. "I don't know. . . ."

"Oh, hell . . . you have someone. An aunt, isn't it?"

"Yes, an aunt."

"You are lucky. But I don't need anyone. A job, paint on Sundays. We are grownups, adults. We can do anything. You know what I really would like to do?"

She sits up and stares at me, her eyes suddenly narrow and hard. "I would like to be in one of the camps for the green ones. To be *their* guard." She rolls back on the bed, hands under her head. "Reversed, you know. That's the way life is. You are up or you are down. Oh, I would not want it for a long time, just a year or so. Just long enough to . . ."

"You don't mean that!"

"What? No, of course not. I wouldn't waste my time!"

Outside it is a deeper blue now. Through the window come singing voices and laughter.

"Would you like to get up and sit by the window?"

"No!" I say it quickly.

Eva turns to me—her eyes fixed on mine—stands up. Her hands clasping the edge of the table, she says, "Listen, I will tell you something. From now on, whenever I will tell you to get up, you will get up!"

"What's the matter with you? Since when do you give me orders?"

"That's what you are used to. I saw the others, they are all the same. They wouldn't get up! And then it was too late, understand? Each day I ask you and each day you say no. We are going to try it. Not tomorrow, but right now! Come on, up you go!"

"No . . . Eva . . ."

"Yes! You can do it."

"Don't pull me. Tomorrow . . . maybe in the morning . . ."

She slowly lifts my hands off the pillow. I feel torn from the warmth, the softness. The cover is thrown off, the abrupt air on my legs.

"Eva . . . you will see . . . it's impossible."

I feel myself being raised and now I sit, my feet touching the floor. Eva is putting Ilse's slippers on me.

"Ready?"

My heart is pounding. Eva's arm under mine, she lifts me to a standing position. I feel very tall and narrow. When I look at the floor, it seems such a long way down. Behind my back the door opens; I stand still, hanging on to Eva's arm.

The voice of Ilse, loud and full: "Well! What do you know? And when *I* ask her, she says no. Good. Good! Let me help you. . . . Here we are."

Ilse is holding me under the other arm.

"All right," says Eva, "you just do what I tell you. It will be easy, you will see. Ready? Your right foot, that's right, put it there, forward. . . . That's it!"

I look down on the floor. On the yellow linoleum, there is one of my feet, in a black slipper with a red pompom, stretched a little ahead of the other.

"Now, the other one; lift your left foot, put it where the other one is," says Ilse. "You want your feet together, don't you?"

My feet together. Is that what walking is? And how easy it seemed in the past. . . . The window does not come closer.

"How many steps to the window?"

"Never mind," says Eva. "Here we go, left foot, right foot."

I cling to them in the darkened room, with the singing coming from the lighted square. Left foot, right foot. It is important now that I reach the window. There is everything outside, the laughter, the voices rising and the evening sky lifting the moon.

There is a bench under the white frame of window. They lower me on it and I turn to look out in the square. There are colored lanterns strung between the trees. In the swing of the lights, the colors shift on the houses, red and blue. Ilse and Eva sit beside me in silence. The sound of harmonicas—couples dance in the center. It must be a dance of their country. The words come to me, absurd and wonderful: "Hands, knees, and bumps a daisy . . ." and they slap their knees and they slap their hands and spin around. Some soldiers in plaid skirts, others in their battle jackets; they turn and whirl around the girls with white arms. A narrow throat above a cotton dress, a flower stuck in the too short hair. Beyond the lamps, couples walk, arms around each other. The music stops to the clapping of hands.

"What are we celebrating?" I say "we" as if a part of me was outside also, turning among the flowers, under the colored lights.

They look at me, then turn to each other. "Didn't you tell her?" Ilse's voice is full of surprise.

"No, I thought she knew. . . ." They are both silent now as if they did not know how to tell me.

"It's the end of the war," says Eva, putting her head down on the window sill.

Ilse's voice breaks the silence. "Now . . . let's go slowly back to the bed." They lift me from the bench. "One, two, one, two . . ."

Back in bed, I repeat to myself, The end of the war, the end . . .

I learned how to walk again, just in time.

The Dress

I open the door to the closet and take out the dress. I hold it out in front of me, then bring it closer against my body. Looking down at the wide skirt with its blue flowers, I think of Ilse. This is her last gift to me. Since last night, Ilse has been gone; gone with the flowers thrown through the evening air, the band playing as the train started to move. The first repatriation train. Garlands of flowers swung from the roofs of the cattle cars. Standing there, her arms full of gifts, she bent down to a soldier and kissed him, and others came to shake her hand, kiss, wave. I stood apart, watching her, and she blew me a last kiss when the train moved. "I'll see you! I'll see you, Tania!"

I pick up a piece of chocolate, the imprint of Ilse's teeth still in it, and crack it in my mouth. The sun is bright. What shall I do now? Eva is in the office as usual. "I will leave with the last train," she said. "You will see, you'll leave before I do." Maybe I will, if I pass the next physical.

I pick up the dress again; I hold it up to the light; I turn it, watching the wide skirt spinning. I look inside the dress and run my finger over the many seams.

I take off my skirt and shirt and pull the dress over my head. I don't know where she got it, but the size is right. I hook the belt in the last hole and think, It fits me well. I slide my feet into the new pair of sandals and think of how easy it is to walk now. I do not walk any more with my hands stretched out to grip the nearest object; I do not measure distances any more: between bed and table, table and closet, closet and door. It was the hall that I feared. I would move close to the walls, brushing them with my hip with nothing to meet my hands.

I comb my hair, light from the sun. Suddenly I feel like singing. A beautiful dress. I try my voice, very low, humming a tune. But my voice is not ready yet. I turn, look back at the room as if I have forgotten something, and walk out of the door.

Outside, Vito is sitting on the steps. "Going for a walk?"

"Yes, you want to come along?"

He stands up and walks beside me. On the square the houses have a deserted look. From an open window a girl leans, pouring water from an enamel pot on the flowers below. The water falls in a thin white stream, with the light of the sun falling down with it. On a lawn some soldiers play cards on a brown blanket.

Along the road we walk on the side of the shade.

"You are going to miss Ilse."

"Yes. It has been such a long time that we have been together. Without her, I might not be here."

"How old are you, Tania?"

"Twenty."

We jump over a ditch and enter the woods. It is cooler here and the air is dark green. A squirrel sits up on his hind legs, under a tree, the little body erect, two paws in front of his mouth; then he runs, the fur of his tail spread light. We stop, watching the curved movement of his body.

"Did you see?"

Vito is not watching the squirrel, but is looking at me without smiling. I pick up a branch and start to talk fast. "I like it here, don't you? We used to pick mushrooms and fry them with eggs. It's very good. I am sure . . . Look, there is one." I point to a mound under a tree. I uncover the moss and there is the brown, soft head of a mushroom, perfect in its roundness, the rich smell mixed with that of the earth. "You see?"

I stand up, my face suddenly close to his. The brown eyes have yellow centers. I do not move but stand still, on my fingers the fresh earth and on my face his lips. I move away, my hands spread in front of me.

"Do you have something I can wipe my hands on?"

He hands me a red handkerchief. The earth leaves small brown dots on it. I look down at the dress, afraid that I might have dirtied the hem.

"I have never seen you in a dress. Who gave it to you?"

"Ilse. Ilse gave it to me yesterday. Do you like it?"

"Yes, I like it." He laughs, hugging my shoulder. "I like it."

There is more light now and soon we come to a clearing with high grass.

"Do you want to sit down for a while?"

He sits down in the grass, a small distance away from me. "It's good here," he says. "We should stay here and never go back. Live on mushrooms. What do you say?"

I put my finger to my lips, then point silently. A shadow moves from the rim of the trees and the shape of a young deer, awkward on his legs, jumps higher than the grass. Turning his head, the pointed ears turn; I see for a second the dark, round eye; then all is lost in the fleeing body.

I lie down in the grass again. Vito reaches out his hand to touch mine, stroking one finger after another.

"Little, little Tania . . ."

"Don't say that! I put on five more pounds! Do you know how much I weigh now? Almost eighty pounds!"

He shifts closer, laughing. "I like every pound of it. And the more there'll be of you, the better."

His hands close to hold my head and he kisses me. I can see the yellow light again inside his eye. He is warm, his mouth, his hands . . . I roll away, get up and brush the dry burrs from my dress.

"Tania . . ."

I am running across the meadow, into the dark trees. I stop and lean against a tree. I wait. I cannot help noticing the green stains on my dress, the rumpled fold. He moves slowly, his eyes reading my face.

"Vito . . . I want to tell you. I . . . I am not ready yet. You understand? I am not ready."

He comes close to me and pulls me into his arms, and I lay my head on his shoulder, looking up through the twisted branches.

"That's all right, that's all right, Tania," he whispers, holding me close, stroking my hair.

I feel good now; I would like to stay like this. With the sound of the forest and the leaves touching from branch to branch; with the wind that comes to move the branches, swaying, and the leaves leaning away, letting through the broken light.

We start to walk back, with the breeze on our faces. I see a patch of clustered leaves and I bend down, my fingers closing over the tight green fruit.

"They are still not ripe, the blueberries."

"It takes a long time," says Vito. There is a softness in his voice and I look at him. He is standing with his legs wide apart, the T-shirt stark white among the dark trees. He is looking down at the berries; then slowly his eyes move to mine.

I straighten and we walk again. "You know what we can do, Vito? We can stop at the kitchen and get some coffee and I have some biscuits. . . ."

"Yes," he says. "That's fine. Let's do that."

We come out on the road and walk faster. The wind ripples the dress and I pull it closer to my body, taking in the looseness. I see now that the dress is too big for me, but it should not be too long before I grow into it.

6

The lands came back with the smell of the plain. The children, pulled by kites across the fields, stopped and flapped their hands at the people sitting in the open freight cars. The trains, strung with flowers along their sides, passed too quick; the children stared at the cars growing small with distance, the kites plunging at the end of long loops across the sky. The trains moved through spring and into summer, the sun followed on the rails.

Some of the people got off the trains where no towns were and walked away under the bend of smoke. At night the moon tilted and the sky was dark. In the mornings the rails parted the land and the sun widened above the hills. Orange smoke lifted from above the steaming river and the houses came out of the trees. Ducks and geese stuck their heads between the quick fences. Houses clustered closer together; towns curved on the hills. At last the rails turned above the river and the city emerged from the deep valley.

Those who long ago walked away in the blue-cold morning of the city came back. They came back to find sidewalks that had not deepened with the prints of boots; to find streets over which the years of war slid like snails over wet leaves.

In the tight streets, they saw the iron shutters rolled up and the shopkeepers dusting their goods behind the windows. They saw the gold towers shimmer as if under water. In the gardens, where the green bushes leaned away from marble benches, they saw the gravel walks leading to the mansions; the closed windows reflected nothing; only the brown grass marked the path of the departed soldiers. At last they came to streets where the houses were standing stiff and close to the curbs. They started to look for the house where they were born, for the school where they had learned something, for the place on the river where they had bathed.

The streets turned and the sun leaned along the high roofs. The memory of those left behind—the shadows in the morning longer than the trees. Slowly lifting their heads to read that number on that house, they knocked on a door and waited. Sometimes there was no answer and sometimes the wrong face in the door. And when they turned away, the turning was heavy. They went back to all places and, through the wandering streets, the ones that did not return now went with them. It slowed their steps. And some talked to the absent ones, trying to lighten their walk:

"K____, why did you drink that yellow water? . . . B____, you had to be a hero, didn't you? . . . D____, that morning, you wouldn't get up and covered your head with a blanket. . . . R____, I told you to wash and you said it was too cold. . . . J____, why did you never learn to move your head in your sleep, so that the rats would not get at your ears?"

Standing on a corner, they watched the crowd. Shining, full bodies passed, the faces dark under the hats. They thought, The dead we know, the living we do not know. The smiles of the women were white, breasts in summer dresses rising as they moved. When a hand brushed along their flanks, it was a warm hand. They remembered flat, thin bodies and felt tenderness—in memory they ripened.

But the women among them saw something else in the passing bodies. They saw the bright, waving dresses, but could not see themselves wearing them. They saw faces that had spent time in front of a mirror and they tried to remember, but could not. They saw the little adornments, bright buttons and rings, a scarf skillfully placed, crisply tied. Of all these things, they felt, it was too soon for them to understand. But one thing they understood at once: the women fat with child. The sight made them wonder, How long before my blood returns?

They moved again, men and women, looking for their city: for the stone horseman on the square, the bronze clock on the tower, the bridge watched over by the headless saint, the castle whose windows of blue crystal always reflected their wonder.

And finally, not knowing exactly where it was, they met someone who had known them before. The face that stopped when they stopped. The Survivor met the Citizen.

CITIZEN: Well! I haven't seen you for a long time. Where have you been?

SURVIVOR: I have been away. I just came back.

CITIZEN: I remember now. They took you! Was it as bad as we heard?

SURVIVOR: What did you hear?

CITIZEN: You know, terrible stories. But it's all over. You are here.

SURVIVOR: I survived.

CITIZEN: Tell me about it.

SURVIVOR: Tell you? There is no method to it, you know. Small things on which life depends. I learned somehow. But you are probably busy. . . .

CITIZEN: Yes, I am a little pressed for time. But, anyhow, how does it feel to be back? Wonderful, eh?

SURVIVOR: I don't know. I would like to shout, but you don't do that here. I would like to laugh, but you cannot laugh alone. Even to cry, I would need a place to go. I would like a shelter . . . but one that I could walk out of. You know, I . . .

CITIZEN: What is it?

SURVIVOR: Look over there, the birds between the buildings; look how the shadows go up the walls and . . .

CITIZEN: Listen, I have to go now. What are you going to do? You'll have to get yourself a job, get settled. Listen, I could talk to my boss. . . .

SURVIVOR: No. There is something I have to find first. I am sure it's somewhere. Maybe in this city, maybe in myself, maybe in the dead. You see? I have to find the answer to . . .

CITIZEN: Yes, of course. We'll talk about it sometime. I'll tell you what! You come for dinner tonight—I just remembered my wife got a goose from the country. That's settled. All right?

SURVIVOR: Yes . . . yes, I would . . .

CITIZEN: Good. You remember the street, don't you? And wait till you see the children, you won't recognize . . . Well, anyway . . . And about that shelter . . . we still have that guest room. . . . I'll see what the wife says. You will come tonight?

SURVIVOR: Yes. I will come tonight. I want to thank . . .

CITIZEN: When my wife goes to bed . . . I have a bottle of plum brandy hidden away. . . . We will get drunk, eh?

SURVIVOR: Yes. We will get drunk.

The returning ones saw the sun slanting down the copper roofs. Their eyes and hands moved slowly; they were tired. Home, that familiar space marked by habit, arranged to be known in the dark, was yet beyond the border they had crossed. They did not see the end of the street and they could not ask what was around the corner.

When the evening lights struck on the lanterns at last, they found a refuge. Some under dark bridges lay down like long children, to sleep on the tilted plain above the river; some behind a warm door found a bed covered with crisp linen. And the last citizens entered their houses.

Darkness covered the city and all sleepers became one size. Above them, the churches rang a thousand bells: one sound.

The Return

The borders are crossed. I sit in the cattle car, swinging my legs in the open door. With the sound of wheels the fields drift by. We move on the rim of the land and the scenes shift: A woman in a small house washes windows, her head turning toward the passing train—I hold her image for a moment, the spread arms across the window, forever motionless. A little girl plays with a stick in a pond, striking white spray from the water. A boy in shorts pedals on a bicycle, alone on a field road; the planted rows spin about a high church at the center of the land. Ducks and dogs, roosters perched on shingle roofs and manure stacked in front of the village houses. The stations with flower pots hanging between the pillars. This is my country.

I lose count of the stations; they merge into a ringing of switch engines as they shunt freight cars to the sidings in the yards. Those small bells sounding in my mind make a music, the words of which are the names on the swinging signs. The names are important—but yet they do not matter: I have been here before.

The people wave. Handkerchiefs flap from courtyards; lips open to greetings that the wind carries away. How different from that other country, where the people stared and the children kept their eyes on the ground. I remember too how the dogs came into the stations, sniffing at our hanging feet.

Tomorrow the city. It is only now that I begin to believe in the returning. I wish the wheels turned faster; at the same time there is too much, too fast, to hold. There will be new faces, new voices. I find myself missing what I left. I see Eva and Vito at the station—Eva waving, Vito not moving, his eyes on my face. Regret. It is a feeling I have almost forgotten. I hold on to their faces and see them again as when the train started to move: becoming smaller and more distant until they were two points; each holding a different part of my love.

I wonder how I will look to those who are in the city. Will I seem strange to them? The sun is going down and I move inside the car. I light a cigarette and listen to the singing voices, humming the same tune. After a while, they settle down to sleep. I lie here, repeating to myself, One more night, one single night. I touch the pocket of my shirt—the paper is still there: my aunt's address. I wrote it down just to be sure I would know where I was going. I wish I had known when I wrote her that I would be coming so soon. It seems strange that no one waits for me there.

I wake up and I do not know where I am. Something is missing—the motion. The train is stopped. The women wake around me, the voices asking, "Where are we? What happened?" We pull the sliding door aside and lean out.

I try to focus on what is there before me. Through the grayness all the colors in my mind appear. All the shapes—guessed at, withheld, denied—form into the one city of this morning.

Lifting above the river mist, orange gables and the arches, the slant of copper roofs and the high windows sharp with light. The river flowing dark under the bridges, the heavy houses stepped to the sky and rising from the hill, the castle. The castle, gold towers round as hands with the jutting spires, fingers pointing to crosses at their tips.

We are solid together at the door, pounding a back, a shoulder. We jump from the open door. We turn in each other's arms, shouting, kissing; we spin about, tripping over the rails, scuffling in the loose gravel. Someone scoops cinders and gravel, kisses them and tosses black pebbles in the air.

From the station five men in wide coats and a sash across the chest come toward us. In quiet voices they read us their welcome. Then they tell us that we will have to wait until a group of other officials arrive and the social workers and the Committee for Liberated Prisoners comes, and then everything will be settled. The ones that have nowhere to go will soon be taken care of. Nothing to worry about. The train is a little ahead of schedule; that is the reason for a slight delay. One man in a top hat pulls out a watch on a gold chain and says, smiling: "To be exact, an hour and twenty minutes early. Please, make yourselves comfortable. Coffee and rolls will be brought to you. But *please,* do not leave the station."

There are more words, but I do not hear them. I go back into the car and pick up soap and towel from a blue canvas bag. The officials are gone now; the women stand in groups, talking. Some sit in the car, hands folded in their laps: through the years of waiting a taut patience. I cross the tracks to where I have seen a faucet. I wash my face and hands. I clean my nails. Drying myself, I see the corner of the main railroad-station building. Now I remember. I left from here once to go somewhere on a trip. I see people moving there with suitcases. They all seem far away. The morning is still cool, but the sun is already in the sky. There is a slight smell of smoke in the air. It will be a good day.

The coffee is brought by six women in white coats. They look like nurses, but maybe they are waitresses. They look very healthy and they do not stop smiling, handing out coffee with milk in it. There is a great heap of rolls on a cart. "Take as many as you want," they keep repeating, still smiling. I eat four rolls with blue poppy seeds on them; the coffee is hot and sweet. I go back to the cart and pick up some more rolls. They are very good, but why do they make them so small? I eat without becoming full. Is it a permanent hunger? No, it is just a big appetite, I think, sinking my teeth into a roll. They wheel the empty cart away, saying, "Good luck to you, good luck."

I step up in the car. I move fast now, opening the canvas bag, putting the towel and soap back into it. I reach to a nail, where I hung my dress, pull my clothes off and put the dress on. I comb my hair, push the skirt and shirt in the bag. I look around the car; I did not forget anything. I step over legs; somebody says, "Where are you going?" I stand, turning to them, but I do not answer. I lift my hand in a farewell sign and jump out of the car.

I walk slowly across the tracks toward the station building. There are crowds of people now. The important thing is not to stare at anybody, not to make myself noticeable. I wonder where they are all going. A group of Boy Scouts comes toward me, with their bare knees showing and with rucksacks over their backs. Now there are some who are leaving for vacation; I see fishing poles and tennis rackets, a cage with a canary in it; a man with a canvas cap on his head, holding a butterfly net, a girl with a stuffed blue rabbit in her arms. There are the porters, pushing carts with heaped luggage. "Attention, Attention!" I freeze. "The train on number five track, leaving in ten minutes, destination . . ."

I cannot go through the main building. I stand, hesitating, then turn and walk alongside the building toward the back. I see a small iron gate, not higher than my waist, swing open. Without turning back, I walk through the gate.

I come out into a street. I knew a street like this once. The sidewalk is made of fitted stones. The sun slants from the windows, people scatter in the street. I turn in the middle of the sidewalk, examining them. Someone bumps into me and I clutch my canvas bag. They look . . . different. They pass with their eyes forward, the women stopping at windows, looking into them, lifting hands to their long hair. Nobody has noticed me and now I feel disappointment. I am turned so many ways that I do not know where I am going any more. I stop and press my face against a window. The dresses are on bodies of wax, the smiles set into white faces. One wax woman has a finger missing. The styles have changed. Farther down the street I pass a shop with a sign: THE-PET-BEAUTY-PARLOR. In the window, rubber bones and leather collars and small knitted boots. THINK OF THE RAINY DAYS, a sign announces. I turn away, following a woman with padded shoulders, tilting on high wooden wedges. Past a shop with pyramids of books—I do not know the names of the authors; they must all be new. Everything is too new in my old city.

I stop at a corner and turn back upon the street. I realize that I have been looking for something: ruins. Where are the ruins? I have been at home in ruins. But this city is untouched. I cross over to a park. I feel tired already, with the sun on my shoulders and the feeling of stone under my feet. Through the park, past old men sitting on benches and feeding the pigeons. Past a small statue in black stone, fishes spouting water from their mouths, the water falling into a pool in a long foam. I would like to sit down but I cannot stay here. Out of the park, into the streets where the houses stand leaning toward each other. I shift the bag from hand to hand. The colors sway before me: the print dresses of women, the shoes flashing white, a flower stand on the corner, with an old woman sprinkling the blue, yellow and white disks of asters. Seeing the flowers and the people strolling, I think of a carnival; I wonder if it is a holiday. An older woman in black passes by. I take hold of her shoulder and say, "Please, what day is it?" At my touch the body jerks away and she stops, staring at me.

"What did you say?"

"Is it Sunday?"

She starts to walk away; then she says, over her shoulder, "Saturday, it's Saturday." I watch her shaking her head and talking to herself.

At the next corner I stop: There is a tramway standing, waiting. The cars are half-red and half-white. The number is eleven. I run across to the island of cement and board the car. I stand on the platform. *Number eleven is the one that goes home. That is the one that goes home.* The cars move with a rattling surge. I look at a passing sign with the name of a street. I know this street so well, but I do not recognize the name in white letters. It must be a new name. Each time the tramway stops, the man in black uniform reaches to the cord above his head and signals for departure. He is coming through the car to the platform where I stand, the bag at my feet. He has a small mustache, his cheeks meshed with broken veins. He is looking at me. Maybe he is the same one I used to ride with to school. I smile at him.

"Well, young lady?"

I clear my throat. Maybe I should say hello to him. I continue smiling, shifting my feet.

"Your fare, young lady?" He is rattling coins in the black bag hanging across his belly.

The heat is in my face. How could have I forgotten?

"I am sorry. . . . I don't have any money; I . . . will get off."

"Where do you think you are?"

"I will get off. I am sorry."

A man inside the car lowers the newspaper he is reading and turns his head toward the platform. Now all the people in the car turn to watch me. I should explain that I did not want to cheat. I just forgot there was money, that is all.

"I forgot about it," I say.

He is looking down first, at my shoes, then up my body. "You from . . ." He waves his hand in the opposite direction. "You just came back, eh?"

"I will get off," I repeat.

He pats my shoulder. "That's all right. For once. So, like that . . . Was it bad back there? I told my woman, when she complained about the butter, you know how they are, I told her many times, you be glad you are where you are, isn't it right?"

"That's right."

"You just stay right here in the corner and don't worry. How far do you go?"

"Vinehill."

He nods his head, saying, "You going to surprise your folks, eh?" and walks away, through the car, to collect the coins.

The tramway goes up the hill. The houses are steep on the sky, the shadows, the shape of roofs, are dark wedges on one side of the sidewalk. A small wind rolls grains of dust and yellow paper over the shadows. A curtain, lifted by two fingers, and a face behind a square of glass. The skirts of women walking up the hill lift round above the white knees; the wind fills the pants of the men. Their legs are shorter and the bodies slant with the street. Two girls play with a red ball, four hands higher than the two points of their blue ribbons, their voices lifting and dropping with the ball. I recognize the square with its squat church, the Park of Roses, the house where Eva used to live. I turn and see the receding door through which I used to pass, running up the steps, taking them two by two, as if there was something that was going to escape at the end.

"Vinehill, Vinehill next!" shouts the man, winking at me from the end of the car.

I pick up my bag and step down. I see his hand reaching to the cord and the cars move away with the sound of a bell.

The name on the corner pole is the same. They did not change it. Even the black plate of the sign is the same, the *i* a little crooked. The old woman selling the pickles is still there, the wooden barrel shorter than I remember. I stop at the movie house and look at the stills. A thin little man standing in a room with pie on his face; the same man leading a village parade in his underwear.

I tell myself, This is the street. The trees rimmed with stones, the grass around them brittle. But it looks narrower than I remember. There is the grocery store where Mother used to shop. They had chocolate figures of small people in a glass jar. I recognize the beer parlor with its zinc bar. The foam of the beer would drip through the small holes and I always wondered where it went when I stood there waiting for my pitcher to be filled—then I carried it through the summer-evening street, back into the house.

There is a new shop, all white from the outside. I press my head against the glass. The lady inside is dressed in a starched pink dress and the walls are pink. There are waffles in a glass container, with a round glass top. I wonder why we never thought of ice cream. I put my bag down and lean against the window. There are large zinc freezers where they keep it cold. In one the yellow, in the others the berry and chocolate. A little girl walks into the shop. I see her lips moving, the woman's head bending above the open freezer, scooping, filling a cone. Exchange of ice cream for coins. The girl comes out, her tongue sweeping around the chocolate mound.

"Want an ice cream?"

Two soldiers stand behind my back. I smile at them. "Yes, please."

I follow them inside. It is cool here, and quiet suddenly, after the noise of the street. These soldiers have different uniforms and speak a language that I can almost understand. The blond one turns to me and says, "What kind?"

I put down my bag. "Oh, vanilla and strawberry." I come close to the counter and lean over it. The lady hands me the cone. I hold it with both my hands, putting my face closer to it, to smell the ice cream. It doesn't smell anything. It starts to drip down my fingers. The soldiers walk by me and sit down at a table. They turn their large fair faces to me and smile; the blond one motions with his hand, and I sit down at the small marble-top table.

"You look tired," says the darker one.

I nod, looking at him. His tunic has a straight, stand-up collar; it reminds me of a Chinese dress. My mouth is full of ice cream. Sweet, cool. I lean back in the chair and think, It is good to be back. The blond one clears his throat. I look up and see them looking at each other. They whisper something in low voices that I cannot understand. But I catch a glance, a direct stare. I continue licking the ice cream, then slowly lower my eyes to where they have been looking. My left arm is on the table and on the sunburned skin the number is clear. I scratch my arm.

"Do you like the city?" I say.

They nod their heads. "Beautiful, beautiful city. Lucky people here. No bombs."

"I was born here," I say.

They nod slowly, as if that was a sad thing. Then, his face brightening, the blond one says, "I think I wish to eat. Do you wish?"

I hesitate. "I am not very hungry, you know. Maybe a piece of cake?"

I eat a piece of chocolate cake and one nut cake and a cheese-filled roll and I drink a tall glass of sweet pink soda water. They tell me they are leaving the city soon and I can see that they are glad to leave, to find their country again. I think of how strange it is that a city that means so much to one is just away from home to someone else.

I shake hands with them and they stand side by side, feet joined, click their heels and walk away.

A green light goes off and the orange blinks, the red flashes on. It is a round eye of glass that gives an order with its color. I watch the people now, all stopping beside me and think of how well they know this. Across this street and one more block. There must have been a time, far back in the days of childhood, when the edge of a sidewalk was a frontier, to cross finally when I was old enough. On green I follow the people. I am locked in the press of bodies, another crowd of strangers coming from the other side. But in this single moment of crossing the street, I suddenly find the sameness in all of us: We all want to get to the other side. On the sidewalk, the people split into their different directions and no one turns after the other.

I am alone again. I walk slower now. No hurry. This is the block. This is the block where I used to throw the ball against a wall of a house, where it struck and rebounded back to me.... *I threw it and it came back. I could always count on it: throw it low and it would bounce back high. Hit it at a slant, and you have to chase it. Street is better than playground. There was a dead man once under a tree in the playground. No horror, but curiosity. Looked asleep without snoring... Somebody lived in this house,*

I don't know who. It's very hot. The schools are out. I must go back to school. They will teach me again. The houses here don't change. There is the one we had to move out of because . . .

What am I doing here? Whatever made me come? Maybe it was too early to go to my aunt; that's why I am here. I will just walk by the old house and not stop. I cannot stop time. Gone, finished. ". . . Wait you will regret, regret . . ." That's what Mother would sing so often. About two lovers. I can see the house now. Just walk by, not stop.

The deep color of stone. The portal of the door carved in a laurel of stone, the branches following the shape of the door. I face the house. I lift my eyes to the apartment on the main floor. I put the bag at my feet. In one of the high windows, the curtains in their color of mauve . . .

The strange colors Mother likes. "Mauve," says Father, "show me one, just one house with mauve curtains." "That's why," she says, "that's why!" She laughs and her laugh comes easily. . . . The reflected color on the pale-blue walls. Mother's special room. The sun slanting in the high corner of the curtain; a square of sky bending on the rounded surface of a vase.

I lean on a tree in front of the house. I look down at the bag at my feet. I know what is in the bag: towel, soap, toothbrush, one shirt and one skirt. Two packages of cigarettes. A notebook. One brown sandal. The other one is somewhere in a meadow. In the pocket of the shirt . . . the address of my aunt Magda. I know exactly what is in this bag. I don't know what is in a house. I should leave. I should not go in and have the curtains explained. I want them blown over the window of my past.

Steps coming from inside the house. A young woman comes through the open door. She poses for a moment, the dress too white against the dark of the hall behind her. She raises her hand to touch the nape of her neck. Brass bracelets ring her wrist. She steps out, the bare shoulders catching the sun. She walks away on high heels and I watch the long black hair swinging across her back. The legs are strong on the spiked heels. . . . How healthy, solid and ready she is. But how can feet walk so high above the ground? I look down at my feet in their flat sandals; between the toes dark lines of dust. I take out my checkered handkerchief and blow my nose. Two women walk by, shopping bags on their arms, heads wrapped in bright cotton. A worker in his new leather cap stops and lights a cigarette, the large hand shielding half of his face. He moves off. Now a dog in its soiled fur stops and lowers his pointed head at my feet. I bend down to caress him and he runs away. They are all going somewhere. . . .

I pick up my bag and enter the house. Inside it is dark and cool, the smell of rugs dampened for sweeping. I turn to the brown door on the right side. The bell in its brass circle; I put my finger on it and press. I shiver in the cool hall. Behind the door the muffled steps. The door opens and a woman stands there. Her hair is tight in curlers and she has a blue and white apron around her waist.

"I am sorry, I think I made a mistake." I back away. Her feet in scuffed red slippers, the hair dark on her legs.

"Whom did you want?"

"I . . . was looking for a family that used to live here. The Andres."

"Never heard of them. Not in *this* house." Her hand goes toward the knob. "You can ask the janitor. Maybe they left an address."

"Yes. You know . . . I recognize the curtains. . . ."

The space in the doorway narrows. "The curtains? They were here when we moved in. What's wrong with keeping them?"

"Nothing. I just remember them."

"Yes, well . . . they sure are a funny color. But what with the war and no material, I kept them."

"Thank you. I am sorry I disturbed you."

"That's all right. You ask the janitor." The door closes; the chain clicks on the other side.

I walk away, down the dark hall. The street is hazed; the people swim in my sight. I turn the first corner and hear music. I see paper heads, turning their blinking lashes on the people stopped along the sidewalk. Behind the masks, two men stumble under the weight of a banner. The banner is too bright. There are words, but I cannot read them. There is a horn opening like a brass flower, twined around the body of a man. The grunt of the tuba, the thumps of the tasseled sticks on the stained skin of the drum, the bugles calling . . . I feel these sounds jarring me; my hands shake. The sound passes, falls away, but the feeling remains—with the traffic coming in now to fill the space the parade has emptied.

Suddenly a sharp pain swells in my belly. I am doubled over, the bag slipping from my hand. It is over before I straighten. The pain leaves me feeling hot all over, and at the same time it seems to me that I can see more clearly now.

I go through streets known, the shops familiar, suddenly a recognized face above a counter. He does not know me, but I know him. I think of how that makes me even more of a stranger: to go to places remembered and not to be recognized.

I would like to take the tramway and go to Magda. I don't even know how much the fare is. I am tired. I don't have the smallest coin of money. What is the smallest coin? I walk slower now, through streets shrill with the horns of cars. The people walk fast and everybody passes me. I see children with their clean hair, women with their bellies full. The street leads to the river and I walk on a bridge, seeing below me the summer river as I always knew it: It moves with slow turns and twisting streams; it flows solidly, changing always and always the same.

Across the bridge I follow the streets; to some I give a name, but when I lift my head to read the sign, it is not the right street. A square with a tall church, the spikes of its towers glittering with sun. I am sure the church stood on the opposite corner of the park. The pain comes and goes, not sharp now, but with a widening pulse. The sun has dipped behind the houses, but the heat is still in my skin. I press my head against a cool pane of glass. A delicatessen shop, with salami hanging on a string, the skin white as if powdered. In the window the herring are rolled with pieces of pickles protruding, a toothpick stuck through their backs. The dark red beans with whites of onions, glistening with oil. A sign gives the cost of each thing and the number of ration tickets required. There is nobody in the shop. Maybe the salami is not real; perhaps it is paper.

I walk on, and the street bends down a slope. This is the street where Magda lives. I start down the slope and I can already see the house, its windows wide. The apartment is on the fourth floor. I put my bag at my feet and lean on a lamppost; I feel that I cannot go any farther. I would like to sit down on the sidewalk. Rest. Prepare myself for the meeting. But if I sat down, they would look at me. I don't know them, but I know what they would think. The metal of the lamppost is cool against my back. The pain comes again and I bend with it, closing my eyes. It will go away like before. And it goes away. I open my eyes, still bent over. And there, between my white sandals—drops of blood. I try to swallow the sound, but the laugh comes, shaking through my body. And with wonder I recognize it: It is the laugh of joy.

I start to run. It is easy going down the slope. I listen to my feet, making that bright sound. I run past the houses, past noises coming through windows. Toys roll away under my feet. I startle a cat and it leaps. I scatter pigeons. I reach the house, still running. Between the bright surfaces of the wide hall, the sound that followed me here, now, with one step, ends.

I stand still in the quiet house and lift my hand to cover the hard knocking of my heart.

Afterword

In April of 1945 the British Army liberated the camp of Bergen-Belsen, and I was able to return to Prague that summer after almost four years of internment. I found my aunt, the one non-Jewish member of our family, and stayed with her and her three-year-old girl, this unknown cousin born during the war. I went back to my old school, sat in the familiar rooms, listened to the remembered voices of my old teachers. I passed my baccalaureate and took on office jobs. When I walked through the city, I was surprised how unchanged, untouched by the war it remained. I felt nothing but estrangement. I did not go to the cemetery to visit the grave of my grandfather. I did not go to the street where we used to live. With the rumor of yet another government change, I left for France. I was twenty-two years old.

I came to life in Paris. In the foreign indifference of the city I felt free. The broad boulevards and avenues offered larger vistas. The city gave me much, without the high cost of painful memories. But there was also the colorful bureaucracy of working permits and the regular visits to the police regarding my domicile, which was then required of all stateless persons. In 1955 I left for America.

In California I met the man I was to marry. I now had a home life, a working life, and I formed lasting friendships. During that first year in America, far from Europe, the idea of this book emerged. I needed to tell what happened to me and to so many others. Through fiction I could distill these experiences, and honor the friendships that helped me survive. I showed the first chapters to my husband, and with his encouragement I continued. In 1961 *Tell Me Another Morning* was published.

During those years I stayed in touch with my aunt and my cousin, who was now a nurse in a hospital. Forty-five years after leaving Prague, I returned. I was drawn back, to this family, to that city. In the face of my cousin I recognized my own. Sitting around the dinner table with my cousin, her husband, and their grown daughter, we talked of everyday life. Soon I started to explore the city, wandering in the Old Town. The sheer splendor of it overwhelmed me with its enduring beauty. I had forgotten the grandeur of the extravagant baroque churches, Gothic cathedrals, Art Nouveau buildings. And above it all, the castle brooding on the hill. I was now ready to accept the beauty of this old part of town, the city that survived two occupations and changes of government. But there was also the constant reminder of years of neglect: peeling paint, crumbling stone, and with the sudden return of June heat, the damp smell from dark cellars.

One day I crossed the Moldau River on the Charles Bridge. The ancient bridge remained the same, carrying its burden of stone saints. Underneath, white swans cut "V" ripples in the river. I moved through the tourists, the street musicians, the stalls of vendors, distances distorted by unreliable memory. Much of what was there during my childhood was gone. But there was also the sharp, sudden point of recognition, knowing where a shortcut would lead. Still, the castle seemed farther away and some streets veered off at unexpected angles.

After the cold formality of the Waldstein Palace gardens, after the too-perfect flower borders that held the smell of ancient earth, I sought out the old orchard of the Vojanov Gardens and sat on a bench. In this humble, deserted place, I rested. All my wandering was a postponement of the pilgrimage I had to make: a return to the street and the house of my childhood.

The next day I set out to find what once was my own part of the city. I caught the tram near the National Museum and it climbed a hill, and went past the Park of Roses, where my brother and I spent our childhood afternoons. I stepped off, across from the Flora Hotel. On the corner of our street there had been a candy store where Mother bought us hard candy the color and shape of violets. Also missing was the movie house where my brother and I went to Sunday matinees.

The once elegant neighborhood was shabby and run down. I approached our block slowly, carefully. The house of memory had survived, but with cracked plaster. Our apartment was on the main floor. As a girl, if I leaned far out the window, I could see Father coming home, his head tilted slightly to the left, as if he were listening to some distant message.

I stood by the old chestnut tree staring at the window that once looked out on a time of such innocence. A little boy walked along the street, stopped in front of the house, pulled out a key, opened the door and went in. I watched him enter and heard the door click shut. There were new families in this house. Life on the street continued. Walking away, I did not look back. I left the house behind.

On another morning I decided to go with my cousin to the Jewish cemetery to visit the grave of my grandfather, who died when I was still a child. We walked through a long avenue of chestnut trees in a vast park of tombstones. In this abandoned place we were the only visitors. Although she had been taking care of the gravesite, she had difficulty finding it. The ground was covered with ivy, looped over and around the headstones. I heard her rustling through the tangle of vines. Finally, there it was. A black stone framed by ivy. I was left alone and I felt a chill. The stone was filled with names added to that of my grandfather. All the names of the family—my mother's five brothers, their families, my brother, my mother, my father—etched in stone, official and final. And I found myself looking for my name, a name that should have been there and was not. I felt excluded from this vast family. Dropping to my knees, I mourned them all. When I stood up, I placed the flowers I brought and a small pebble on the gravestone.

As we left the cemetery, holding hands, my cousin reminded me that we were going to the State Opera House in the evening to hear Verdi's *Masked Ball.* We were to meet at the statue of St. Venceslav. These many years later, I still see her running down the square, pushing her way through the crowd of tourists. She arrived, breathless. We hugged, my hand on her damp, cool neck. This was the child I held on my knee upon my first return to Prague, in 1945.

I have lived in three great cities: Prague, Paris, San Francisco. It is now 2007. I live on the northern coast of California, among the redwoods, with my husband and a cat. I remain in touch with "Ilse" and "Eva," my teenaged companions who are fictionalized in this book. The friendship that helped us to survive continues.

About the Author

Zdena Berger was born in Prague in 1925 and attended school there until the German occupation. She spent the war years as a prisoner of the Germans in several concentration camps, including Theresienstadt, Auschwitz, and Bergen-Belsen. Freed finally by the British Army in 1945, she returned to Prague to complete her education, and then moved to Paris, where she worked for the United States Army and the American School. In 1955 she immigrated to the United States. She is married and lives in California.

Acknowledgments

Paris Press offers bountiful thanks to the many individuals who made the publication of this book possible. They include Margery Adams, Jon Budish, Sara Budish, Fay Chandler, Daniel Chess, Aaron Feinstein, Mary Fitz-Gibbon, Mindy Fortin, Elaine Freeman, Anne Goldstein, Sonja Goldstein, Tzivia Gover, Ivan Holmes, Elizabeth Lloyd-Kimbrel, Eleanor Lazarus, Richard Lilly, Patricia McCambridge, Jeanne Roslanowick, Eva Schocken, Judythe Sieck, Dorothy Tegeler, Michael Thurston, and Linda Weidemann. Special thanks to Emily Wojcik.

Paris Press offers deep gratitude to the Lasko Family Foundations, the Schocken Foundation, the Shapiro Family Foundation, and the Massachusetts Cultural Council for their generosity in support of this important project and Paris Press.

Zdena Berger expresses her gratitude to Bill Broder, a long-time friend, who always thought her out-of-print novel should find a new generation of readers, and sent it on its way. She also thanks Jan Freeman of Paris Press, who passionately believes in the importance of bringing *Tell Me Another Morning* back to life.

About Paris Press

Paris Press is a not-for-profit, independent press publishing neglected or misrepresented literature by ground-breaking women writers. Paris Press values work that is daring in style and in its courage to speak truthfully about society, culture, history, and the human heart. To publish our books, Paris Press relies on support from organizations and individuals. Please help Paris Press keep the voices of essential women writers in print and known. All contributions are tax-deductible.

Paris Press books include Bryher's *Visa for Avalon, The Heart to Artemis: A Writer's Memoirs,* and *The Player's Boy;* Muriel Rukeyser's *The Life of Poetry, The Orgy,* and *Houdini: A Musical;* Virginia Woolf's *On Being Ill;* Elizabeth Cady Stanton's *Solitude of Self;* Ruth Stone's *Simplicity* and *Ordinary Words;* Jan Freeman's *Simon Says;* Adrian Oktenberg's *The Bosnia Elegies;* and *Open Me Carefully: Emily Dickinson's Intimate Correspondence with Susan Huntington Dickinson,* edited by Martha Nell Smith and Ellen Louise Hart. To contribute to the Press and to order our books, please visit www.parispress.org or write to Paris Press, P. O. Box 487, Ashfield, MA 01330.

The text of this book is composed in Stempel Garamond.
Cover and text design by Ivan Holmes Design.
Calligraphy on cover and in text by Judythe Sieck.
Typesetting by Linda Weidemann, Wolf Creek Press.
Painting on cover, "Girl with Hearts Falling," by Charlotte Salomon